PRAISE FOR PETER SAVAGE NOVELS

"I would follow Peter Savage into any firefight."
–James Rollins, *New York Times* bestseller of *The Demon Crown*

"Edlund is right at home with his bestselling brethren,
Brad Thor and Brad Taylor."
–Jon Land, *USA Today* bestselling author of the *Caitlin Strong* series

"This **compulsively readable** thriller boasts
a whiplash pace, a topical plot, and **nonstop action**.
Edlund fans won't be disappointed."
–Publisher's Weekly
Praise for *Lethal Savage*

"a near-perfect international thriller"
–Foreword Reviews
Praise for *Guarding Savage*

"With **a hero full of grit and determination,** this action-
packed, timely tale is **required reading**
for any thriller aficionado."
–Steve Berry, *New York Times* bestselling author,
Praise for *Hunting Savage*

"**Crackling action**, brisk pace, timely topic…"
–Kirkus Reviews
Praise for *Deadly Savage*

Unforgiving Savage

A Peter Savage novel

UNFORGIVING SAVAGE

A PETER SAVAGE NOVEL

DAVE EDLUND

Light Messages
Torchflame Books

Durham, NC

Published 2021, by Light Messages
www.lightmessages.com
Durham, NC 27713
SAN: 920-9298

Paperback ISBN: 978-1-61153-410-8
Ebook ISBN: 978-1-61153-411-5
Library of Congress Control Number: 2021938482

This is a work of fiction. All characters, organizations, and events portrayed in this novel are either products of the author's imagination or are used fictitiously.

For Scott Hale—my friend, my brother.
We've made some great memories.
Love ya bro.

ACKNOWLEDGEMENTS

THIS IS THE EIGHTH PETER SAVAGE NOVEL, and it's been a long and rewarding journey to arrive at this point. So much work goes into producing a novel, and I want to recognize important contributions from those who have worked tirelessly to bring *Unforgiving Savage* to life.

Light Messages Publishing. Your support and encouragement are appreciated more than words can say. It is indeed a delight to work with such a talented and dedicated group of professionals.

A special shoutout is due to my editors, Elizabeth Turnbull and Ashley Conner. Your contributions in taking a rough manuscript and turning it into the finished product are nothing short of miraculous. Your patient and thoughtful feedback is greatly appreciated. Thank you.

The medical details in this novel could not have come together without the advice and instruction of my good friend Dr. Scott Hale. Yes, the *real* Dr. Scott Hale. Our friendship goes back to our first meeting when we were in high school and competing in a national science fair. Although we lived in different cities (Sacramento for me, and Fresno for Scott), we stayed in touch through the years, our friendship growing stronger with time.

Thank you, Scott, for helping me get the trauma details correct. I hope you enjoy the fictional Dr. Hale as much as I do.

The legal issues presented in this novel, particularly related to the "zone of death," benefited greatly from the expert advice of my good friend Alex Gardner. As former District Attorney for Lane County, Oregon, and now the Director of the Oregon State Police Forensic Services Division, Alex provided valuable insight into crime scene investigation, as well as the legal conflicts of venue and vicinage created when Congress placed all of Yellowstone National Park under Federal jurisdiction (notwithstanding that the park falls within the boundaries of three states). Thank you, buddy.

Every author I know dislikes public relations and promotion, although it is a necessary step in trying to get one's work before a reading audience. Fortunately, I have the help of the talented Jori Hanna for everything related to book promotion—graphics, endorsements, even social media coaching. Thank you, Jori.

Of course, none of this would have any relevance if not for you, the fans of Peter Savage, Diesel, and colleagues. Without an audience to read these novels, there would be little reason to write them. Please continue to share your comments and post reviews on Amazon, Goodreads, and other social media sites. And if you want to reach me directly, I'd love to hear from you, either through the contact page on my website (www. DaveEdlund.com), or via email at dedlund@LightMessages. com.

AUTHOR'S NOTES

THIS STORY PICKS UP where *Valiant Savage* ended. Nevertheless, I endeavored to make this a standalone novel. The inevitable references to *Valiant Savage* are abbreviated in content in an effort to avoid spoilers. That said, if you are a fan of Peter Savage, I would recommend reading *Valiant Savage* first, then follow with *Unforgiving Savage*.

The pulsed-energy, antipersonnel (PEAP) weapon system is featured again in this novel. Developed by EJ Enterprises, under funding from DARPA, the handheld weapon is about the size of a conventional carbine, and it fires a micro-second burst of laser radiation. Since light is, practically speaking, unaffected by gravity, the PEAP carbine is a formidable weapon and ideal for extreme long-distance engagements.

I was inspired to introduce the PEAP carbine in *Valiant Savage*, based on the many public reports of vehicle-mounted laser weapons under development by the Department of Defense. Those weapon systems fire a continuous beam of high-intensity light at the target. However, the PEAP is different; it fires a short burst of energy, like the blasters in *Star Wars*, and an example of fiction departing from reality. Or so I thought, until February 2021 when a short report appeared in the public domain, describing the Tactical Ultrashort Pulsed Laser. According to the report, this weapon will emit a high-intensity and extremely short laser pulse lasting only two hundred femtoseconds. The US Army expects to begin testing the weapon in 2022. Could this be an advancement of the PEAP carbine first developed by Peter Savage and EJ Enterprises?

Human nature, being what it is, will inevitably cause humankind to bring advanced weapons to bear for mixed purposes—good and bad. History teaches that when weapons are developed with the intention of ending conflict, they only give rise to new and terrifying levels of fighting. Examples are dynamite, the machine gun, and the atomic bomb. Each of these weapons was invented with the intention of making further conflict so horrible that warfare would cease.

If only it had. Sadly, conflict escalated with bloody consequences after each of these inventions. Rather than being more peaceful, international warfare has become deadlier.

In this story, I wanted to examine this topic using the PEAP carbine as the next major advancement in arms. For Peter Savage, this is probably the most personal novel yet.

I hope you enjoy.

—DE

CHAPTER 1

BILLY REED HAD READ THE ARTICLE TWICE. It was published in the national section of the local newspaper. In five days, President Taylor would honor a man and his dog with the Presidential Medal of Freedom. Give me a friggin' break. His dog? The ceremony was to take place in the Rose Garden.

Billy wanted to be there, although he knew the chance of receiving an invitation was exactly zero. He didn't breathe the same rarified air as the elite politicians and power brokers of Washington. Obscurity- wasn't the problem. He was fairly certain that at least the president and his chief of staff knew his name. Being number one on the FBI's Most Wanted list had removed him from the shadow of anonymity and thrust him into the national spotlight—attention he preferred not to have.

Billy reasoned that if he couldn't attend the ceremony, he'd have to devise an alternative plan, which is exactly what he did. He phoned his friend Travis Hewitt from the militia. Travis had an ultralight aircraft and occasionally spoke of flying it low and fast over the Snake River, at times only five feet above the rushing water.

"I sh-shouldn't be talking to you Billy. You know that." Travis spoke in a slow cadence, and his face contorted as he struggled to get his words out. "Ever since the m-militia disbanded, we've been ordered to lay low. W-what if our phones are t-t-tapped?"

"Don't panic or say something stupid. There's no harm in two friends getting together and just talking."

"Depends on what you want to talk about. I'm done, m-man. So don't t-try to talk me into join—"

"Shut up. I'm not talking about joining anything."

"So w-why did you call?"

"Let's meet at the fork in the river in two hours."

"What for? I don't know. I don't think this is right. I'm not d-doing nothin—" Travis struggled to keep his voice calm and his words flowing.

"Just relax, Travis. Okay? I'm not asking you to do anything illegal. It's been a while since we got together and tipped some beers, right? What's the harm in having a picnic?"

Travis didn't answer, and after a long moment, Billy said, "Unless you don't like me anymore. But I've always been your best friend. Just putting it out there."

"You m-mean my only friend," Travis replied.

Billy knew Travis wasn't the star of any social scene, but he didn't realize it was that bad. Billy attempted to cheer him up.

"What about that young guy with the shaved head and goatee I saw you talking to on the range a couple weeks ago?"

"I was trying to help him. He was jerking every time he p-p-pulled the t-trigger. He got m-mad at me and called me a queer. Then he laughed at the way I talk. Everyone laughs at m-m-me."

"Come on, Travis, you know that's not true."

"Yes it is!" He sounded childlike, and Billy wondered if he was in tears.

Travis continued, "You're my only friend. You d-don't laugh at me."

"And you're my friend, Travis. Cheer up, man, you sound pretty down. Look, I'll see you in two hours."

They both road quad ATVs to a meadow where the Salmon River merged with the Snake River. As promised, Billy delivered a six-pack of beer on ice and sub sandwiches stuffed with a double portion of cheese and sliced meats. He picked this remote location at the edge of the Wallowa–Whitman National Forest, knowing it was unlikely that the FBI could have followed them without being spotted.

Travis had calmed himself and was enjoying the companionship and easy conversation. He never felt defective or inadequate in Billy's presence, and he was smiling and laughing as they passed the time.

Although Travis was a bit slow, he suspected there was something important Billy hadn't shared yet.

Travis said, "So w-what is it you want from m-me?"

Billy feigned surprise. "I don't know what you mean. We're just talkin' and drinkin' beer. Haven't seen you in a while. Why do you think I want something?"

"B-because you always do. Th-that's why you c-call me."

Billy crushed the empty can. He grabbed the last two from the cooler and handed one to Travis, then popped the top of his beer and took a long chug. When finished, he wiped the back of his hand across his lips and chin.

"All right, I'll be straight with you. I need you to let me borrow your ultralight. It's only for a few days."

"Oh, that's all? And w-when did *you* learn to fly?"

"Well, that's the other part. You have to give me lessons. I have two days to learn how to fly and land."

Travis stifled a smile. "Really. You want me to t-t-teach you to fly my airplane in two days? Why so much time? I mean, how about I j-just show you how to turn the engine on and where the throttle is, and then she's yours."

Billy's eyes widened. "I thought there was more to it than that."

"Of course there is. I'm being sarcastic." Travis laughed at his own joke. "But I had you going." He laughed again.

"Oh. But you can teach me in two days?"

"No. And what's the hurry, anyway? You never t-t-told me about any interest in flying before."

Billy took another swig of beer. "It's for a job I need to do."

"W-what job?"

"I'd rather not say."

"Then I'd r-r-rather not lend you my ultralight."

"Look, man. I need your help."

"And I'd like to help you, Billy. I truly would."

He turned away from Travis, facing the cold, clear water of the Salmon River. His curly black hair, cut in a mullet, was held down with a thin knit skull cap. A full beard, angular cheek bones, narrow pointed nose, and chiseled jaw gave him a ruggedly masculine appearance. The child of a biracial marriage—his father Caucasian and his mother African American—he was often confused for Hispanic or Middle Eastern.

Billy took his time considering his options, and finally came to the conclusion that he really didn't have any options.

"Okay," he said. "But you can't say anything, not even to your wife."

Travis frowned. "Don't w-worry. She left me. Three d-days ago, right after the FBI raided the militia headquarters."

Billy nodded understanding. "I'm sorry."

"Don't be. She'd been looking for a b-b-better man for a long time. One who could at least t-t-talk right."

Travis took a long draw from his beer. Finished, he squished the can with a satisfying crinkle of aluminum, expending a miniscule fraction of his pent-up humiliation and anger.

"Now, are you going to tell me what the job is?" he said.

Billy looked at him squarely in the eye, fixing his gaze.

"I'm going to finish the mission."

Billy didn't blink, and after many long moments, Travis replied, "You're serious."

"Damn right I am."

"How? You can't just w-walk up to the White House and off the p-p-president. I mean, you can't even get close enough to see the man."

"I can't. But *we* can."

Travis cocked his head. "You want me to fly you over the W-W-White House? Is that it?"

"Hell no. That would be suicide. They have Stingers, and probably other missiles on the roof, and a bunch of snipers. They'd have no problem shooting your slow-moving plane out of the sky."

"She may be slow," Travis said, "but she's highly m-m-maneuverable."

"They'll still shoot your ass out of the sky."

"Okay, genius. If we can't fly over the White House, then why do you want my plane?"

Billy paused, using the moment to weigh how much he trusted Travis. They'd met on the target range while in the militia, and developed a friendship through hours of drills and training exercises in the Idaho wilderness. Many of the other guys made fun of Travis behind his back because of his stutter, but it didn't bother Billy. Travis seemed like a nice guy, and he'd never lied or cheated—at least, not that Billy knew of.

Still, Billy had lived a hard life and survived many harsh lessons. His number one rule: never trust anyone—never.

"To get me close," Billy replied. "The rest, I'll tell you when it's time."

"The rest you'll t-t-tell me now, or it's no deal. You can go talk some other sucker out of his airplane. We're either in this together, or I'm not in at all."

Billy drew in a deep breath and slowly exhaled.

"How do I know you won't sell me out?" he said.

"It's up to you, m-man, but you called me. I'm an ex-con. I've been running around these mountains with a bunch of anti-government militia, shootin' rifles I ain't s-supposed to own. So tell me, why I would have a relationship with the FBI?"

Billy stood and walked a half-dozen paces to the edge of the Salmon River. There, he knelt and splashed some cold water on his face. He hadn't shaved in a week, and the facial hair still felt odd to his fingers.

With his back still to Travis, he said, "You know, I love these mountains. Here, a man is truly free."

"Yeah," Travis said. "I've spent m-more than ten years of my life in county jails and prison. When you've lived like that, you really understand what it means to be free. To go where you want, w-when you want to. To breathe fresh air and be surrounded by beauty rather than hate."

Billy turned to face the other man. "What were you in for?"

Travis had his knees pulled up and his arms clasped around his shins. His dishwater blond hair was stringy, looking greasy and unwashed. Which was pretty much in keeping with the rest of his appearance. His clothes hadn't been laundered in a good long time, and he smelled like he hadn't showered in a week. He was looking off to the side, toward the juncture of the two rivers.

"Armed r-robbery." His voice was soft, not like the voice of a man proudly proclaiming his accomplishments. "It was a s-small gas station and mini-mart in Boise. I was just a kid.

Nineteen years old. I'd dropped out of high school to support m-my girlfriend and our b-baby."

He shifted his arms, drawing his legs in closer to his chest, then continued.

"I'd worked there for t-ten months, pumping gas. The pay wasn't much, barely enough to pay rent and buy food. Had no car, so I walked to work. Our apartment stunk from the m-mold in the carpet, and the dog and cat piss. But it was our home. Then one day, this guy drives up in his Corvette and tells me to fill the t-t-tank. With p-premium, he says. And I did. He gives me a fifty, and I walked inside to ring it up, came back with his change. Then he starts screaming at m-me, saying I shortchanged him. He tells the m-manager that he gave me a Ben Franklin, and demands another f-fifty in change."

"Did you?" Billy said.

The simple question seemed to break Travis out of his trance.

"Huh?"

"Did you shortchange the man?"

"Hell no, I didn't!" Travis didn't stutter much when he was angry.

He calmed himself a bit, but the fire in his eyes still smoldered.

"I never cheated anyone! And I don't plan to start anytime soon."

"So what happened?" Billy said.

"The manager gave him fifty dollars from the till. Just to make him calm down, I thought. But at the end of my shift, the manager paid me my wages and told me not t-to come back."

"So you robbed the store."

Travis tilted his head down and nodded. "Used a t-toy gun that looked real enough."

"Why not get another job? Why did you have to rob the store?"

Travis snapped his head up, facing Billy with eyes that burned with bitterness and regret.

"Because when you don't have a GED, and w-when you talk like I do, no one w-wants to help you."

Billy stared back in silence. He understood what it was like to be alone—truly alone in a society where the rules were against you.

"I had to do something. For m-my girlfriend and my baby."

They sat there for a while, neither man saying another word. Billy knew the rest of the story, as if it were a movie he'd watched a dozen times. Travis was swiftly arrested, tried, and found guilty. The judge, prejudiced by Travis's lack of education and speech impediment, gave out a harsh sentence. Instead of taking care of its citizens, the system had thrown away another soul, a man whose real crime was being both poor and different.

"All right," Billy finally said. "So you do your time, and you get out of prison. Tell me, how do you end up owning an ultralight? I mean, those planes aren't cheap."

"I got l-lucky and got a job working for the general taking care of his property and the outbuildings. It's not really m-my plane, but I know how to fly it really good. It belongs to the militia. Or whatever is left of the organization. When the FBI r-raided the general's ranch, they arrested everyone. But not me. I slipped away." Travis displayed a proud smile.

After all the time Billy had spent with Travis, he never knew his story. Truth was, he never wanted to know. He didn't want to be close, because Billy knew that being close to someone was a vulnerability, a chink in his armor. Now that Travis had shared his history, it explained a lot, but not everything.

"If we do this," Billy said, "there's no going back. You do understand that?"

"Is that supposed to scare m-me or something? I've got nothing to go back to."

"You've done your time, and the militia is finished. You can go where you like. Start over, if you want."

Travis shook his head. Then he stood and squared his shoulders with Billy's.

"This country and the people who live here have done n-nothing for me. In their eyes, I'm a f-f-freak. I say we complete the mission. It's t-time for some real change."

CHAPTER 2

TRAVIS AND BILLY DROVE IN SHIFTS, stopping only for gas and fast food. At Billy's suggestion, Travis had showered and changed into clean clothes prior to leaving Idaho.

After clearing Denver, they took Interstate 70 across the Heartland, making good time with little traffic, the ultralight loaded on a trailer towed behind Travis's pickup. In the small city of Hays in central Kansas, Billy stopped to top up the gas tank and use the restroom. Travis took the wheel. He drove in silence for a short while.

Seeing Billy staring into the distance, out the side window, rather than sleeping, Travis said, "W-why?"

"Why what?" Billy said, without turning his head to face Travis.

"Why are you doing this?"

"I have my reasons."

"Yeah, but I d-deserve to know."

Billy turned his head. Travis had his eyes on the road, occasionally checking the mirror for trailing cars.

"Suppose you do," Billy replied. "Just like you, I've got a

score to settle with the system. Because of what they did to my mother and father."

Billy told the story of how his father was murdered in prison while serving a stiff sentence for possession of a small amount of marijuana. The judge, a middle-aged blonde with political ambitions, felt it would help her election bid if she threw the book at Billy's tattooed father.

"After that, it was just me and my mom. We lived in a rundown one-bedroom apartment in a poor neighborhood of Portland. I slept on the couch, and Mom had an old mattress on the bedroom floor. I don't know how she could do that, sleeping on the floor. The carpet was dirty and smelled of cat piss. Anyway, she cleaned local businesses at night, working hard to scrape together enough to live on. It was seldom sufficient."

Billy was staring out the side window again, as if in a trance. He continued, saying how he helped out by working odd jobs that usually paid cash, or collecting cans and bottles for the deposit money. Consequently, he was seldom at school. But that didn't mean he was stupid. He said how he especially liked history and mathematics, and had learned on his own by reading the textbooks.

One night, about seven months after his father died, he came home and gave his mother all the money he'd received from turning in three large bags full of foul-smelling cans and bottles. It was enough to buy a few groceries, maybe even some fresh fruits or vegetables.

"But I knew she would go to the corner market and spend the money on the cheapest bottle of red wine and some cans of beans, or maybe ramen noodles. I'm still sick of noodles and beans."

"Really?" Travis said. "R-ramen noodles and b-beans? I'd expect you'd at least have cheap burgers or tacos from the drive-through."

Billy shook his head. "You can't just go around spending money you don't have. I never wore new clothes. Mom knew a couple ladies who worked at the thrift store. That's where my shoes and clothes always came from. The ladies who worked there, they wouldn't charge mom the full price. They were just trying to help, but it hurt Mom. She was very proud and didn't want assistance. She never got food stamps. Said there was always someone else worse off who needed that help more than we did. Anyhow, that night she went to the corner market, I was stretched out on the couch, reading my history book from school. I guess I lost track of time. There was a knock at the door, and it was two police officers. I could tell they really didn't want to be there. They said my mother had been killed during an attempted robbery of the market. The gunman took her hostage, and the policeman just shot everyone—the robber and my mother."

"W-why would they do that?" Travis said.

Billy shrugged. "They said they didn't mean to, but she was in the way."

"That's terrible, man. I'm really s-sorry."

"Don't matter much now. I didn't have money to buy food, so I stole what I could. Within a month, I was kicked out of that crappy apartment. I had nowhere to go. No family, no friends. So I lived on the street." He turned toward Travis. "You know what the worst part of living on the streets is?"

Travis shook his head. "No."

"You can never get clean. So after a while, there's this stink of sweat and piss. And you don't notice it, because you're always smelling it. But everyone else does. And they know you're homeless. People cross the street to avoid walking near you. And they won't look you in the eye. I hated that. I was homeless for almost eighteen months, when a social worker found me and gave me a check. A big check."

"F-For what?" Travis said.

"It was from the City of Portland. The police department never said they were wrong in shooting my mother, but they paid me a bunch of money anyway. Probably just to keep me quiet. So I started to think about getting even."

"No kidding," Travis said. "I can understand why you'd w-want to kill that bitch judge. And the city m-mayor. But why Taylor?"

"I'll take care of the judge and city officials when the time is right. As for Taylor, he's the president. It's like he's the father of the government. And just like I lost my father and mother, it's time for the country to feel that pain."

⊕

Billy was wearing dark sunglasses and a hoody when they arrived in the Washington, DC Metro Area with a couple days to spare. He hoped the disguise, plus his full beard, would be enough to avoid recognition, at least by casual observers.

He insisted they forgo staying in a motel. Besides, it was less likely that someone would try to steal the trailer with the ultralight if both men were sleeping in the truck.

Every night, they moved to a different location. And on the evening of May 23rd, they parked near Marshall Hall boat ramp in Piscataway National Park. Just off Route 227, on the east side of the Potomac River, the boat ramp was about sixteen miles south of the White House, still well within the no-fly zone. But Billy had a plan to deal with that.

As the sun was setting, Travis conducted his pre-flight check of the Challenger ultralight. The aircraft was powered by a sixty-five-horsepower engine, and was equipped with floats, which is why they were at a boat dock.

"Everything is f-fine," Travis said.

"Is the gas tank full?" Billy replied.

"Yep. I t-topped it off before we left Idaho."

With the preparation completed, the men set two folding camp chairs next to the aircraft. Travis unhitched the trailer and then drove off to buy dinner. They agreed that Billy would guard the plane. The weather was mild, and the hooded sweatshirt was adequate to keep him comfortable.

Close to an hour later, Travis returned.

"S-sorry. There was a long line at the drive-through."

He opened the bag and then shared the contents with Billy—cheeseburger and French fries, with a large soda. Both men ate in silence. Twice, other people walked over to ask about the ultralight, but Billy remained silent and disinterested, keeping his head down, and Travis provided short answers. His message—Go away and stop bothering me—was received, and the visitors soon left.

Shortly after sunset, Travis returned to the truck and fell asleep. Alone, Billy sat in his chair and studied a map of Washington, DC on his phone, preferring the satellite image since that's what he would see tomorrow from the airplane. Over and over, he went through the steps, memorizing where they would take to the air, how far from the White House they would circle, where the Rose Garden was located, and how they would exit.

His plan required surprise to achieve success. He just hoped that no one had ever tried what he and Travis would do in the morning.

CHAPTER 3

THE DAY STARTED WITH AN EARLY morning departure from Portland, Oregon, for Washington, DC. During the flight, Governor Kathrine Bingham stayed busy reviewing notes and various reports as she prepared for an important meeting with the president and other Northwest governors. In her mid-fifties, she maintained a trim figure through regular exercise, and when she could carve time from her busy schedule, adventure vacations such as white-water rafting, kayaking, and rock climbing.

She'd inherited the office when the former governor resigned under accusations of self-dealing and abuse of power. Although Bingham had tried to build trust with the voters, allegations that she was misusing her official expense account for personal gain left a cloud over her administration. She hoped to use the forthcoming meeting with President Taylor to boost her approval rating and distract from the negative press.

Midway through the cross-country flight, she allowed some time to converse with Peter Savage and his fiancée, Kate Simpson. The governor also pulled two dog biscuits from a pocket, which Diesel, Peter's red pit bull, devoured.

The rhythmic hum of the engines on the executive jet—courtesy of a group of the governor's wealthy supporters—soon had Peter's eyelids closing. As he napped, Diesel was curled in the adjacent seat, snoring. The plane flight—not his first—didn't seem to bother the pit bull at all.

After Peter adopted Diesel from the shelter, the two bonded completely. As a result, Diesel was receptive to learning many commands—both voice and hand signals—and this ability to communicate, albeit rudimentary, allowed Diesel to interact in the human world at an unusually high level. Daily, Diesel would travel with Peter, completely under control without requiring restraint. But on some occasions, Diesel's martial training was called into play.

Sitting across from Peter, Kate used the quiet time to reflect on the past several days. So much had happened: the marriage proposal, the invitation from President Taylor. Growing up in a blue-collar family—her mother working retail, while her father had a factory job—she never imagined she was destined for anything more than a modest lifestyle. She graduated from Central Oregon Community College with an associate of general studies degree but decided not to advance her education further. While attending the college, she met Peter. And now her life was anything but pedestrian—it was perfect.

She gazed upon Peter's face. An adhesive bandage was pressed on the side of his forehead. The stitches had been removed only yesterday. The doctor proclaimed that the laceration, caused by a ricocheted bullet, was mending well. His left arm, wrapped in a soft cast, was still tender from a hairline crack in the ulna, and a full recovery was expected soon.

Kate thought about how peaceful he looked resting in the seat, his head tipped slightly backwards and supported by the headrest. Her gaze traced the hard edge of his jawline, and she noticed how his thick brown hair always seemed to fall in place. As she studied his features, Kate realized that what set him apart from other men she'd known was the simplicity of his appearance. There was no pretense, no charade in his countenance.

The lines on his face were less pronounced in his slumber. Still, two prominent horizontal creases on his forehead appeared over two vertical lines between his eyebrows—a T-shape, and a perfect symbol for this man who she knew to be true. And that was why she loved him so deeply. Because there was nothing complicated about him. Just an ordinary man who would do anything for his family and friends. There was no façade she had to break through. Peter Savage was everything he appeared to be, and his virtues and his failings were there for anyone to see, if they took the time to look.

A bump and jostle of the cabin was followed by an announcement from the co-pilot that some turbulence was expected for another half-hour. He encouraged his passengers to buckle their seat belts. Peter stirred at the interruption. He opened his eyes to find Kate studying him like he was some new puzzle to be solved.

His lips drew into a smile. "Is everything okay?"

"Couldn't be better." She leaned forward, and Peter met her halfway to share a kiss.

⊕

The landing at Ronald Reagan National Airport in mid-afternoon was smooth, and they quickly deplaned, each pulling a roller suitcase. It would be a short trip of only a couple days.

Governor Bingham was in the lead, flanked by two Oregon State Police officers from the Dignitary Protection Unit, one man and one woman. Peter and Kate followed closely. On a short leash, and trotting in between the newly engaged couple, was Diesel.

At the curbside, two black SUVs were waiting in a no-parking zone. The engines were idling and two suited men, replete with sunglasses, were standing alert, one beside each vehicle. Although a marked police cruiser was only thirty feet away, it paid little attention to the illegally parked cars.

As the group approached, a man near the lead SUV nodded acknowledgement to Governor Bingham. He stepped forward, closing the gap, and introduced himself.

"Agent Kolb of the Diplomatic Security Service. My partner over there is Agent Vaughn. We've been tasked with escorting you to Blair House."

He opened the door for the governor while one of her bodyguards placed all the luggage in the back. From a short distance, Peter observed a brief conversation between the DSS agent and the two DPU officers. Their voices were too soft for him to make out the words, but he saw one of Governor Bingham's bodyguards pat his waistline, presumably answering the question as to whether he was armed. Whatever he was carrying was covered by an oversized sweater.

Agent Vaughn loaded Peter and Kate's luggage into the SUV. Kate climbed in first, followed by Diesel dragging his leash, and then Peter. The interior of the vehicle was cool from the operating air conditioner, but Diesel was panting anyway. Vaughn glanced in the rearview mirror and took note of Peter's steel-gray eyes. He'd seen those eyes in other elite warriors, and knew there was more to this man than what had been shared in his briefing.

He said, "I can turn up the AC if you'd like?"

Kate shook her head, and Peter replied, "Thanks, but we're good. Diesel is just a little stressed, that's all. He'll calm down once we reach Blair House and I can take him for a short walk."

"Nice-looking dog," Vaughn said. "Must be pretty special.

Not that often that a canine is considered a visiting VIP. In fact, this is a first for me."

Peter and Kate rode in silence for the remainder of the drive, watching the sights pass by through the heavily tinted windows. The two SUVs traveled together, north on George Washington Parkway, then took Interstate 395 across the Potomac, and used 14th Street to cross the National Mall.

The Mall was teeming with people. Peter assumed many were tourists taking advantage of the shoulder season to avoid the crushing crowds who would be visiting the monuments and museums once school was out for summer. But there were also a fair number of joggers as well as professionals dressed in business attire, strolling along. All, no doubt, taking advantage of the sunny day and mild temperatures. In another month, the oppressive heat, combined with high humidity, would turn the city into a sauna.

After passing the White House on the left, the pair of SUVs eased to a stop in front of the stately house. The presidential guest house comprised a central beige building that was flanked by brick structures, the result of four separate townhomes being combined into the one building.

The section of Pennsylvania Avenue in front of Blair House was blocked to normal vehicle traffic, creating a pedestrian walkway. While the governor stood next to the SUV, absorbing the sights, Peter approached her.

"Pretty impressive," he said.

She raised her eyebrows. "You got that right. An overnight stay at the president's guest house is extremely exclusive. You know, they don't even allow tours of Blair House. This is a treat."

"Indeed." Peter gazed up to the US flag hanging over the front entrance. "This still doesn't seem real to me."

Bingham chuckled. "Well, believe me, this is as real as it gets."

Peter smiled, and Kate walked up to his side with Diesel, his leash slack.

Bingham said, "I hope you and Kate will excuse me, but I have a full agenda today preparing for my meeting with the president later this evening."

"Of course," Peter said.

Kate said, "Other governors from the Northwest will also participate?"

"That's right. The governors from Washington and Idaho. We plan to cover a range of issues important to our states, including the huge income and social gap between urban and rural populations, and funding shortfalls. Ever since the downfall of the timber industry, there's been a shortage of tax revenues that were tied to it."

"Good luck with your meeting," Kate said. "I hope some good comes from it."

While Governor Bingham was escorted inside, Peter and Kate stood in awe at the base of the steps. With Blair House behind them, they looked across Pennsylvania Avenue to the Eisenhower Office building. Diagonally to the left stood the White House and the immense surrounding grounds.

Agent Vaughn said, "You can go in and get yourselves unpacked. I believe the staff has you staying in Mrs. Truman's Bedroom. Someone will show the way."

"Why don't you go ahead," Peter told Kate. "I'm going to take a short walk with Diesel."

"Okay." She leaned close and kissed Peter on the cheek, catching him off guard. "Have I ever told you that I love you?"

"You have." He wore a mischievous smile. "But I never tire of hearing it."

⊕

After unpacking, one of the resident staff members gave

Peter and Kate a tour of the guest house. With it being more than 60,000 square feet, and having 120 rooms, Peter thought it was more a mansion than a guest house. After the tour, the couple took Diesel on a stroll around the White House. Kate spoke of the wedding planning, which had only just begun. Peter tried his best not to make fun of her work, which Kate clearly took seriously. For Peter, all he needed to know was where to be, and when.

After finally overcoming his fear of rejection and proposing to Kate only nine days ago, he felt a wild mix of emotions. He was overwhelmed with his love for her, and giddy with the idea of sharing the rest of his life with her. He thought these emotions had died, vanished when his first wife, Maggie, had passed years earlier. Until recently, the ghost of Maggie seemed omnipresent, haunting him with memories of what they'd shared. But now, that ghost had been exorcised from his soul. He felt at peace knowing that Maggie would want him to be happy—and he was happy, for the first time in a very long time.

It was late afternoon when they returned to Blair House and retired to Ross Garden to share a loveseat. Being behind the house, the garden was secluded, surrounded by the brick walls of neighboring buildings. The garden itself was immaculately maintained and in full bloom.

A waiter brought a bowl of water with floating ice cubes for Diesel, and then delivered cocktails and hors d'oeuvres on a silver tray.

"I could get used to this." Kate drew her lips into a smile of contentment.

Peter wrapped his hand around hers, and in his best impersonation of Russell Crowe as an Englishman, he said, "All I can offer, my lady, is a roof over your head, a meal when you hunger, and my heart."

"And with those gifts, I'll be the richest woman in the world." She laid her head on his shoulder.

They sat there in silent contentment for many long minutes, each thinking about the possibilities the future offered, and happy to share the present.

After an hour, and two more cocktails later, they dined in the Lee Dining Room. Like the other rooms they'd seen, the formal room was exquisitely decorated. In the center of the room, the antique mahogany table was surrounded by six chairs, although it would only be Peter and Kate at the table— Governor Bingham was still working with the other governors.

While Peter enjoyed a porterhouse steak grilled to perfection, and Kate had fillet of sole, Diesel was given a range of beef trimmings mixed with peas and diced carrots.

"You're going to spoil him," Peter told the waiter, earning an ear-to-ear grin in reply.

After sharing a bottle of 2014 Frog's Leap Merlot from Napa Valley, they took Diesel out for one more walk before returning to their suite. After settling the pit bull down on a thick foam pad covered in terry cloth, courtesy of the staff, Peter dug into his daypack and pulled out a James Rollins novel.

"What do you think you're doing with that book?" Kate said.

"Just going to read a bit. Kowalski's in a tight spot, and I can't wait to see how he gets out of it."

"Can't wait, huh?" She wrapped her arms around Peter's neck and kissed him, softly at first, and then passionately.

Peter dropped the book on the floor. "It can wait."

CHAPTER 4

FOLLOWING BREAKFAST, DSS Agents Kolb and Vaughn drove all of the visitors across the street to the White House, and stopped under the portico at the West Wing. Peter and Kate felt refreshed following a good night's sleep, but Governor Bingham had bags under her eyes that her makeup could not cover. No doubt she had worked late into the night.

Peter wore slacks and a lightweight sport coat over a polo shirt. Kate had skillfully applied makeup to hide the angry red line on his forehead, all the way to his hair line. His left arm was wrapped in an elastic bandage, hidden by the jacket sleeves.

An officer of the United States Secret Service Uniformed Division was standing at a podium, checking the IDs of invited guests and confirming their invitation. He wore a short-sleeve, pressed white shirt, and black trousers, with black loafers. A radio was fastened to his utility belt, with the mic clipped to his shoulder strap.

Peter and Kate stood before the officer and presented their IDs while Governor Bingham held back with her two bodyguards. The officer returned the IDs, checked his list, and gave them visitor badges.

He said, "The dog is not allowed to proceed."

"Excuse me?" Peter said.

Sensing a potential conflict brewing, Bingham stepped forward to stand beside Kate.

Peter was holding Diesel's leash, and presently the canine was sitting beside his master, his amber eyes gazing up at the police officer.

"You and Miss Simpson are free to enter. But there is nothing on my guest list about a dog."

Peter said, "Well then call—"

"Excuse me, Officer," the governor said in her most pleasant and diplomatic tone. "Both Mr. Savage and his dog, Diesel, are to receive the Presidential Medal of Freedom this morning."

"I'm sorry, ma'am. I have Mr. Peter Savage on my guest list, but no dog. I'm just following procedure."

One of the Dignitary Protection Unit officers stepped forward and joined the escalating debate.

"This is Governor Bingham," he said. "You will address her respectfully, as Governor."

Bingham turned to her bodyguard and placed a hand on his forearm.

"It's okay," she said.

The White House officer must have decided tensions were rising, because he keyed the mic and began talking on his radio.

Kate leaned toward the man. "I was on the phone call with President Taylor when he specifically invited my fiancée *and* Diesel be present so they could be recognized. Do you know what they did?"

As the commotion ensued, no one was paying attention to Diesel, who stood, walked to the end of his leash, and then raised his leg and peed on the pant leg and shoe of the officer. As the warm liquid soaked through his trousers and sock, he looked down, then jerked his leg back and swore.

Peter and both of the governor's bodyguards craned their necks to look around the podium, then all three burst into laughter. Peter caught his breath just long enough to call Diesel.

Over the mirth, the officer's radio screeched the reply to his query.

"Mr. Savage and his pet canine, Diesel, are both confirmed as honored guests."

The officer shook his foot while replying, "Roger that," then tipped his head toward the doors opening into the West Wing.

Once out of earshot, Kate told Peter, "That police officer is a pompous ass. I clearly heard President Taylor, and he said both you and Diesel were invited."

"Don't get worked up, Kate," said Governor Bingham. "He's just doing his job. Still, I believe Diesel didn't think too highly of him."

"Yeah," Peter smiled. "He's a good judge of character."

The group headed toward the West Wing and then exited to the Rose Garden. There, Peter saw Commander James Nicolaou. Peter and Jim had a strong friendship going back decades, to their youth.

He caught Jim's eye and nodded. Jim broke away from his interview with a member of the media and strode to his friend. He extended his hand, and Peter readily accepted.

"Jim, this is my fiancée, Kate."

Jim shook her hand. "It's a pleasure to meet you. I feel like I know you already, from what Peter has shared."

Kate gave Peter a coy look. "Talking about me behind my back?"

"I told Jim about our wedding plans and—"

"Peter is fortunate to have you in his life," Jim said. "And I'm looking forward to the wedding. Nothing short of a nuclear exchange will keep me from being there."

They all laughed. After the banter, Kate already felt at ease with Jim.

She said, "I understand you two have been friends for a long time."

"Yes, ma'am. Peter and I attended Hiram Johnson High School together in Sacramento. When Peter went on to college, I joined the Navy. We reconnected several years ago."

Peter said, "Jim commands the Strategic Global Intervention Team, or SGIT."

"Ah," Kate said, still facing Jim. "So you are the reason my fiancé disappears for weeks at a time, only to come back bloodied and bruised."

The smile had left her face, and her eyes reflected a brewing storm.

Jim held his hands up in mock surrender. "I plead the fifth." Then he laughed to lower the tension. "I'd like to introduce you both to Colonel Pierson. He's my boss, and the founding force behind SGIT."

The trio crossed the lawn to a distinguished-looking military officer with four rows of campaign and service ribbons above the left breast pocket of his dress uniform. Pierson sensed their approach and turned to face them. He was just shy of six feet, with silver hair parted on the right. His face bore the many deep creases earned from years of command. Presently, he wore a stern expression, and Peter assumed that was the resting state of his visage.

"Excuse me, sir," Jim said. "I would like to introduce Mr. Peter Savage and his fiancée, Kate Simpson."

Colonel Pierson drew a broad and genuine smile. "Mr. Savage. We finally meet."

They shook hands, and Peter noted how firm the colonel's grip was.

"Yes, sir," he replied.

Pierson faced Kate. "Ma'am, it is truly a pleasure to make your acquaintance."

Kate smiled. "Why is it I feel you all are sharing a secret that none of you will let me in on?"

Peter averted his gaze to the ground, and Jim turned toward his commanding officer. Only Pierson held Kate's inquisitive gaze.

"You're right, ma'am. There is much that Mr. Savage has been involved in—unofficially, of course—with Commander Nicolaou's team at SGIT. I regret that, due to reasons of national security, none of us are allowed to share those accounts with you."

"I see," she said, but clearly she didn't agree with Colonel Pierson's assessment.

⊕

If the news reports were to be believed, the ceremony in the Rose Garden would begin in forty minutes. Billy and Travis pushed the Challenger ultralight down the boat ramp and into the Potomac River. The aircraft was built with the wing over the cockpit, and tandem seating for two. Although it was equipped with a plexiglass windscreen, the sides of the cockpit were open. Seated behind Travis, Billy had unobstructed views out both sides of the aircraft.

They motored slowly up the Potomac, just like any other recreational boater. Only, their boat had wings. With twin V-shaped wakes trailing the pontoons, the unusual watercraft was an attention-getter. Many speed boats and party barges passed the slower float plane, with the bathing-suit clad passengers shouting and waving at Travis and Billy.

They motored at a measured pace, the pusher engine behind Billy purring at moderate revolutions. On the water, movement was unrestricted. Once Travis took to the air, it would be a different story.

Commercial jetliners flew in low and directly overhead, their engines roaring against an otherwise tranquil morning. The approach to Reagan National was the narrow corridor above the slow-moving water. Airspace on either side of the river was restricted, and Joint Base Andrews was close by, in the event that enforcement of the no-fly zone was required.

Following 9-11, the military was much more prepared to put armed F16s into the air to defend against a threat to the capital. Even if that threat was, again, a passenger plane. No pilot wanted that mission, but they were all prepared to execute if given the order.

Inside the Challenger ultralight, Travis was listening to ATC chatter from Reagan National, while Billy was following a local news channel on a portable radio. The coverage had just switched to the White House, with a reporter in attendance at the Rose Garden. She was describing the scene, filling airtime with nothing of significance while waiting for President Taylor to arrive and begin the award presentation.

The float plane crossed under the Interstate 495 bridge, and Billy leaned forward and tapped Travis on the shoulder.

"We're just under six miles from the White House, and the medal ceremony hasn't started yet. Better slow down a bit or do circles."

Travis nodded and pulled back on the throttle. The plane slowed, and Travis maneuvered to the east side of the river, staying out of the way of faster boats.

After motoring almost a mile north of the I-495 bridge, the river widened. The east bank gave way to a tributary stream named Oxon Run. Travis reduced the engine speed to idle and began steering in a large circle. The plan had been drilled into him yesterday. He was to loiter at the mouth of the small bay. The land south of Oxon Run, all the way to I-495, was wooded and undeveloped.

Although the event was scheduled to begin at 10:00 a.m., Billy knew that to be an educated guess. The vagaries of the president's schedule made it near to impossible to pin down the start of an event that was really about nothing more urgent than reinforcing public relations.

Once Billy gave Travis the signal, he would power up the engine and fly the Challenger ultralight at a low altitude, just clearing buildings, trees, and power lines. Initially, Travis didn't like this part of the plan. But when Billy explained the importance of staying off the military radar at nearby bases, as well as the radar that was sure to be atop the roof of the White House, along with short-range ground-to-air missiles, Travis nodded agreement.

The news reporter at the Rose Garden droned on about the assembled guests. She noted that three governors were in the front row. And on the stage were the two recipients—Peter Savage and his dog, Diesel, along with Peter's fiancée, Kate Simpson. The reporter pointed out again that a dog had never before received the highest civilian award from the president.

As the minutes slowly passed without President Taylor arriving, it was clear the reporter was running out of useful commentary. Ever resourceful and drawing from experience, she resorted to describing the audience, pointing out high-ranking members of the military, and many members of the president's cabinet. She also noted, with a touch of irritation in her tone, that the audience was getting restless. Paper programs were folded by many and used as makeshift fans under the morning sun. Then she commented on the vivid blue of Kate's conservative dress, as well as the pale-gray suit jacket worn by Peter.

⊕

A woman from the White House staff corralled Peter and

Kate, informing them that they should be in their seats on the stage.

Peter, Kate, and Diesel were directed to chairs on the low platform behind the speaker's podium. Governor Bingham took an assigned chair in the middle of the front row. The other Northwest governors were seated on either side of her. Other dignitaries filled the second and third rows, with the invited press taking the remainder of the seats. Cameras, mounted high on tripods to provide an unobstructed view of the ceremony, were at the rear, behind the seated guests.

The security detail, most belonging to the Secret Service, but including bodyguards for the three state governors, were milling around the perimeter of the assembled guests and reporters.

Everyone waited for President Taylor to arrive. There were murmurs, and the air was charged with anticipation. Peter sat with his palms on his pant legs, trying to keep them dry.

For his part, Diesel didn't seem fazed at all. He sat still next to Peter, his tongue protruding just a bit as he panted to stay cool.

Without warning, President Taylor entered the Rose Garden from the Oval Office. Everyone rose as he stepped up onto the dais and then stood behind the speaker's podium. He paused, scanning the crowd, and then made eye contact with the row of governors while his speech was loaded onto the autocue. The words would appear simultaneously on two angled glass screens, each mounted to the end of a stand and positioned slightly to either side of the podium. Whichever direction President Taylor cast his gaze, he would be able to read the prepared address.

"Ladies and gentlemen," he said, "and distinguished governors. All too often, the job of the president involves difficult choices. Rarely a day goes by when I'm not required to make a decision that affects dozens, if not hundreds or thousands, of people. Sometimes these judgements have life and death consequences. I am happy to say that this ceremony is not one of those times, although it springs from terribly frightening events that occurred not quite two weeks ago, when Air Force One was assaulted in an all-out attack meant to kill yours truly and decapitate the United States government.

"Were it not for the heroic actions of many, but one man in particular, the militia that launched that attack would have, in all probability, succeeded. That man is Peter Savage."

President Taylor turned sideways and extended his hand toward Peter, who stood to applause. After the ovation quieted, Taylor continued while Peter remained standing.

"Awarding the Presidential Medal of Freedom is always an extraordinary event. But today, this ceremony is unique in two respects. Never before has a president been afforded the honor of bestowing the Nation's highest civilian award upon one person for thwarting a presidential assassination attempt. I am privileged and humbled to be standing here today to recognize the man who most certainly saved my life. But what makes this observance exceptionally special, is that Mr. Savage was aided by the gallant actions of Diesel, his red pit bull."

A chorus of laughter rippled through the audience, followed by applause.

"In fact, I am told by those who were in a position to observe the battle, including Kathrine Bingham, Governor of the great state of Oregon, that Diesel demonstrated extreme determination and discipline when facing overwhelming forces. If Diesel were a person, I'd say he exhibited remarkable valor risking his own life to save others. Some of the facts surrounding the militia attack on Air Force One on May twelfth have made it into the public record. Many other facts have not, including the valiant actions of this human-canine pair. In time, I believe the full story will come to light once the investigation has been completed. In the meantime, the attorney general has reminded me to be sparing in making public all the details of that horrific day. Thus, I cannot share the whole story at this time. However, I expect an entire wing of my future presidential library to be devoted to this failed assassination attempt, and the role played by these two heroes. I have no doubt that the documents to be stored there will provide rich material for historians, years from now."

Again, a round of laughter emerged from the assembled guests.

"Nevertheless, I believe I can be quite comfortable saying that their ingenuity in the face of superior firepower and near certain death, and the brave actions of Mr. Savage and Diesel, allowed most of the crew and passengers onboard Air Force One to escape. Sadly, many did not survive that day, including Vice President Vince Nagashima; Speaker Dorothy Maybridge; and Colonel Norton, Captain of Air Force One."

The president paused for a moment of reflection.

"This nation, its government and citizens, owes an enormous debt to Mr. Savage. And so it is with great pleasure that I am bestowing the Presidential Medal of Freedom, with distinction, to Peter Savage and to Diesel."

A standing ovation followed on the heels of the president's words, and continued for two full minutes. Once the assembled guests and reporters were seated again, President Taylor asked Peter to come to the podium with Diesel. While Peter stood, Diesel sat on his haunches, and president Taylor leaned over and slipped the blue ribbon over the canine's head. The wide ribbon slipped down Diesel's neck and came to rest against his broad shoulders, the heavy white star centered on his chest.

Next, the president clasped the ribbon behind Peter's neck, then shook his hand. Although no one in the audience could hear it, President Taylor thanked Peter again.

The president returned to the podium and continued his address while the honorees remained as they were.

"There is a personal footnote to this story that I want to share, because it is an important lesson for all who value freedom. Ten days ago, I phoned Mr. Savage to express my gratitude, and to invite him to this ceremony."

Oh God, Kate thought. *He's going to embarrass me with that phone conversation.*

"During that phone call, I had the pleasure to speak with Miss Kate Simpson, and I learned that she and Mr. Savage are engaged to be married."

Clapping filled the pause in his speech.

He continued, "Kate, will you please step forward and stand next to your future husband?"

With flushed cheeks, she stood next to Peter and slid her arm around his, pulling in close enough that their shoulders were touching.

"This remarkable young woman had the courage to remind me that, time and again, it is a few extraordinary individuals who act spontaneously and selflessly for the benefit of others. Many times, these individuals risk it all, and sometimes the price they pay is dear. It is not fair. But I believe this is a defining characteristic of Americans. This is the primary reason that I chose to award the Medal of Freedom, *with distinction,* to this extraordinary gentleman and his—"

Taylor's words caught in his throat as a searing pain lanced across the side of his neck, just above his shoulder. He slapped his right hand over the injury. His eyes, registering confusion and surprise, scanned the people sitting and standing in the Rose Garden, but nothing seemed out of the ordinary.

Two of the nearest Secret Service agents advanced toward the president. The first one to reach him wrapped an arm around Taylor's shoulder while the other agent closed from the opposite side.

Had the President been stricken ill?

Peter overheard President Taylor say, "I don't know. Just, suddenly there was a burning pain across my neck." He removed his hand, and it was red with blood.

While Peter watched, there was a sudden pop, like a firecracker, and one of the Secret Service agents fell to the stage.

CHAPTER 5

BILLY'S HEART RATE QUICKENED when he heard the reporter's words: "And President Taylor has finally arrived. Everyone is standing as he's walking onto the stage."

Applause carried over the radio transmission, threatening to override the reporter's own words.

Billy tapped Travis again. "Let's go. The president's on the stage."

The engine roared to life, and the little plane shot forward. Before Billy realized it, the craft was airborne. Travis flew north, only feet above the surface of the river. Soon, Reagan National Airport was on the left and the Anacostia River branched to the right. Travis turned, following the smaller waterway. The White House was 2.3 miles to their left. As Travis gained altitude, Billy shouldered a futuristic carbine so radically new that it was the only sample in existence. The weapon was fitted with an 8x to 80x variable magnification March rifle scope. The exceptionally high magnification was necessary since the weapon fired a laser pulse, lethal at thousands of yards.

At five hundred feet, Billy found the White House and the West Wing out the left side of the ultralight. The laser weapon was powered by a replaceable battery. A tiny LED on the stock where only the shooter could see it was either green if the battery charge was good, or red if the battery was drained of power. Right now, the light illuminated green, but Billy had no idea how many shots he could get off before the battery was dead.

"You have to go higher," Billy shouted to be heard over the whipping wind and roaring engine.

The plane climbed again, leveling off at one thousand feet. Travis was flying north, and slowly banking so the White House would be off the left side of the aircraft, allowing Billy time to steady his aim.

At the highest scope magnification, Billy saw the guests in the Rose Garden as if they were only fifty yards away. But the magnified image was jittery, causing the crosshairs to bounce all around the target. He rested his right arm and the weapon against the airframe. The image of President Taylor filled his sight picture. He was standing behind a lectern, addressing the audience. Billy hurried to move the crosshairs onto the president and squeezed the trigger.

There was no explosion accompanying the firing of the laser gun. Instead, Billy felt a small vibration in both hands as a mechanical striker within the weapon slapped a steel plate. Had it not been for the noise of the aircraft, Billy would have also heard a faint snap, like a breaking matchstick.

With no recoil, time wasn't wasted to reacquire the target, and Billy fired a second shot before his sightline was blocked by trees.

CHAPTER 6

THE POP!, SOUNDING LIKE A FIRECRACKER, and simultaneous with the Secret Service agent going down, was instantly recognized by Peter. He launched forward, wrapping his arms around the president and the second agent as if he were executing a football tackle. The trio collapsed to the deck, triggering a panic as the audience en mass tried to exit the Rose Garden for the safety of the West Wing and the White House.

The jarring collision sent a sharp spike of pain radiating from Peter's healing arm bone. Commander Nicolaou and Colonel Pierson were shielding some of the cabinet members with their bodies, pinning them to the lawn. Three more Secret Service agents took to the stage, surrounding the president, who was still held down by Peter. The agents all produced H&K MP7 machine pistols which hung from their shoulders by a nylon strap. Peter overheard radio chatter indicating the agents were communicating with snipers on the roof of the White House. No one had spotted the gunman. And then two more pops in rapid succession and two agents went down, blood flowing from chest wounds.

Peter shouted, "Kate! Get down!"

But she was already laying on the deck.

Then Peter said, "Diesel—guard!"

The pit bull had bonded to Kate some time ago when she became a regular part of Peter's life, and the command probably wasn't necessary. But Peter issued it without thinking.

The back edge of the stage was only ten feet from Kate, and she methodically crawled toward it. Diesel was pacing her, mimicking her movements. In a handful of seconds, she was at the edge. She rolled off onto the lawn and then shimmied under the deck, the canine by her side.

Pop! The third agent fell, the machine pistol still within his grip. His face was covered in blood and gore, the top portion of his skull blown away.

Another pop!, though not as sharp as the previous ones, and Peter felt a searing pain in his leg. He hazarded a glance and saw smoke wafting upward from his pant leg near his left calf. He was able to move his foot, and concluded that his calf muscle was still functioning.

"We have to get the president to cover," Peter said to the agent helping to shield President Taylor.

"If we get the president onto his feet, he'll be killed," the agent replied.

Peter cast his gaze across the stage. Nothing but chairs, a few bodies, and the dais. *That's it—the podium.* He twisted his prone body around until he could reach up and grasp near the top of the wood stand. With a grunt, he pulled, leveraging his weight to destabilize the dais. It crashed to the deck with a thud, missing the agent's head by inches.

"Give me a hand," Peter said. "We need to the pull the stand over the president."

"Bullets will go right through that," the agent said. "It won't offer any protection."

"Yes, it will. Those aren't bullets being fired. They're energy pulses. And they won't go through the wood podium."

Together, Peter and the Secret Service agent edged the dais parallel with the president's horizontal figure, taking care to shield the president with their own bodies.

When the positioning was done, the agent said, "Mr. President. We are going to roll the stand onto you."

He was lying face down, with his hands covering his head.

"You'll feel the weight, but it won't hurt you."

"I understand," Taylor replied.

Peter and the agent rolled the dais onto the president's back, retreating as they did so.

"It's heavy," Taylor said.

His head was beneath a shelf near the top of the stand, and all the mass was distributed across his back, buttocks, and legs.

"Are you okay, sir?" Peter said.

"I'll be fine until you can get me out of here."

Peter raised his head, peering across the makeshift shield, across the Rose Garden, but he failed to see any assailants. And then, right before him, two points of gray smoke erupted from the wooden dais, immediately followed by seconds of yellow flame before the fire naturally extinguished.

"Stay down," Peter said to the agent.

The bodyguard was on his radio, his voice clearly communicating frustration that the snipers on the roof of the White House had been unable to find whoever was shooting at them.

"Damnit," the agent said. "We can't stay here indefinitely. We have to get Eagle to safety."

"We have no targets," the voice said over the agent's earpiece.

Neither Peter nor the president could hear that message.

"No audio signature either, no report. We can't triangulate to the sniper's position."

Minutes ticked by without anything eventful happening.

Finally, Peter ventured his head up again. Nothing.

He said, "I think it's safe now. Whoever was shooting has probably left."

"You can't be sure," the agent said.

Peter rose to a knee and then stood. He looked around.

"Kate? Kate?"

"Over here."

Her voice filled him with relief. He turned and saw her face rising above the edge of the stage. And then Diesel jumped up and trotted to his master.

While Peter helped to lift the podium off the president, the surviving Secret Service agent rushed him to the Oval Office, where he would be safe behind bulletproof glazing while security regrouped.

A swarm of Secret Service agents flooded into the Rose Garden and secured the perimeter. Peter rushed to Kate. He hopped off the stage, favoring his left leg, and embraced her.

"I was worried you'd been shot."

"I'm fine." She held him tight.

He winced at the pressure on his arm.

"You all right?" she said.

"Yeah, just a bump."

Together, they looked to where the audience had been seated ten minutes earlier. The chairs were all empty, many knocked over and scattered as people had stampeded to get away from the assassination attempt. Several of the expensive TV cameras were also laying on the lawn.

"I don't understand." Kate rushed the words between breaths, her voice shaky.

"Someone tried to kill President Taylor."

"But how? There weren't any gunshots. And the Secret Service didn't shoot back."

Peter sighed. "Whoever did this was a long distance away.

And they were using the energy weapon that was stollen from my shop two weeks ago."

Kate gasped and placed her hand over her mouth.

Peter said, "That weapon was used by the militia—the Cascadia Independence Movement—to assassinate the vice president and Speaker of the House the same day they also tried to murder the president."

From the West Colonnade, a voice called, "Mr. Savage, please come inside."

It was the same Secret Service agent who had helped Peter protect President Taylor.

Holding Kate's hand, Peter took a step forward and nearly collapsed. He caught his balance with help from Kate.

She called out, "He's injured. We need help!"

CHAPTER 7

TRAVIS BANKED SHARPLY and completed a second gun run, during which Billy fired the PEAP six more times before the charge indicator light turned red. He was out of juice—no electrons to fire the lasing mechanism.

"D-did you get him?" Travis shouted over his shoulder.

Billy lowered the carbine. "I can't be certain. I had good hits on three Secret Service agents, but the president was still shielded. Even with the magnification of the scope, I couldn't see if he was still alive. I'm pretty sure I hit him, though, on the first shot." He doubled-checked the weapon. "The battery is dead. You better get us down, and fast. Those shoulder-fired air defense missiles they have on the roof of the White House can shoot us down easily."

The small ultralight dropped altitude so fast that Billy thought he might lose his breakfast. It was like being at the highest point on a roller coaster and then dropping at a 120-degree dive. Seconds later, Travis leveled out and Billy estimated they were flying well above the normal cruise speed of ninety-five miles per hour. A couple more sharp banks that had Billy gripping the airframe to keep from being tossed from side to side, and they were flying level about ten feet above the

Anacostia River and then merging over the Potomac.

Although Billy couldn't hear it, the air traffic controllers at Reagan National were fuming that whoever was flying the small aircraft was also not responding to their persistent calls. But as soon as he dropped to the deck, the radar could no longer track him. They knew he was over Washington, nearly at the epicenter of the no-fly zone, but what he was doing and where he had departed to, the radar evidence would offer no clues.

Travis hopped up and over the I-495 bridge. Otherwise, he stayed just above the surface of the river, all the way back to the Marshall Hall boat launch. There, he reduced speed and executed a perfect water landing.

"You really think they have m-missiles on the roof of the White House?" He taxied the plane toward shore.

"They'd be stupid not to. If it were me, I'd have a whole bunch of the latest and greatest Stingers. Maybe some Javelins, too."

Billy instructed Travis to beach the ultralight near the boat ramp. Anyone watching might think they planned to go out again later in the day. Instead, they strolled to Travis's truck, unhitched the trailer, and drove away.

"I still d-don't think it was necessary to ditch the plane," Travis said.

"Trust me," Billy replied. "The feds aren't stupid. You were high enough that radar had to have picked us up, even if only intermittently. They'll soon piece it together and figure out that someone was shooting at the president from the sky. And the radar will tell them your air speed, which is way too slow for a conventional aircraft. So by process of elimination, they'll suspect it was an ultralight. And then your truck driving across the country with your small plane in tow will be a red flag attracting a lot of attention we don't want. Got it?"

Travis frowned and merged onto Maryland Route 210 South.

"You d-don't have to talk down to me. I'm not st-st-stupid."

Billy ignored the complaint. His mind was replaying recent events. He clearly saw the president raise a hand to his neck following the first shot. Was it fatal? Two agents crowded the president, and then Billy was certain he killed one of them. And then the guy getting the award tackled the president and the other agent to the ground. Even if the laser pulse struck the side of Taylor's neck, it could have severed the carotid artery. *Maybe President Taylor bled to death on the stage.* Maybe that's why he didn't see the Secret Service get the president to his feet and usher him to safety.

"Just keep driving," Billy said. "Follow the signs to I-95 and Richmond. In a day and a half, we'll be back in Idaho."

CHAPTER 8

INSIDE THE OVAL OFFICE, Peter and Kate sat side by side on an antique Chippendale sofa. A member of the president's medical staff had examined the injury to Peter's left leg—a nearly two-inch long burn that cut through the subdermal layer of tissue. The laceration was perfectly straight.

"We can put a bandage over that," she said, "but I'd prefer a few sutures to pull the edges of tissue together. It will heal faster that way."

Peter consented, and after lidocaine shots to numb the injury, the doctor stitched it and covered it with an adhesive bandage. The whole procedure took less than five minutes.

That was forty minutes ago.

The elastic bandage wrapped around his left forearm to lend support to the healing ulna had been removed and reapplied. The pain had diminished almost completely, and Peter declined to have an X-ray taken.

They sat there alone, other than Diesel. A silver tray of snacks—various finger sandwiches and cookies, plus coffee, hot water, and an assortment of tea bags—had been delivered and placed on the coffee table while Peter was having his wound attended to.

Neither he nor Kate were hungry, but Peter offered a finger sandwich to Diesel. It had some type of white cheese, and what looked like sliced turkey with mayonnaise. Diesel gulped it down, and Peter gave him a second one. He was still petting Diesel's head when President Taylor entered. The president was followed by two men.

Kate and Peter started to stand, but the president motioned with a hand.

"Please, just relax. You've both been through a lot."

Peter raised an eyebrow. The flesh-colored bandage on the president's neck was clearly visible, but from a distance would be difficult to discern.

Taylor lowered himself into a leather club chair opposite his guests. He noticed Peter staring at his neck.

"It's nothing to worry about," he said. "A grazing wound. Should be healed within a week or two." He nodded at Peter's leg. "I've been told you were also wounded. Several stitches?"

Peter nodded. "It's nothing."

President Taylor took in his guest, noting the wrapping on his left arm and the slit trouser leg where a dressing covered his most recent wound.

"Seems like you're collecting a lot of injuries while protecting me." He paused, seeming to reflect on his words. "Maybe I should have you on the White House medical policy?"

Kate and Peter chuckled.

"This is my chief of staff, Gavin Gutowsky." The president indicated the balding middle-aged man with wire-rim glasses, seated in the chair to his right. "And this," he motioned to his left, "is Grant McLuskie. Grant is the Secret Service special agent in charge. That means he's responsible for security at the White House."

In contrast to the academic appearance of the chief of staff, Grant McLuskie gave the impression of a seasoned warrior.

From the moment he entered the room, he focused on Peter and Kate, like he was sizing them up: ally or enemy? He did not have the belly roll common to many men who wore a suit as a uniform. The only visible concession to his age was the gray hair at his temples.

Pleasantries were exchanged, and Peter didn't sense any egos at play.

President Taylor said, "I regret that this is how your first visit to the White House turned out. A terrible tragedy. Grant has shared with me that four of his agents were killed. I'm glad to report that none of the members of the audience were injured."

Peter said, "I'm sorry about your agents. Commander Nicolaou and Governor Bingham, they're okay?"

President Taylor nodded.

Peter couldn't help but notice how remarkably composed President Taylor was. He'd just witnessed four murders. He himself was wounded and nearly killed. Even under intense stress, he had a knack for remaining calm and tactful.

"We all know what killed those men," Taylor's gaze bore into Peter. "What wounded you and nearly took my head off."

"It was the PEAP carbine," Peter said, surprised that the security detail had figured it out so quickly.

"What's a PEAP carbine?" Gutowsky said.

Clearly, he hadn't been read-in on all security matters.

"It stands for pulsed energy antipersonnel," Peter replied. "My company developed the prototype with funding from DARPA."

McLuskie turned his head to the chief of staff. "What Mr. Savage invented is a shoulder-fired laser gun."

"Under less dire circumstances, I'd think you were joking."

Peter's shoulders slumped. "I assure you, Mr. Gutowsky, this is no joke. Together, with my chief engineer, we developed the prototype. Just over two weeks ago, following a successful live-fire demonstration, the carbine was stolen." He turned to the president. "That's the part I don't get, sir. I mean, that was a one-off prototype. There were no others. And based on what little information has been shared with me, that gun was used to commit multiple murders in Boise only three days after the theft. I was told the weapon was recovered, so it should be in the possession of the FBI or DARPA."

"There's more to the story." Taylor glanced to the man on his left. "Grant, please fully brief our guest."

"Excuse me, sir. This is highly classified information."

"I think Mr. Savage has earned the right, don't you?"

"And Miss Simpson?"

Peter said, "Whatever you have to say to me, Kate also deserves to hear."

President Taylor gave a curt nod. McLuskie shifted in his chair. Although he held a notepad on his lap, the screen was dark.

He said, "The events you just shared are mostly true. But a key piece is missing. The Boise Police were the first to arrive at the crime scene, and they sealed it off. By that time, everyone knew the crimes would fall under federal jurisdiction, so the local cops preserved the scene and waited for the FBI.

"It didn't take long for the Bureau to arrive—less than fifteen minutes. After photos were taken, an agent by the name of Rigby was tasked with securing the weapon in its hard-side case for transportation to Headquarters, less than a mile away. Problem is, Rigby never made it."

CHAPTER 9

"I DON'T UNDERSTAND," PETER SAID.

"What Grant is telling you," President Taylor replied, "is that the PEAP weapon *and* the federal agent never arrived at FBI Headquarters. The gun should have been checked into evidence and locked away, but that didn't happen."

Peter said, "Which means..."

"Which means," said McLuskie, "that the PEAP carbine is out there in the hands of God-knows-who."

Understanding dawned on Kate. Peter had kept her in the dark on the details, and now she grasped why the project he'd been working on for months was veiled in secrecy.

She said, "I don't understand how the FBI can just lose a top-secret gun. There's still something you haven't told us."

Gutowsky leaned forward, his eyebrows pinched, and glared at the special agent in charge.

"I'd have to agree," he said. "I think we *all* deserve to know what's really going on."

"Please go on, Grant," said President Taylor. "You have my permission."

"Yes, sir." McLuskie drew a deep breath. "On May twelfth, hours after the murders, the PEAP carbine was removed from the clock tower in Boise, by Agent Rigby. Several witnesses all stated that they saw Rigby place the case containing the PEAP inside the trunk of his car. He was driving a government vehicle, and that vehicle did not return to FBI Headquarters in Boise."

"So what happened to it?" Peter said.

"Twenty hours later, the car and Agent Rigby were found in Cottonwood, Idaho."

"Never heard of it," Peter said.

"I'm not surprised. No reason you would. It's a small farming town in North Central Idaho. A little more than two hundred miles north of Boise. Population is less than a thousand. It's perhaps best known for a B-and-B that's built in the shape of a large beagle. On the early morning of May thirteenth, the agent's car was found in a dirt parking lot next to the football field. Rigby's body was lying next to the car. He'd been murdered. The trunk lid was closed but not latched, and the vehicle was unlocked. Keys were still in Rigby's pocket, as was his wallet. His Glock was still holstered on his hip. In fact, nothing appeared to have been stolen."

Kate blinked. "I'm sorry. You've lost me."

Peter said, "What he's saying is that the PEAP carbine should have been in the car, but it wasn't."

"That's right," McLuskie said. "Whoever killed Agent Rigby took the weapon."

"Who's the suspect?" Gutowsky said.

"There's very little to go on. Whoever did this was careful. The few prints on the car that did not belong to Rigby have been dead ends. The crime lab has fiber samples from the trunk that may be helpful if we can identify a suspect. But otherwise, that evidence is meaningless. Based on the condition of the body, he was likely killed between three a.m. and five a.m."

Peter said, "In the early morning like that, it would have

been pretty quiet in a small town. Someone must have heard something."

"The Bureau talked to almost everyone in Cottonwood, but no one heard anything unusual."

"What was the cause of death?" Gutowsky said.

"A deep puncture at the base of his skull." McLuskie pressed his finger to the back of his head, just above his neck. "The coroner said the wound was consistent with a narrow double-edged blade. Probably a dagger."

Peter leaned back in the Chippendale sofa and looked at President Taylor.

"So whoever killed the FBI man and took the PEAP carbine is trying to kill you."

"So it would seem. Question is, who is out for my head?"

Kate said, "Well it must be someone from the militia. What do they call themselves? Cascadia something?"

"Cascadia Independence Movement," McLuskie replied. "However, with the leadership and most of the members either dead or locked up, it's doubtful they're behind today's attempt."

"Then who?" she said.

"We don't know. It goes without saying that this is the highest priority for the Bureau."

Peter said, "Well, until they find the assassin, I suggest the president cancel all public appearances. This is a good time to stay home. With the curtains drawn."

"We need your help, Mr. Savage," said Taylor.

"Oh no," Kate said. "He's done enough already. You need to find someone else to risk his life."

"I understand how you feel," the president said. "But what I am asking will not place your fiancé at risk. We just need information, that's all."

Peter held Kate's hand. "Of course. Whatever I can do.

But I've never worked law enforcement. I can't help you find whoever did this."

McLuskie said, "You know more about the PEAP weapon than anyone. What are its capabilities? How can we protect the president?"

"The weapon fires an ultraviolent laser burst only a few microseconds in duration. It's not effective against metal, and it won't penetrate other materials like a bullet would. The energy pulse is designed to be effective on material containing water."

"Like human tissue," McLuskie said.

"Yes. But as you saw, the laser radiation will burn through a few layers of fabric, and it can even burn into wood, just not very far."

"What is the maximum range?" McLuskie said.

Peter scrunched his mouth to the side. "Hard to say. We didn't get that far in testing."

"Then tell me what range it was designed for," McLuskie said.

"A long way. Far enough to make conventional sniper rifles obsolete."

"How far, Mr. Savage?" McLuskie's voice hinted at his growing irritation.

"Under optimum atmospheric conditions, five miles. Maybe more."

"That's ridiculous." Gutowsky leaned back in his chair, shaking his head. "No one can shoot that far."

"They can, with good optics," Peter said. "You see, the laser pulse has no mass, so it's not affected by gravity or wind. And since it travels at the speed of light, literally, all the shooter has to do is place the crosshairs on the president's head at the same time he pulls the trigger. You asked me what the effective range is. It's limited by the optics."

McLuskie said, "The crime scene reports said the PEAP

carbine was fitted with a forty-five-power Leupold competition scope when it was found in the clock tower in Boise."

Peter frowned. "All the shooter needs is a clear line of sight."

"Then explain what happened in the Rose Garden," Gutowsky said. "That space is designed so no sniper can get a shot at the president. The trees in the garden, and other structures, provide an effective screen from the roof of any building in the city."

"That's an important point," Peter said. "And one I've been thinking about. There's only one possibility."

"An aircraft," McLuskie said. "The shooter was in an airplane."

"My thought exactly."

"The airspace above DC is restricted," Gutowsky said. "No way a plane could get close enough."

"Commercial aircraft fly in and out of Reagan National Airport on a regular basis," Peter said. "And let's not forget about American Airlines flight seventy-seven, which was flown into the Pentagon on 9-11."

"Still," McLuskie said, "for the sniper to get off multiple aimed shots, the plane would have to be circling. Our radar on the roof didn't pick up anything remarkable."

"Better keep looking," Peter said. "I'd think a slow-flying ultralight would be a good sniping platform. I don't know what the radar cross section would be for such a small aircraft, but it's gotta be tiny."

McLuskie was nodding. "You could be on to something. I'll have my team dig deeper. We can also check the radar recordings from Reagan National and Andrews."

President Taylor stood and looked at the special agent in charge. "Please keep me informed." Then he faced Peter and Kate. "You are welcome to stay at Blair House. Gavin will work out the details with you. A driver is waiting at the West Wing entrance. He'll take you anywhere you wish to go in the city. I hope you will accept my invitation."

Peter and Kate both stood and thanked the president. Gutowsky and McLuskie followed the chief executive out the door, leaving the couple alone in the Oval Office, with Diesel still sitting obediently near Peter's feet.

CHAPTER 10

AGENT VAUGHN WAS OUTSIDE the West Wing entrance, leaning against the idling black SUV, and typing into his phone. From his peripheral vision, he saw Peter and Kate walking toward West Executive Avenue.

"Hey!" he shouted, and jogged to catch up. "I've been assigned as your driver. I've got the AC running."

"Thanks," Peter said. "But I think we're just going to take a walk down the National Mall."

"No problem. I can drive you there. If you want to go to one of the museums, I'll drop you right at the entrance."

Kate smiled. "Thank you, Agent Vaughn. But we don't want to keep you from important work."

"Oh, it's no problem at all." He faced Peter. "And with that leg wound, you should take it easy for a few days."

"Really," Peter said, "I appreciate the offer. But we'll be fine. We just need to decompress."

The Secret Service agent held up his hands in appeasement.

"Okay, I understand. If you change your mind, or just get tired of walking, give me a call." He handed his business card to Peter. "Oh, and if any of the park service officers gives you a problem about Diesel, just call me. Or better yet, tell the officer to call me."

They took their time walking the short distance to the Mall. Peter felt the tension of the stitches in his calf, but it wasn't too painful. They stopped frequently to let Diesel sniff and occasionally mark a tree or garbage can. It was easy to navigate—they just walked toward the Washington Monument.

With the tall stone obelisk immediately in front of them, Kate looked both directions. To her left was the Capital. She scrunched her nose and looked right. Off in the distance was the Lincoln Memorial. That was the direction they went.

They detoured through the World War II Memorial. Peter thought he knew the history of that conflict fairly well, but the engraved lists of major battles reminded him of the enormity of the geographical scope and the vast number who were killed.

He took a seat in partial shade on a long, curved stone bench near the central fountain. The spray of water cooled the air noticeably, and he and Kate sat there in silent contemplation. Diesel stretched out his body in the shade underneath the bench seat.

After many long minutes of silence, Kate whispered in a conspiratorial voice, "Do you think any of those people are spies?"

She was referring to the wave of tourists ebbing and flowing past the circular fountain and pool.

Peter snorted a laugh, thinking it a silly question. And then he realized it wasn't a crazy question at all. Any foreign agent worth their salt would be trained to blend in and be inconspicuous.

"Hard to say," Peter replied. "What brought that up?"

"Just people-watching."

Her head was slowly moving as she tracked an Asian man as he strolled by, hands clasped behind his back. He was wearing mirrored sunglasses, an off-white Panama hat with a navy-blue band, dark gray slacks, and a blue short-sleeve shirt. A high-end digital camera hung around his neck.

Once he was out of earshot, Kate whispered, "See that man who just walked by, wearing the hat and blue shirt?"

"Yes," Peter said. "Probably here with a tour group."

"Look around. There are no tour groups here. And besides, he's got a nice camera but isn't taking any pictures."

Peter craned his neck and saw the man standing in front of the southern arch memorializing victory in the Pacific. He appeared to be reading the inscription, but just as Kate had observed, he was not holding his camera.

"Maybe the batteries are dead." Peter stood and offered his hand to Kate. "You're getting paranoid."

She stood. "That's a real laceration on your calf, and that was a real attempt to kill the president."

Yes. And four men died.

They ambled onward, Diesel shuffling along, sniffing occasionally.

Midway along the Reflecting Pool, they commandeered a green bench that had just been vacated by a mother-daughter pair. Peter gently extended his leg. Pigeons assembled in a group only ten feet away. The boldest occasionally strutted up to their feet, only to be startled to find a motionless dog eying them. But Diesel never broke his sit.

"Part of my brain won't accept that what happened today is real," Kate said. "But I know it is. And yet I'm sad more than I am frightened."

Peter studied her face, reading her emotions. She had said little about the attack, and he knew she needed to release her pent-up emotions. Rather than responding, he opted to let her talk, hoping it would begin the healing process.

"Is that normal?" she said. "Is there even such a thing as a normal response to seeing four people murdered?"

He held her hand and twisted so he could gaze into her eyes.

"Listen. What happened is terrible. I never wanted you to see violence like that."

"You could have been killed." Her eyes glistened, tears gathering and ready to trickle down her cheeks.

"I wasn't, though. And neither were you."

"But those four agents who were killed—"

"They died in the line of duty. They saved President Taylor. It was more than just their sworn duty. Those men protected the president because they believed it was the right thing to do. There will always be bad men doing evil deeds. And there will always be good men to stop them."

Kate wept, her head buried in Peter's shoulder. He held her gently, knowing he'd cheated Death again. But it was more than that. Kate was only feet away, and her life was also in grave danger. He knew he couldn't live with himself if she was killed. By allowing her into his life, he was placing her in danger.

That was unacceptable.

After many minutes, Kate raised her head and sniffled until Peter handed her a travel pack of tissues. She blew her nose and dried her eyes.

People walked past as if they had not a care in the world. If anyone noticed the crying woman, they said nothing.

The pair sat there on the bench, Kate leaning into Peter. The shadows grew longer, but there were still a few hours before the sun would set. Both Kate and Peter were alone with their thoughts, neither speaking for some time.

Finally, Kate said, "Doesn't it bother you? I mean, what happened?"

Peter was taken aback. "Of course it does." He paused, trying to understand the unspoken message. "I didn't want any of this to happen."

"I know that. What I mean is that you invented that new laser gun, or whatever you call it. Seems to me that gun has only one purpose: to assassinate people and get away with it."

The accusation cut deep and stung more than any physical injury he'd received.

"I…that's not true. You've always known what my business is. I've never attempted to deceive you in that respect, or any other. What we do at EJ Enterprises is design and manufacture military weapons. They are sold only to the US government, and they help to keep American troops safe. I can't control how people will use a weapon made by my company."

Kate's features appeared strained, her mouth downturned.

"I'm sure you believe that. But there is no denying that the weapons you make are designed for one purpose…"

Peter knew what was coming, because he'd heard it before. He steeled himself for the blow.

"…to kill."

He felt like he'd been sucker punched, the wind knocked out of his lungs. The worst part, though, was that he knew she was right.

⊕

The walk back to Blair House took an hour. An hour of almost complete silence. The only words spoken were either to Diesel, who blissfully avoided the intense spat, or so trivial as to amount to the small talk one might share with a complete stranger.

The situation didn't improve as they dressed for dinner.

Upon their arrival at the Lee Dining Room, the mood was lightened a bit when one of the wait staff presented a large plush pillow for Diesel to lay his bulk on, as well as what appeared to be a ceramic pie dish with a small portion of raw vegetables—

peas, carrots, and green beans. He was also given a large bowl of water.

"Looks like you scored, buddy." Peter ran his hand over the red pit bull's head.

Kate even chuckled.

The meal began with bay shrimp cocktail, and several of the shellfish were given to Diesel, sans spicy sauce.

While Peter filled their flutes with a sparkling Chardonnay, Kate said, "I'm sorry this turned out to be a horrible, lousy day. It was supposed to be a celebration for you."

"It wasn't all bad," he said.

Kate replied with an inquisitive look.

"Anytime I can be with you is good in my book."

She smiled, but Peter knew the tiff from earlier wasn't resolved. The fire still smoldered, waiting for just a puff to reignite the blaze.

Peter fidgeted with his hands, then drained and refilled his glass. He thought he'd overcome his reticence to speak openly with Kate, to lay bare his emotions. But once again he found himself unable to get the words he wanted to say past his lips. A lump was building in his throat, and his pulse quickened. He took another long drink of wine.

"What's wrong?" she said.

"Nothing." He felt his anxiety escalate.

"You've got a funny way of showing it. You've hardly spoken three sentences since we left the Reflecting Pool."

"I…I just don't want to argue."

"I wasn't arguing." She reached across the table and held his hand. "It's just that I'm an emotional wreck. You may have experienced things like this before, people being killed." Her eyes moistened, and she fought back tears. "But it's new to me. I just told you what I was feeling. What I am feeling."

He dug deep and summoned the courage he needed. *Why*

is this so damn difficult?

Peter cleared his throat. "I want to tell you something."

It felt so hard to formulate a coherent sentence, and he paused to order his words.

"Yes?" Kate said. "Tell me what?"

"When Maggie died, I thought my life was over. If it wasn't for the kids, it probably would have been. I didn't think I could ever love another woman again. Eventually, I gave up trying. In part because it felt like I was unfaithful to her by thinking of anyone else."

"Oh, Peter." Kate squeezed his hand. "I didn't know Maggie, but I'm sure she would have wanted you to move on and—"

"Please. If I stop now, I don't know if I'll be able to tell you. It's hard, but I need to share this."

She nodded, encouraging him to continue.

"Life became an existence, nothing more. Once Ethan and Joanna became adults, I poured myself into my work. But my life was empty. And then I met you."

Peter lifted his napkin and dabbed the corners of his eyes. Then he stared at the sparkling wine flute, twirling it between fingers and thumb.

"I love you, Kate. You complete me." He raised his gaze and locked eyes with Kate. "I never thought I would feel this way again. And then today, I thought I might lose it all once more."

"I don't understand. I love you, too, Peter, and I want to marry you. Why would you think you would lose me?"

"Because of what happened today. Because of *who* I am, and *what* I do. You said it yourself. I build weapons that are designed for the singular purpose of killing people."

Kate stood and walked around the table to where he was seated.

"Come here," she whispered.

Peter stood, and she looped her arms around him and drew him close.

With her head turned sideways on his shoulder, she said, "I'm sorry. That was a cheap shot."

"Cheap or not, I know you're right. And I could read the disappointment in your face. I'm sorry. This is who I am."

"For a brilliant man, you couldn't be more wrong. I know exactly who you are and what you do. You are honorable, loyal, and faithful. You are brave and courageous. And you're not afraid to fight to protect the innocent, just like you did today when you saved President Taylor—*again*. This is why I love you. You're not going to lose me."

They shared a kiss, then returned to their seats just before the main course arrived—steak and lobster.

After the plates were placed and they were alone again, Kate said, "There is something I would like for you to do."

Peter cocked his head.

"Since you saving the president is becoming a habit, I think you should ask to be put on the payroll. A pension, at the very least."

They both laughed, and with the emotional tide subsided, they enjoyed their meal at a leisurely pace. Talk was mostly about plans for the wedding. Kate wanted to keep it small, with only family and close friends.

"Maybe we can reserve Shevlin Park and have the ceremony and reception there?" she said.

Peter listened and offered suggestions when asked. But his mind was working overtime on more dire questions. Whoever tried to kill the president still had the PEAP, and there was no reason to believe the killer wouldn't try again.

CHAPTER 11

SEATED IN A BOOTH AT A DINER on West Main Street, Travis and Billy were enjoying a hardy breakfast of skillet potatoes, scrambled eggs, and hash. They'd driven straight through from Washington, DC. It took two days, and they didn't have any encounters with law enforcement, which served to bolster their belief that they'd made a clean getaway.

Grangeville was small enough, Billy figured, that they were unlikely to run into any sheriff deputies. And even if they did, with a full beard and sunglasses, would the local law officers recognize Billy as a fugitive?

Just outside of Lexington, Kentucky, they'd heard on news radio that President Taylor had survived the assassination attempt with minor injuries. He wasn't even hospitalized, and was still conducting his duties. Full recovery was expected within two weeks. Four Secret Service agents had been killed, and a civilian by the name of Peter Savage of Bend, Oregon, was also wounded.

Travis and Billy were disappointed, but Billy wasn't surprised. He'd seen the difference between a one-shot kill with the agents, and the grazing hit on the president. Next time, he vowed, he would not merely nick the commander in chief.

As they entered the Midwest, Billy began to worry about the ultralight they left behind. Although it did not have a tail number to be unambiguously identified in flight, with no other civilian aircraft flying near the White House, the leading hypothesis would certainly be that it was this ultralight that had been observed from Reagan National Airport and picked up by radar.

He was certain there were no incriminating fingerprints inside the cockpit or on the fuselage—both he and Travis wore gloves, and he'd wiped the plane with ammonia-based glass cleaner prior to their mission. The cleaner would remove prints and denature any traces of DNA from their fingers.

But there was the issue of the aircraft serial numbers on the airframe and on the engine block. Once the manufacture's records were checked, the FBI would learn that the aircraft had been sold to Stuart Denson, former leader of the Cascadia Independence Movement. Denson was in custody and would be questioned. But there was nothing he could reveal since he had no knowledge of Billy's mission. No one did, other than Billy and Travis.

"Why are you s-so quiet." Travis drained his coffee cup.

Billy was deep in thought. He kept working the question over and over. How could the FBI trace the ultralight back to either Travis or himself? And there was only one answer he came up with.

"Look, Travis," he said, between bites. "You have to get rid of your truck."

"W-why?"

Before Billy could offer a reply, the waitress marched up to their booth. Printed on her name tag was, Hi! I'm Courtney. Her red hair was tied back, and her green eyes were bright and cheerful. Her red lips parted in a smile. Without asking, she filled both cups with coffee.

Then she said, "How are you, Billy? Haven't seen you in a while. I like the beard. Almost didn't recognize you."

Billy frequented the diner, and he always sat in Courtney's zone. Over time, they grew to know each other a little, to the point where he considered her a casual friend. He was even considering asking her out, but hadn't quite worked up the courage. And no way in hell he'd ask her in front of Travis.

Billy smiled. "I'm doing fine. Just real busy. You know how it goes."

She rolled her eyes. "You can say that again. Been working ten-hour shifts until the owner can hire another waitress."

A shout came from the kitchen, "Order up!" ending the brief banter.

Just before Courtney turned away from the booth she said, "You let me know if you need anything, okay?"

"I th-think she likes you." Travis grinned.

"Yeah, maybe. I don't know." Billy gazed at her backside while she was loading up plates of food. "That doesn't matter. Like I was saying, you have to get rid of your truck."

"You still haven't told me why."

"Because someone at the boat ramp may have noticed your license plate. Trust me on this. If the feds get that information, they'll be all over you, and then me."

"S-so. They can question me, but I'll never give up anything. Besides, I don't have the money to buy another truck."

Billy flashed a brief smile. Despite his internal defenses, he had grown to genuinely like Travis. The guy was solid, dependable. And life had dealt him a crappy hand. Billy felt sorry for Travis, and that only made him more determined to inflict pain upon the nation, and by extension, upon society. The ruling class—politicians, the wealthy—had become too complacent, too comfortable in their status with their own rules that ensured people like Billy and Travis would always be underdogs.

Time for a revolution.

"Hey, it's cool," Billy said. "I'll help you get another truck. And I know I can trust you. I wouldn't have brought you into this otherwise. But I've been thinkin' it over. There's only one potential clue that could lead the FBI to us. We get rid of that clue, and they've got nothing. So we lay low for a while. And then, when the time is right..."

Travis was drinking his coffee when he heard this, causing him to grin, and for coffee to run down the corners of his mouth. He lowered the mug and dabbed his mouth with his napkin.

"Yeah. And this time, we won't miss. Isn't that right, B-B-Billy?"

"Shhh. Keep your voice down." Billy surreptitiously glanced around the diner.

The other patrons were all involved in their own conversations, and no one appeared to be paying any attention to the two would-be assassins.

"Finish up," Billy said. "I'll pay the bill. Drive your truck out to that place on the BLM land where we used to shoot. You know the place?"

Travis nodded. "Yeah. By the b-big boulder that's split."

"Exactly. I'll meet you there. Remove the license plates and anything you want to keep."

"The b-battery is new. I want to keep it."

"Sure, no problem. I'll finish my breakfast and be right behind you."

Travis slid out of the booth and left the diner. Billy watched through the large windows as Travis pointed his pickup onto West Main Street and drove away. He was still looking out the window, watching two motorcyclists also leave the diner parking, when he felt the seat cushion sag from someone's weight. He turned his head, and two Asians had slid in—one next to him, uncomfortably close, and the other, a woman, on the other side of the table where Travis had been seated. Her raven hair cascaded to her shoulders like a silk scarf. But it was her hazel eyes that held Billy's gaze. It was like looking into twin pools of honey. He'd met her before, and knew she was Korean. Her name was Cho, although she had insisted that Billy address her as Miss Cho.

"Where were you last night?" Her voice was melodic and beautiful, as were her features—petite nose, plump lips, and flawless skin. "We waited two hours. You didn't show."

Billy started to answer, then stopped as Courtney strolled over with a pot of coffee and two mugs. She filled both, then topped up Billy's mug.

"Anyone want to see the menu?" she said.

"No," Cho said politely. "Just coffee."

Courtney faced Billy. "Are you all done?"

He nodded.

"You didn't finish everything. Was it all right?"

"It was delicious, as always. And now I'm full."

Courtney picked up the plate. "Okay. But if you change your mind, just let me know."

She turned and continued her rounds through the diner.

Billy returned his attention to Cho. "I was busy."

"Busy? What could be more important than our deal?"

"Well, Cho," he said, knowing addressing her that way would irritate her. "You see, I don't think I want to do the deal anymore."

The other Korean sitting close to Billy—a medium-sized man with thick arms and cords of muscle joining his neck to his shoulders—had remained silent. His gaze bore into Billy with a degree of malevolence that made Billy feel uneasy.

"Where is the merchandise?" Cho said.

"As you can see, I don't have it."

"Is it in your vehicle? Maybe your home?"

"I don't have a home," Billy said.

He lived a nomadic life in a used travel trailer, usually parking on federal land away from civilization.

"And before you indulge your fantasy of tearing apart my truck out there in the parking lot," he said, "take a moment to imagine how you will explain your vandalism to the local police. Not to mention all the cell phone videos the patrons here will shoot of you and your minions."

Cho sipped from the mug and then tapped the tips of her nails on the table, her eyes never leaving Billy's.

Finally, she said, "We entered into a bilateral agreement in which you willingly participated. You offered an item for sale, and I agreed to buy it. You cannot unilaterally terminate the agreement. I have made certain representations to my government, and in turn, my government has made certain plans based on acquiring the item you have offered to sell. If I fail to deliver the goods, my government will be quite unhappy. That is not a position I want to be in."

Billy shrugged. "Not my problem."

Cho smiled. "Oh, but it is."

Billy felt a sharp point just below his belt, next to his genitals. There was a sting as the steel pierced his skin, just barely. He froze, fearful that if he moved, the blade might inflict serious harm with a flick of the man's muscular arm.

"By the look on your face, Billy, I know you feel the tip of Mr. Sung's dagger. I'm sure you would prefer he removed the knife gently, yes?"

Billy's mind ran through his options, and settled on the one he believed had the best chance of a good outcome in which he retained his manhood, not to mention his blood.

He turned his head to face the Korean man. "I'd be careful if I were you, Sung. You see, if you kill me, you don't get the *article,* and the boss lady here is going to be very angry with you. Probably the Supreme Leader, too. I hear he has a nasty way of carrying out capital punishment. Tell me, would you prefer to be shot to pieces by antiaircraft guns, or thrown into a tank of piranhas?"

Sung's gaze moved just a bit to the left so he could see Cho. She was glaring at Billy, calculating her next move.

She said, "Seems like we have a standoff."

"I don't think so. I'm going to leave now." Billy started to stand, but doing so drove the knife tip deeper into his flesh.

He winced and returned to his seat.

"Billy," Cho said. "You will carry out your part of the agreement. Don't make the mistake of thinking we have no leverage. I've seen Mr. Sung peel half the skin off a man without killing him."

"I don't respond well to threats."

"Call it what you want. I'm simply a businesswoman trying to complete our transaction. One which you invited us to. Then you'll never see me again."

Billy's phone rang. It was sitting on the table next to his mug. He glanced at it. The caller ID said it was Travis.

"Go ahead," Cho said. "Take the call. Put it on speaker."

Billy followed her instructions, a sense of foreboding engulfing him.

"Hello," he said.

"B-Billy. What's going on? Two Asian dudes riding m-motorcycles followed me out of town. Once I turned off the highway onto the gravel road, they pulled guns and started shooting."

"Are you all right?" Billy whispered.

A new voice came over the phone speaker. "Your friend is okay. For now."

"Let him go," Billy said, as much to Cho as to the man on the other end of the connection.

"When you deliver the merchandise," she said.

After a moment of hesitation, Billy said, "Okay. When and where?"

"Tonight. Same time, same location. And don't be late. Your friend is depending on you."

"If you kill Travis, the deal is off, and you'll never get the weapon."

"Oh, please, Billy. I have no wish to harm your friend. But if you attempt to deceive me, or if you fail to complete the transaction, your friend will wish we had killed him."

"I'll be there. Just make certain you bring the money, and Travis."

CHAPTER 12

BILLY LEFT THE DINER AND DROVE EAST out of Grangeville, then turned south on Mount Idaho Grade Road, which made a series of turns that took him past scattered houses and ranches, toward Mill Creek. His old Dodge Power Wagon took the turns with ease. He followed another narrow gravel road that he knew came to a dead end. At the end of the road, he parked in the shade of a small copse of evergreens. There, he waited. And watched.

From his hide, the road extended in a straight line a quarter-mile back in the direction he'd driven, then took a sharp turn. Any vehicle following him would have to expose itself. But none did. After thirty minutes, he was confident no one had pursued him.

Behind the truck seat was the PEAP carbine, wrapped in an old towel to protect it from rattling between the seat back and the cab. He was surprised his bluff had worked. If Cho had searched his vehicle, they would have found the PEAP almost immediately.

Billy grabbed the weapon, keeping the towel wrapped around it. He left his Dodge behind and set off trekking cross-country through the woods. His destination was only a couple miles away. He crossed Mill Creek, and soon found his first marker—a ten-foot wall of metamorphic gneiss, probably cut ages ago by surging storm runoff. Working around the exposed rock, he climbed the sloped bank.

A hundred yards distant, he saw the jagged stump of an old pine tree. It appeared the tree had suffered a genetic defect that caused the trunk to separate into a Y-shape about four feet above the forest floor. Over decades, the twin tree trunks grew equivalently, but they could never overcome the inherent weakness of the split trunk. Eventually, whether due to internal rotting or a gale, the tree split. One trunk lay where it fell, and the other was still rooted in the soil. But the wound where the trunk had cleaved left the evergreen open and vulnerable, eventually to succumb to disease. Now, the weathered remains provided shelter for forest inhabitants such as racoons, squirrels, and jays.

Rather than moving directly toward the dead tree, Billy skirted it and hiked beyond for another fifty yards, and then settled behind a few gnarly manzanita bushes. Although he was wearing tan jeans and a lightweight, gray zippered sweater rather than camo, he doubted anyone would easily spot him if he remained still. A more serious handicap was that he didn't have a spotting scope, or better yet, a pair of good-quality binoculars. Either would have been helpful in spotting someone at a distance before they saw him.

Exercising an abundance of caution, bordering on paranoia, he walked past the weathered tree as if it meant nothing. Soon, he would know if he was being followed.

He sat on the ground and worked his buttocks into a comfortable position, making certain he had a clear field of vision between the twisted manzanita branches, back to the snag. He cradled the PEAP carbine across his lap.

He sat perfectly still, watching and listening. Even the

occasional fly buzzing his face was left to carry out its annoying habit, for fear that the twist of his head or flick of his fingers might give away his position.

After many minutes, the natural forest sounds began to return. First, it was the chirping of nuthatches and finches. Then the scolding jeer of jays, followed by the chatter of tree squirrels. As the minutes passed, chipmunks popped from burrows and dashed across open ground for another hole, some stopping atop a rock to chew a pine nut while surveying the landscape.

Other than the native creatures, there was no movement. But it was possible that someone could approach unseen if they were wearing camouflage clothing.

He waited longer, using time as his defense. It was human nature to be impatient, and waiting was difficult for most to accept. A pursuer might stop for one or two minutes to listen and look for clues. But after failing to notice anything of interest, it was likely they would continue on.

Billy had to be more patient. He had to wait longer, his senses attune to a flash of movement or the snapping of a twig, maybe the brush of a tree limb or bushes against clothing.

After some period that Billy judged to be long enough, he rose from his concealed position. Standing tall and still, he again scanned left and right.

Nothing.

He advanced on the snag. It had stood in the face of the elements long enough that the bark had flaked off and piled around the base, leaving the wood surface to gray from exposure.

With each placement of his sneakers, he was careful not to set his weight on a dry stick that might snap, or a loose rock that could roll and cause him to twist an ankle. These were skills that had become second nature, a product of spending time in the forest, honing his skills as a woodsman and shooter.

The sapwood, long ago dried and hardened, retained the jagged edge produced when the trunk broke, while the inner heartwood had rotted. Enterprising critters had hollowed the pithy center away, leaving a convenient deep cavity.

After removing the battery from the PEAP, he wrapped the weapon again with the towel. He planned to search for a replacement battery. Next, he secured the cloth with a section of paracord he'd carried in a pocket, and then stuffed the package down the hole. It just fit.

As the final act, he placed a few pieces of bark and dried pine needles gathered from the forest floor, across the broken section of tree to hide the cloth.

Satisfied, he marched back to his truck.

⊕

At a quarter past eleven, he turned the engine off and waited in the alley behind the Blue Fox Theater. He watched as several young men stumbled to their cars parked next door behind the Pizza Factory, no doubt having consumed many pitchers of beer. They were boisterous but harmless, and none paid any attention to him.

With a screech of burning rubber, they left, and the alley once again fell silent. He had worked out his plan, accounting for all the variables he could think of. He arrived at the meeting location early, just in case Ms. Cho decided to send some of her team to set a trap.

Billy was armed with a Smith & Wesson Model 66. Years earlier, he'd bought it on the street, paid cash, and naturally, had no background check. The gun had most likely been stolen, but that wasn't important. What *was* important was that the gun could not be traced to him.

The revolver was old school, but extremely reliable and

formidable. It was loaded with six .357 magnum rounds, each cartridge capable of sending a 125-grain hollow point bullet downrange at a blistering speed and inflicting serious damage on flesh and bone. The round was legendary for its one-shot stopping capability.

He didn't trust Cho any more than she trusted him, which was not at all. The challenge was to get out alive with Travis and the PEAP carbine.

The only illumination in the alley came from lights above the back doors of the theater and the pizza joint. It wasn't much, but Billy still chose a spot in the shadows to park the old Dodge Power Wagon. With the windows rolled down, he listened for any sounds that might equate to a threat. There was nothing but the *tick-tick* of the engine block cooling.

With nothing much to pass the time, Billy thought back to his first meeting with Cho, a little more than two weeks ago, and the beginning of this ordeal. He knew he would be the one to use the PEAP to assassinate high-level government leaders. So why not make some extra money after that job was completed? He reached out to someone he knew in the militia who was knowledgeable in the dark web. With some direction, and hours of searching, he made a connection to a guy in Seattle who introduced Billy to Miss Cho.

At first, the communication was only through a chat room on the dark web, and this made Billy nervous. He knew little about computers or the Internet, and the dark web was something else entirely.

After a couple chat sessions, and a picture Billy shared of the PEAP weapon, Cho agreed to a face-to-face meeting. It was in Boise, at the Whiskey Bar on West Main Street. Billy liked the rustic interior with weathered barnwood planks paneling the walls, and a moose head hanging high over the one pool table.

Cho was alone for the meeting, and they sat in a corner, sipping some specialty cocktails that he couldn't recall the name of. Billy's senses were on high alert. At this point, he had no idea if the beautiful Asian woman sitting with him was a fed. He needed her to incriminate herself to prove she was legitimate.

Finally, after dancing around the subject, Billy said, "You requested this meeting Miss Cho. What do you want from me?"

"Just like an American. Direct, almost to the point of being rude."

"Look, lady, I don't know you. For all I know, you could be working undercover, trying to trap me. So I'll ask again—what do you want from me?"

She smiled. "Maybe I have the same suspicion of you? Maybe *you* are the federal agent trying to trap *me*? If you remember, I responded to your offer posted in the chat room. Maybe that was just bait to draw in foreign agents?"

"Are you?" Billy said.

"Am I what?"

"Are you a fed?"

"No. I came to do a deal. Now, we can either get on with it, or I'll be on my way to more important things, and you can sit there and enjoy your drink. It's up to you."

Billy sat in silence, thinking about what she'd said. Was it enough that his lawyer could argue entrapment if she was lying?

Cho pushed her chair back and stood to leave.

"Wait a minute," Billy said.

She lowered herself into the chair. "Yes?"

"You're familiar with the object I'm offering?"

She ran her fingers across her forehead to push stray hairs back in place.

"Yes, I know what it is," she replied. "My government places value on this type of technology. My job is to serve as a broker. Kind of like a broker of fine art. I search for such unique objects, and when I find them, I share the details with my government. If they are interested, they authorize me to negotiate the purchase and arrange delivery."

Billy nodded. "Delivery. As in delivery to the Supreme Leader? What's his name? Kim?"

"I'm sure you know. The news media in America perpetuates a biased perspective of the Supreme Leader to bolster public support for your government's warmongering."

"Sure," Billy said. "Whatever. I have little interest in politics."

"Is that so? I believe you have a great deal of interest in politics. Or should I say, altering the balance of power in your federal government."

Billy tried too late to hide his surprise, and Cho didn't miss the cues in his body language.

"You really think I don't know how you came into possession of this *unique* object?"

He tried to maintain a poker face. "What you know, or think you know, really doesn't matter. I have it, and you want it. All we have to do is agree on a price."

"And what do you have in mind?" Cho said.

"Five million."

Cho snorted a laugh. "Let me rephrase my question. Within the realm of reality, what price are you asking?"

"I told you."

"Then we have nothing to discuss. Thank you for the drink." For the second time, Cho stood and stepped away from the table.

She had taken only two steps toward the door when Billy said, "Come on back."

She returned to the table, making a point of displaying her irritation. She'd done negotiations like this a dozen times, and Billy was clearly an amateur. The only question was, how much to squeeze him? If she pushed too hard, she risked losing the deal. And there were other governments equally interested in this technology who would think nothing of dropping five million to acquire it.

"I'm listening," she said.

"Two million. In small bills. Nothing larger than a fifty."

"That's a lot of bills. How are you going to carry that?"

"I'll manage," Billy said, feeling more confident.

"One million. Not a dollar more."

Billy mulled over her offer, spinning his glass, causing the ice cubes to clink.

"Make a decision, Billy. Yes or no. But if I get up a third time, I'm not coming back."

Billy remained silent and pensive. Another minute passed, and Cho pushed her chair back.

"Okay," Billy said. "One million." After a pause, he said, "Do you have the money?"

"Money is not a problem, but it will take a few days to get it in small bills."

Billy gave her the meeting date, time, and place. They even shook on the deal before departing the bar.

So much had happened since that initial meeting. Billy focused his attention on the business at hand. The deal was not going down smoothly, and it was his fault. He had to get Travis back, unharmed, and renegotiate the deal. With President Taylor still alive, he wasn't ready just yet to give up the weapon.

Another ten minutes passed, and a Jeep Wrangler rolled into the alley, then turned off its lights. It stopped about twenty yards away. There were a half-dozen parked cars, and Billy's truck was snugged between two other pickups. He thought he could make out four people in the Wrangler. That seemed about right, considering that Cho was supposed to have Travis present, and she would certainly have brought additional muscle.

The driver's door opened, and a man stepped out. In the dim light, Billy couldn't see clearly enough to know if it was Sung or another person. Then Cho slipped out the other side.

Billy waited several moments, expecting the others to also exit from the Jeep, but they remained inside.

The dome light in his truck was switched off, and he opened the door. He lowered his foot to the pavement, then eased his body out. He wore an oversized chamois shirt, unbuttoned, over a short-sleeve tee. His revolver was in a hip holster hidden under lose shirt tails.

In the darkness, Cho didn't immediately see Billy. Not until he stepped in front of the grill of the Dodge pickup. He stood there, arms limp by his side.

"Good to see you, Billy," Cho said.

Her companion stood to the side and a half-step behind her.

Billy said, "Where's Travis?"

Cho turned her head toward the Wrangler. "Sung. Bring out our guest."

Sung slid out first. As soon as Billy's friend cleared the door, Sung grabbed him by the collar and pressed something against Travis's neck. It was impossible to tell if it was a gun, or something else.

From twenty yards away and in the dark, Billy couldn't be sure if Travis had been injured.

"Are you all right?" he called.

Travis nodded. "Yes, I'm okay. J-just give them what they want."

"You should listen to your friend," Cho said. "I hope you brought the PEAP."

It was the first time Billy had heard her refer to the weapon specifically. It felt oddly refreshing. The practice of calling it the merchandise or object was phony, something he expected in a cheap novel or a B-grade movie.

"Travis first," he said. "Let him go."

"I'm more than just a pretty face," Cho said. "You have to do better than that, or Mr. Sung will slice your friend's throat."

As she spoke, Billy caught a glint of light reflecting off Sung's narrow blade, likely the same one he had used to threaten Billy at the diner.

"Let's see the money," Billy said, stalling, looking for an opening.

Cho tipped her head, and the man behind her strode to the Jeep and returned with a large suitcase. It was obviously heavy. He took five paces, then laid it on the ground and pulled the zipper open. Easing back the cover, Billy could see the case was full of something. Paper, maybe. Money, hopefully.

"Take a look," Cho said.

"First tell your goon to step back."

The man returned to Cho's side, and Billy approached the case. In the light cast by his phone, he saw bundles of notes— tens, twenties, and fifties. He picked one up and fanned the bills. It all looked legitimate. But moving it quickly was going to be a challenge. He estimated it weighed at least forty pounds.

"I've shown you mine," Cho said. "Now, time for you to show me yours."

Billy walked back to the Power Wagon and retrieved a hard-side gun case from the bed. With confidence to his step, he placed the gun case on the pavement next to the suitcase full of money. Then he retreated to the pickup.

Travis remained within Sung's grip, and the steel blade never wavered from his throat. The second man came forward again. He knelt in front of the case, released the clasps, and folded back the cover. His eyes widened in surprise at what he saw, and he turned his head to Cho.

Before he got a word out, Billy had the stainless steel Model

66 in his hands. He aimed as best as he could in the darkness and squeezed the trigger.

The explosion of the gunshot shattered the calm night, echoing off the buildings lining the alley. Billy's ears were ringing, effectively rendering him temporarily deaf.

Everything that followed happened simultaneously. The Korean tumbled backward. Billy saw the blade enter Travis's throat and then rip forward, followed by a gout of blood. Travis slumped to the ground. The wounded Korean rolled to his back, some type of pistol in his hand.

Through the ringing in his ears, Billy heard the gunshots as the Korean fired at him.

Billy was on the move.

Travis was dead, or soon would be.

After dropping beside a new Subaru, Billy pointed his revolver at the wounded Korean and fired again. The hollow-point bullet ripped through his abdomen just below his ribs, and blasted a fist-sized hole where it exited his back, killing him instantly.

In the frenzy, Cho and Sung glimpsed inside the open gun case delivered by Billy.

Empty.

Sung grabbed Cho by the arm and yanked her to the Jeep. They piled inside, Sung behind the wheel. He gunned the engine and raced down the alley, away from Billy.

In the distance, a lone siren wailed, and Billy knew the police would arrive soon. The back door of the Pizza Factory was open, and several people were standing there, cameras flashing. By morning, Billy's picture would be circulating among Idaho law enforcement.

Ignoring the witnesses, he holstered his gun and walked up to Travis. He dropped to one knee and looked into his friend's lifeless eyes. A large pool of blood was still spreading from the wicked gash that had nearly severed his head.

He placed a hand on Travis's chest. "I'm sorry. It wasn't supposed to go down this way. I thought I could get you freed. Guess I really screwed up. But I can still make it right."

With a sigh, Billy rose and strode to the suitcase. He zipped the lid closed before carrying it to his truck and tossing it in the back.

Then he drove away.

CHAPTER 13

BEND, OREGON
MAY 28

PRESIDENT TAYLOR HAD QUIETLY directed Chief of Staff Gavin Gutowsky to have a plane ready to fly Peter, Kate, and Diesel back to Bend when they were ready to return home. Taylor intuited that, under the circumstances, they would not want to stay in DC, preferring the comfort of their home to heal the body and mind. And so it did not come as a surprise when Peter informed Agent Vaughn that the couple planned to fly home following breakfast.

"Would you drop us off at Reagan Airport?" Peter said.

Vaughn informed Peter that air transportation had already been arranged.

Their last meal at Blair House was a celebration put on by the staff. Mimosas were served in antique Venetian crystal flutes said to have been given to President Theodore Roosevelt. Breakfast was a multicourse affair beginning with fresh fruit and followed by the chef's secret recipe for country scrambled eggs, French toast, homemade fennel pork sausage, hickory-smoked pepper bacon, grits, freshly baked croissants with an assortment of jams and marmalade, and skillet potatoes with heirloom tomatoes and both yellow and green peppers. Diesel also enjoyed a sampling of everything on the menu, other than the fruit, which he refused to touch.

Agent Vaughn drove them to Andrews Air Force Base, Kate and Peter each sipping coffee from commemorative Blair House travel mugs. Diesel, belly full, was laying on the passenger seat, snoring.

The black SUV stopped at the gate long enough for Agent Vaughn to present his ID and badge. The guard checked a list of names and then waved them through. The vehicle coasted to a stop near a wheeled stairway leading up to the cabin door of a C-37B. The sleek Gulfstream business jet was painted white with a blue belly. The words United States of America appeared in black above the passenger windows spanning the middle third of the aircraft.

Peter and Kate each shook Agent Vaughn's hand and expressed their appreciation for his service. Peter concluded with an invitation to visit, if Vaughn ever made it to Bend.

Cruising at forty-five thousand feet, the flight to Oregon was smooth. They flew the breadth of the country nonstop, and landed at the Bend Municipal Airport in the early afternoon.

After arriving at Peter's loft residence near the Deschutes River in the Old Mill District of Bend, he suggested Kate spend the night.

"But I really should unpack and do my laundry." Kate feigned objection. "And my apartment hasn't been cleaned in close to a week."

Peter reached for her hand. "You have clothes here. Or I'll take you shopping, if you'd rather."

"Trying to bribe me?"

He drew her closer. "I don't want to be alone tonight. Or ever again."

"Me neither," she said in a husky voice.

⊕

Shortly before 1:00 a.m., Peter rose from bed, unable to go back to sleep. Quietly, to avoid waking Kate, he descended the spiral staircase from the master bedroom to the great room. His loft-like home was on the second and third floors of an old brick powerhouse, complete with the three original smokestacks. On the ground floor was EJ Enterprises. Although the exterior had been largely preserved, the interior was gutted and rebuilt to modern standards.

The large great room dominated the living space and connected to the front entrance as well as the dining and kitchen spaces. The floor was wide-plank pine aged to a rich honey color. The space was cavernous, with brick walls extending twenty feet up to the ceiling, supported on rustic wood beams. One wall was dominated by a massive hearth, while the wall opposite supported a bookcase that spanned from corner to corner, floor to ceiling. The bookcase was entirely natural-finished oak, with a library ladder made of matching wood to provide access to the upper shelves. In the center of the wall, surrounded by the bookcase, was an oversized arched passage that led to the kitchen and dining room.

The décor was decidedly masculine, with a pair of overstuffed lounge chairs upholstered in distressed tobacco-colored leather opposite a matching sofa. The sitting area was located in front of the hearth. The mantle above the huge masonry firebox was a single, massive, aged timber reclaimed from the original construction.

Peter lowered himself into one of the lounge chairs, Diesel asleep before the hearth. Occasionally, a leg would twitch as the faithful canine dreamed of past or fictional chases where he no doubt was victorious in catching his prey.

As he watched Diesel peacefully rest, he couldn't help but recall when they first met. Diesel had been turned over to the Central Oregon Humane Society, having been rescued from a dog fighting ring south of Bend, outside the small town of La Pine. The puppy had been used as a bait dog, and when Peter saw the little fella, he was in the far corner of his holding pen, trembling in fear. His nose, ears, and neck all bore witness to his horrible existence—fetid wounds from frequent maulings by larger and more aggressive dogs being trained to fight to the death.

The director of the Humane Society explained that the little dog had been severely traumatized, and might never fully recover from the emotional scars. For this reason, they would not allow the puppy to be adopted by a family with children or other pets for fear that the dog could become dangerously aggressive. Once Peter explained he had neither young children nor other animals, he was allowed to meet the terrified little red pit bull.

At first, the dog would not approach Peter, preferring to stand in the farthest corner of the pen, shaking uncontrollably, tail between his legs and head lowered in submission. His amber eyes, wide with fear, refused to meet Peter's. He kept his distance and lay on the cold concrete floor, his head on his folded hands. Eventually, curiosity overcame fear and the little pit bull puppy cautiously approached and pressed his damp nose to Peter's lips.

Peter insisted on adopting the puppy, and over time, their bond grew. Peter was Diesel's pack, the only family the once terrified and abused dog knew. And when Kate entered Peter's life, Diesel readily accepted her into the fold. Peter knew that Diesel would guard Kate with his life, just as Diesel had done for Peter many times before.

Wishing to dispel his melancholic mood, Peter rose from his

chair and retrieved a bottle of Oban single malt Scotch from a bookcase shelf. He poured a shot into a small tumbler, warming the glass in his palm. His gaze moved to a picture of Kate taken shortly after they'd begun seeing each other regularly. She was sitting on a blanket beside Todd Lake, enjoying a picnic they were sharing. She wore a wide smile and her eyes beamed with joy. Just looking at her face brought a grin to Peter.

He sipped his Scotch and reached for a book on one of the shelves, when he heard a cry from upstairs.

"No!" Kate screamed.

Peter bounded for the spiral staircase, taking the steps two at a time. Diesel was right behind him.

He dashed into the bedroom and turned on the switch. Light flooded the room. Kate was sitting bolt upright in bed, one hand mostly blocking the light from her eyes. Even so, Peter could see the tears streaking her cheeks.

He rushed forward and sat on the bed, his arms reaching for her.

"Are you all right?" he said.

Kate was wide awake.

She nodded. "Yes."

"What happened? I heard you scream."

"It was a dream, a nightmare." She leaned forward and Peter wrapped his arms around her.

"I'm sorry. Are you okay?"

"I'm fine. It was just so real."

"It's been a long day. You should try to get some rest."

"I don't want to go back to sleep. I'm afraid I'll have the same dream again."

"Sometimes it helps if you talk about it." Peter used the heal of his hand to wipe away her tears.

"It was about you," she said. "We were in the Rose Garden. It was so real, just like it was for the ceremony. And President

Taylor was shot, and you ran forward to protect him. You turned with the president, shielding him with your body. You looked right at me. And then…" She began to weep again.

"It's okay. You're safe here."

"In my dream, you died. Right there, while I watched." She was shaking and sobbing uncontrollably.

"It was only a dream. I'm fine. We all are."

Peter held her close for many minutes while she calmed down. Once her sobbing ceased, she eased herself from Peter's embrace. Her eyes were bloodshot, and her nose was running.

"I know we are," she finally managed to say, between sniffles. "But what if it happened differently? You can't always be lucky."

CHAPTER 14

May 29

WHEN KATE WANDERED INTO THE KITCHEN, Peter was placing pan-seared ham onto a plate next to a tall stack of pancakes.

"Good morning," she gave Peter a kiss on the cheek while he continued to plate the food.

As she helped herself to a mug of coffee she said, "I didn't hear you come back to bed last night."

"I was having trouble sleeping, even before your nightmare, so I sat in front of the fireplace with Diesel and had a Scotch. When I came back upstairs, you were sleeping soundly. No more night terrors, I hope?"

"No, none at all. I think your suggestion worked. Talking it over seemed to dispel those thoughts from my mind."

"Good. Well, as you can see, breakfast is ready."

They sat on stools at a counter opposite the cooktop.

"It smells heavenly," Kate said, and they both heaped food onto their plates.

The talk was cheerful, mostly about ongoing plans for the wedding. They agreed to have the ceremony at Riverbend Park since Shevlin Park, their first choice, was not available. It would be a small and informal occasion—close friends and family only. Although Kate had already picked out a wedding dress, she allowed Peter to surprise her with his attire.

They agreed that Peter's longtime friend and chief engineer at EJ Enterprises, Todd Steed, would officiate the ceremony.

"Is that legal?" Kate said.

"Indeed it is. Todd is an ordained spiritual leader. Don't ask me exactly what that means, or why Todd chose to pursue that, but it is totally legal."

"Good. I thought you might be setting up a sham wedding so you could dump me in six weeks and steal my fortune."

"You never told me you have money," Peter said, and they both laughed.

After piling the dirty plates in the sink, Peter went to his office and returned a minute later with two pieces of paper and two pens.

"While we're on the subject, let's make our lists of who we each want to invite. We need to get invitations out soon."

"I don't want to mail formal invitations," Kate said. "Can't we just call or email people?"

Peter raised his eyebrows. "Really? You're okay with emailing Uncle Joe and saying, Hey, getting married. Want you to be there."

Kate laughed. "Yes. You are officially off the hook on this one. I take full responsibility if anyone feels slighted because they didn't get an expensive piece of custom printed paper."

It didn't take long, as neither had much family or a large circle of friends. Peter slid his list in front of Kate. As she scanned down it, her gaze stopped on one name near the bottom.

"Jade? Who is this? A former girlfriend?"

"No. I met her about the time we started dating. She's just a friend."

"Uh-huh. Let me translate what you just said. You see, guys speak a different language from us gals."

"What are you talking about? She's a friend. Nothing more."

Kate was trying to stifle a smile. She knew she had Peter.

"So what you said sounds perfectly normal and innocent to a guy. But to a woman, you just said Jade was a romantic interest and she dumped you."

Peter flushed. "What? That…that's not true."

Kate couldn't hold it back, and burst out with laughter.

"Oh, that's just mean." Peter smiled.

"That's what I love about you, mister. You are so honest, and so innocent. There has never been I time when I thought I couldn't trust you. I'm lucky to be with you."

"Ditto. But there is something I need to tell you about Jade."

"Okay, here it comes." Kate rolled her eyes.

"It's not that at all, and I'm serious. Will you please listen to me?"

"Okay, I promise." She moved her fingers in the sign of a cross over her chest.

"After I met Jade Lim, she was kidnapped. Her mother insisted I help to find her daughter. I didn't want to, but to make a long story short, I eventually ended up in Brunei, searching for Jade."

"What happened? Obviously, you found her."

"Yes, we did. I had a lot of help, as you might guess. But what I what you to know is that Jade's uncle is the Sultan of Brunei."

Kate's eyes widened to the size of saucers, and she placed a hand over her mouth.

Once she regained her composure, she said, "No. You're kidding, right?"

Peter stared back, unblinking, eyebrows raised and lips pursed.

"You're not kidding."

"Nope. So…be prepared to be embarrassed by some outrageously expensive and totally useless wedding gift from her uncle."

Kate again placed a hand over her mouth as she drew a deep breath of air.

When she exhaled, she said, "So that's how you got the Rolls Royce you used to drive. I thought you landed a major contract and got a huge bonus at work. But that wasn't it at all."

"Nope. The sultan wanted to thank me for saving his niece and—well, there was more to it, but I can't share that—and he paid for the Rolls."

"Oh my God. You should tell him it got wrecked. Maybe he'll give you another one."

"Look, I don't want you to make a big deal of this, okay? She's a friend, that's all."

"No, no. I get it." After a pause, Kate said, "Having the Sultan of Brunei as a friend. Man, that's huge."

"Please, can we move on?"

Over the next half-hour, they had reviewed and critiqued both lists. With the head count completed, each agreed to either phone or email everyone on their lists later that day. And Peter promised to speak to Todd in the morning about officiating.

Diesel wandered into the kitchen and whined. He was ready for a walk. Together, Peter and Kate walked the red pit bull to a bike path that paralleled the Deschutes River. Between the trail and the water was a thick buffer of wild vegetation that ducks and geese nested in. The variety of scents always held Diesel's attention, and Peter had no trouble imagining that the canine found it exciting to explore.

After many minutes of silence, Peter said, "There's something I want to tell you."

Kate looked at him with curiosity in her eyes.

"It's about last night and what happened in Washington."

"Yes?"

Peter felt the familiar lump develop in his throat.

"It's hard. I don't know why." He swallowed, trying to get his courage back, along with his voice.

"What's hard?" Kate stopped and forced him to look at her.

"Whenever I have something important to tell you, I don't know why, but it's like I can't get the words to come out." He averted his gaze toward Diesel, still sniffing the tall grass.

"Peter, look at me."

He did. Kate saw fear and pain in his eyes.

"Peter, I love you. Don't you know that? There is nothing you could say to me that would change that. Please trust me."

"I don't want to hurt you," he said.

"Stop it. Whatever you have to say won't hurt me half as much as you are now. Talk to me, please."

He nodded and summoned his courage.

"I know I've hurt you."

"By doing what? You're not making any sense."

"You said as much by the Reflecting Pool four days ago. What I do, my job, and my company. We make weapons to kill people." He blurted out that last part so quickly and matter-of-factly that it even surprised him to hear it.

"Peter, listen to me. I told you I was sorry I said that. It was wrong."

He shook his head. "No. You were right."

"Peter—"

He held a hand up. "No. You *are* right. I've been blind for too long. Always justifying my work, on the grounds that it makes America safer. That the weapons I make save the lives of our soldiers. All the while ignoring that I'm just an arms merchant, peddling death."

"No. You're being too hard on yourself. And I was wrong for criticizing you."

"Well, I can fix this."

Kate tilted her head to the side and pursed her lips. "What are you talking about? There's nothing to fix."

"For you and me, yes there is. I can't risk losing you because of my work. I love you, Kate Simpson, and I don't want to live without you. I can't change what I've done, but I can choose a different path going forward. One we can both be proud of."

She didn't know what to say. Everything was happening too fast, and she was afraid Peter had made a rash decision.

Finally, she said, "What are you planning to do?"

"I'm going to sell the business. It will take some time, but I think I can convince one of the big players, maybe Colt or SIG, to buy it. The revenue is steady, and it would give them technology they don't have. I'll retire. I won't invent new and deadlier weapons anymore."

"But it's your passion."

Peter smiled. "Wrong. My passion is being with you. I've got enough saved that with the sale of the company, we'll be fine."

"What about the employees? They're your friends."

"Yes. And that's the tricky part. I will make it part of the deal that employment contracts and full benefits be given to every employee of EJ Enterprises. No more death dealing. No more treks to save the world, as you put it."

"I'm sorry," she said. "I didn't mean to be so harsh with my words. I see it hurt you, and I never wanted to do that."

"I want to live the rest of my life with you. And it's not fair that I cause you to worry that I could get killed. I want to change my life. I want to be your husband, your lover, your friend and partner, for the rest of our lives. I've been playing dice with the devil for many years. I don't want to do that anymore. I don't want to be an embarrassment to you, and I don't want you waking up screaming in the middle of the night. I have no idea what you ever saw in me. I'm not much to look at, and I'm not famous or wealthy. But I love you, and I'm not going to do anything to hurt you or drive you away."

Kate's eyes glistened as she looked upon Peter.

"You can't drive me away. Like it or not, you're stuck with me."

Peter pulled her close. "I do like it. Very, very much."

CHAPTER 15

BILLY HAD SPENT ALL OF THE PREVIOUS DAY collecting his thoughts and working to devise a plan. Once back at his trailer, he examined the contents of the suitcase. Beneath the top layer of bundled bills were stacks of paper. A real twenty-dollar bank note was on the surface to make each bundle look legitimate. But, in fact, the million-dollar payout was just shy of three hundred thousand.

He wasn't surprised. Cho was conning Billy as much as he was lying to her.

When he first connected with the Koreans, he honestly did plan to sell the PEAP carbine and pocket what he figured would be enough money to live on for a long time. But then he got ambitious.

After hearing that President Taylor had survived the first assassination attempt in Oregon, he just couldn't let it go. He had to correct that mistake, and he required the PEAP weapon to do it.

He had failed again. With two attempts on the president's life, security would be cinched tight. He'd have to wait many months, possibly a year or more, before attempting again. So selling to the Koreans no longer suited his needs.

Cho should have simply let it go, as if the deal had never been agreed to in the first place. And she'd made it personal by slitting Travis's throat like he was a hog to slaughter.

It took nearly a day for Billy to calm down enough to think clearly. Every time he pictured Travis lying in his own blood, with his head nearly severed, Billy became enraged. At first, all he wanted to do was kill Sung and every member of Cho's team. But that would be difficult and risky. He didn't even know how many men were working for Cho, or where to find any of them.

After the disastrous meeting, Billy figured that even Cho knew the deal was over. Whatever consequences she had to face with her Supreme Leader was her problem. And he wouldn't shed a tear if she was cut to ribbons by large-caliber gunfire, or executed in some other diabolical method.

He had retrieved the PEAP carbine from the hiding location inside the hollow tree. It was now on the table. He was examining the battery, since he reasoned that eventually he would either have to charge the battery—if that was even possible—or replace it.

The windows of the trailer were covered with heavy curtains so no one could see inside, on the off chance that someone walked by. He was far from civilization, hiding on public land near the Nez Perce Indian Reservation.

His phone rang, and the screen showed that the caller's number was blocked. He answered out of curiosity.

"Hello."

"Billy, I'm disappointed in you."

It was Cho.

His throat constricted as if unseen hands were clamping down on his trachea.

"Are you there, Billy? Don't be shy."

"I'm here. What do you want?"

"The product, of course. You made a deal. You promised to deliver the product."

"And you promised to pay for it. The suitcase was mostly filled with worthless paper."

Cho chuckled. "You had no right to take that money since you did not fulfill your end of the bargain. But you did, so consider it a down payment."

"You murdered Travis."

"It was you who attacked Mr. Bak first! After you reneged on the deal."

"Like I told you before, the deal is off. You forfeited the money. That's your loss."

"Perhaps. But…"

"But what?" Billy said.

"You haven't looked inside your truck recently, have you?"

Billy's pulse accelerated as he moved a curtain to glance out the window. The Power Wagon was still there, and it wasn't on fire or anything.

"So," he replied. "Should I?"

Billy was already out the door of the trailer, striding to the pickup, phone against his ear. Cho was laughing, as if a joke had been shared but Billy was left out of it.

She said, "I had my men leave something for you. Consider it a gift. Go on, take a look. I'll wait."

Billy jerked the driver's door open and gasped, nearly dropping his phone. There on the seat was an upright human head. The red hair was still tied back away from her face. The upholstery where the head rested was saturated in blood.

Billy was trembling now. He knew that if he pushed open the eye lids, he'd see Courtney's green irises. He retched and nearly dropped his phone, the vile sound carrying over the connection.

Cho said, "I see you discovered my present. Tell me, did Mr.

Sung do a nice job with the presentation? I instructed him to be...artful."

"You bitch! She had nothing to do with any of this!"

"I sent you a message." Cho's voice was hard, no longer touched with mirth. "A message that even you should be able to understand. You will deliver the weapon, or you will be next."

"You kill me, and you get nothing."

"You fool. You really think I care? Are you so stupid that you can't figure it out? Either way, I win. If I deliver the product to the Supreme Leader, he will reward my loyalty and resourcefulness. And if instead, I deliver your head, he will reward my loyalty and ruthlessness." She paused again, to let the message sink in.

Billy was in full panic, turning circles, searching for assassins in the shadows of the tall trees.

Cho said, "Now that I have your attention, what will it be? The weapon, or your head?"

CHAPTER 16

BILLY WIPED THE BACK OF HIS HAND across his mouth, trying to remove the rancid puke.

"Okay. I'll give it to you."

"Good," Cho said. "There's a junkyard about three-quarters of a mile out of Grangeville, just off Highway 95, on the way to Cottonwood."

"No, no, no. You come here. This is where the weapon is, and you obviously know where I am."

"Do not treat me like a fool. You have a reputation as one who is proficient at shooting long distances. It would be easy for you to pick off my team as we approach. Be at the junkyard in thirty minutes."

"Not enough time. I need an hour. The PEAP is stashed in a secure location where you'll never find it. I need time to retrieve it."

Cho considered Billy's claim. It seemed reasonable that he wouldn't have left it in his trailer or truck, where one of her men could have easily found it.

"One hour," she said. "Not a minute more. You know where the junkyard is?"

"I'll find it."

"You better not try to trick me again, or I'll hunt you to the ends of the earth. There is no place you'll be able to hide. No one who will be able protect you. I will find you. And when I do, you will suffer beyond anything you can imagine. Every second of every minute of every day will be a living hell. There will be no mercy, no pause. When you pass out, you will be brought back to consciousness. The torture will continue. You will beg me to put a bullet in your head. But I won't. Do we have an understanding?"

"Like I said, I'll be there."

With the call ended, he took a black plastic garbage bag to his pickup. Looking at Courtney's head, he almost vomited a second time, but somehow managed to slip the bag over the ghastly object. When he lifted the bag, the head dropped to the bottom, nearly jerking the plastic from his trembling fingers.

He backed away from the truck just in time—he heaved again until his stomach was empty.

Although Billy had shot and killed men, he always believed those acts were justified. He could even rationalize the murder of Travis as retaliation for his shooting of the Korean. But Courtney was innocent. For him to hold her disembodied head in a garbage bag was surreal, terrifying. He was experiencing certain emotions for the first time, and it unsettled him.

He carried the bag to the base of a tall tree. He didn't know how to impart any respect or dignity to the action, so he just did it. There was no time to dig a hole and bury it, nor could he think of a good reason why he should do so. She was dead, and that was a fact. How her remains were treated didn't matter.

Cho's men had found him. *But how?*

Billy searched the Dodge pickup for a tracking device, running a hand inside the steel bumpers and wheel wells. *Nothing.*

He'd run out of time. In the next several minutes, he had to gather a few items and split.

It was likely the police had figured out that Billy was involved in the shooting of the Korean named Bak. And when the severed head was eventually found, Billy would likely be the prime suspect in Courtney's murder too.

As he gathered his essential belongings, a stunning realization came to him like an epiphany: he was living on borrowed time. Maybe it was inevitable. Maybe it was Karma. Maybe it was just bad luck. Whatever the reason, he had one thing to do. One objective. And he was determined to see this last mission to the end.

⊕

Dust kicked up from the primitive dirt trail as Billy drove for the main road. Behind him, yellow flames from ten gallons of burning gasoline consumed his old travel trailer. When the propane tank blew, he felt, as much as heard, the deep *whump!*

The PEAP was snugged between padding in a hard case, and tucked behind the seatback. He had minimum possessions in a daypack, and the suitcase with the cash he'd taken from Cho was on the passenger seat. The blood-soaked cushion was covered in a blanket. He had to focus on other things, on getting away, to keep his stomach from churning.

As he turned onto Graves Creek Road, he was rewarded with the sight of a blue Chevy sedan in his rearview mirror. He'd expected a tail. The car accelerated to catch up, and was soon close behind Billy's Dodge pickup. In the mirror, he saw two men in the car—the driver, plus a passenger. He figured they intended to run him off the road and steal the weapon. But they could just as easily pull alongside and open up with pistols or a machine gun.

Either way, he was certain they intended to kill him and take the PEAP.

He pressed the accelerator, the twin exhaust pipes rumbling their appreciation as the Power Wagon pulled away from the sedan. But soon, the Chevy was right back on his tail. He slammed on the brakes and cranked the wheel hard to the right. The rear tires screeched and skidded on the blacktop, but the nose of the old truck obeyed and left the pavement for a gravel turnout.

Behind him, the sedan swerved to the left and came close to rolling. But the driver demonstrated his skill by reigning the car back under control. He did a U-turn across the center of the deserted two-lane road and raced after Billy's truck.

A cloud of dust marked the spot where the Dodge had darted into the trees along an old logging road. The road soon turned to a deeply rutted and potholed path, barely wide enough for one vehicle. It was a path that Billy knew, having scouted this trail on several occasions. His old four-wheel-drive pickup could never outrun a modern automobile on a smooth road. But on a primitive road, it would be impossible for the car to follow.

The network of old logging roads would eventually take him back to Highway 95, several miles south of Grangeville. Once back on the highway, he would travel south to the junction with Interstate 84 at the city of Ontario, on the Oregon border. After gassing up, it would be a straight shot to Bend.

CHAPTER 17

THE NIGHT SKY WOULDN'T BEGIN to lighten for another two hours, and Billy was exhausted. After filling the twin gas tanks in Ontario, on the Oregon-Idaho border, he followed Highway 20 due west. About three hours later, he cruised into Bend.

He saw a motel on the east side of Bend. The sign said, Vacancy, so he stopped. He booked a room for two nights and paid cash. With key card in hand, he retrieved the PEAP still in the hard-side case, the suitcase filled with money, and his daypack. It was risky to get a room, but he was exhausted, and needed rest to clear his mind. He gambled that he would not be easily recognized, especially by a night clerk at a hotel far from the scene of the crime.

Events over the previous two days had quickly spiraled out of control. One friend had been murdered in front of him, another decapitated.

Billy had intended to bring pain to the socio-economic class that occupied seats of power in the courts, the banks, and in government. He'd fantasized about sparking a revolution.

But his plans had failed. The government remained in control. President Taylor was still alive.

As he ruminated, he came to the realization that all he'd accomplished was to bring violence and death to two people he truly cared about. For the first time, he saw with clear eyes how his own suffering, and that of his mother and father, had driven him to follow a course of destruction. Now, he saw that many people he'd encountered, and most especially the leaders of the militia, had manipulated him, amplifying his anger and desire for revenge. Only, it wasn't to serve Billy's goal, but rather to satisfy their own lust for power.

Revenge.

It seemed to Billy that that word embodied the one constant in his life since his mother was killed and he was forced to live on the streets. With the murders of Travis and Courtney, with the failure of his grand plan for political change that would bring about social and economic equality, revenge was all he had left. It had become his purpose for being. Nothing else mattered.

He lay on the bed and closed his eyes. Soon, he would savor the taste of retribution. But first he would need to forge an alliance with an unwitting partner.

After hours of deep sleep that reinvigorated Billy's body and mind, he awoke to the sound of a vacuum being operated in the hall outside his door. Just before he fell asleep, he had closed the blackout draperies, so the room was still pitch black. He faced the clock—9:27 a.m.

Billy stretched and rubbed the sleep from his eyes. With his mind sharp again, he realized he needed to secure the cash. Much of it he crammed into the safe at the back of the closet. The remainder fit inside his daypack. He placed the empty suitcase out of the way, in a corner of the room.

After a quick shower, he exited through the lobby, stopping

just long enough to choke down a much-too-sweet Danish and fill a paper cup with burnt black coffee. He climbed in his truck and cranked over the engine, allowing it to idle while he checked his phone for messages. Cho had called him twice, leaving two expletive-filled messages that made her intensions clear: she was going to kill him in the most agony-filled manner imaginable. *No surprise there.*

Next, he activated the navigation app which displayed the most direct route to EJ Enterprises, and he drove out of the parking lot.

The traffic was light, and fifteen minutes later, Billy arrived at his destination. Rather than parking in front of the business, he drove on to a parking lot a half-mile away. With his Model 66 revolver in a hip holster covered by a baggy sweater, and his daypack hanging from his left shoulder, he walked back toward the small-arms business. There was a limit to the type and detail of information he could glean from Google maps, making the recce a necessary step in his planning.

The three smokestacks ahead towered above the old brick building occupied by EJ Enterprises. Across the two-lane street from the old powerhouse was a pocket park, and then rows of upscale stores mixed with restaurants. This was the Old Mill District of Bend, and tourists, as well as locals, were meandering along the sidewalk, mostly window shopping, some clutching bags of merchandise.

With the sun shining on his shoulders, Billy sauntered along. He stepped inside a clothing store on the opposite side of the street from the large brick structure. While pretending to be shopping for blue jeans, he studied the business through the plate glass window of the store he was in.

In front of EJ Enterprises, there were a half-dozen parking spaces reserved for visitors. None were occupied. There was no large, glitzy signage identifying the business—only simple black lettering on the glass front door. On the other side of the door was a lobby and a desk, behind which sat the receptionist. Given the foot traffic, it was difficult for Billy to clearly see the woman, but he could make out blonde hair. She appeared middle-aged—*probably knows how to handle visitors.*

Billy left the clothing store and crossed the street, then entered the business. He strode up to the blonde woman. A name plaque on the desk read, Nancy. She looked up as Billy approached.

"Good morning." She smiled.

"Hi," Billy replied. "I'm here to see Peter Savage."

Nancy consulted the calendar on her monitor. "I don't see anything on his calendar. Do you have an appointment?"

"No. I was in the neighborhood and thought I'd stop by."

"Well, I can schedule an appointment later this week, if you'd like. May I have your name and company?"

"I'm from out of the area, and just passing through."

Nancy frowned. "I'm really sorry, but—"

"It's rather important and won't take long. I have something Mr. Savage lost. I think it's important."

"Oh, I see. You can leave the item with me, and I'll see that he gets it later today."

"It's quite important, from what I can tell. But I'm not an expert on these things. Anyway, I really need to see if what I have is something he lost, and if he wants it back."

Nancy thought about the request. It was the first time she'd ever heard such an entreaty. *Guess there's a first time for everything.*

She dialed Peter's office. "There's a visitor in the lobby. He says he has something important to return to you."

⊕

Cho and two of her team members, both beefy men, were

at the North Korean safe house in Boise. Her government maintained several safe houses in many cities across the US. Although she didn't know how many fellow agents were in America, serving in sleeper cells, she assumed it was many times more than the ten men and women in the cell she commanded.

The cell operated under military protocol, and to avoid any misconception that their relationship was anything other than commander and soldier, she referred to those under her command by their last name. Discipline was tight. To disobey a directive would bring personal shame. A serious infraction would result in the offender being sent back to North Korean. Prison, or time in an indoctrination camp, were common sentences. The most severe punishment was meted out for disloyalty to the Supreme Leader. The penalty was death—for the family of the convicted, too.

Cho was studying her computer monitor while Mr. Ahn and Mr. Moon were both scrolling through postings in a chat room, searching for coded messages from the Reconnaissance General Bureau, or RGB, a North Korean intelligence agency.

"Get the car prepared," Cho said. "The tracking icon has been stationary since early this morning. It appears Billy Read has stopped running."

"Where?" Ahn said.

"Bend, Oregon. We can be there in six hours. Maybe less."

Ahn and Moon logged out and turned off their laptops. They descended the narrow wood steps into the basement of the safe house to gather supplies. Ahn stood to the side, clutching a heavy-duty duffle bag, while Moon spun the dial on a large, commercial gun safe. The double doors opened to reveal an arsenal of modern Chinese-made small arms: submachine guns, pistols, assault rifles, cases of ammunition loaded into magazines, one block of plastic explosive, detonators, and small incendiaries.

Moon ignored most of the weaponry, instead focusing on the suppressed pistols and submachine guns. The mission was to eliminate one civilian, and they would likely execute their mission in an urban environment. Assault rifles and explosives were not required.

He placed several pistols, submachine guns, tactical vests, and a dozen magazines into the bag.

"That should do it," he said.

Ahn zipped the bag closed.

CHAPTER 18

PETER ENTERED THE LOBBY and saw a lone man sitting in one of two black leather Art Deco chairs, thumbing through a local tourism magazine. He walked up to the man and extended his hand.

"Hello. I'm Peter Savage."

Billy jumped to his feet and extended his hand.

"Joshua Jones. Congratulations on receiving the Presidential Medal of Freedom."

Peter raised an eyebrow and cracked a lopsided grin.

"Yeah, well, it wasn't such a great experience."

"You mean the assassination attempt on President Taylor?"

Peter nodded. "Yeah. Was right there in the middle of it with my fiancée."

"That must have been terrifying."

"It was a moment to remember, that's for sure."

"Well, glad you made it out okay."

"Thank you." Peter narrowed his eyes and tipped his head to the side. "You look familiar. Have we met before?"

Although he didn't recognize Billy's bearded face, there was something familiar about his eyes.

"No, I don't think we have," Billy replied. "I'm sure I'd remember."

Peter nodded. "Nancy said you believe you have something of value to me?"

"Yes, I do."

"And?" Peter said, growing annoyed.

He had important work to get back to.

Billy made a point of casting his gaze around the lobby.

"Is there somewhere we can go that's a bit more private?"

"Mr. Jones, I have work to do. I would appreciate it if you'd get to the point."

"All right. I have an item that was taken from your business on May ninth. A rather valuable item."

Peter's eyes grew wide.

"Now that I have your attention…is there someplace we can talk privately?"

Peter checked his watch. "Okay. I've got thirty minutes. Let's go to my office."

"I've got a better idea. That coffee shop across the street looks inviting."

Peter looked to the coffee shop, then back at the bearded man.

"How about I call the police," he said. "Whatever your story is, you can share it with them."

"Sure, you could do that. Ain't no way I could stop you. But if you do, you'll regret it for the rest of your life."

After a moment of thought, Peter relented. Together, they walked into the little café. Peter knew the barista reasonably well, and there was no line to order.

"Two lattes please." He paid the cashier while Billy took a seat at a table in a quiet corner.

With a cup in each hand, Peter crossed to the table and sat across from the stranger.

"I'm listening, Mr. Jones. Or whatever your name is."

"My name doesn't matter. What does matter is what I have."

"Go on."

"I think this item is of great value. I'm not admitting to any wrongdoing. And I want a finder's fee."

"For what? You're gonna have to be more specific."

Billy sipped the latte, then leaned back in the chair.

"For a blaster," he said. "Right out of *Star Wars*."

Peter's heart skipped a beat. He glanced over his shoulder, making sure no one was within earshot.

"Tim McMullen stole that after he murdered two people. How did you get it?"

"Does it matter?"

"Yes, it does. Were you working with McMullen?"

"No." After a pause, Billy said, "Not directly."

"Not directly? What the hell does that mean?"

"Exactly what I said. Look, you got one shot at this, so don't waste it. I could just as easily auction it to the highest bidder."

"Then why don't you?"

Billy considered the question. It was fair to ask, but not easy to answer. Indeed, he felt conflicted. His mind whirled over different objectives before settling on one.

"I have my reasons," he replied.

"Don't tell me you suddenly grew a conscience."

Billy didn't like the probing questions. But he felt he had to answer. And as he did, he felt guilt lifting from his shoulders.

"Too late," he said. "Whatever conscience I had, has been replaced by remorse."

Peter said, "You want to sell *my* weapon back to me so you can sleep better at night. Is that it?"

"No. So *you* can sleep better at night. I don't think you're comfortable with that weapon in circulation. You know what it's capable of…in the right hands."

"I suppose you're speaking from experience?"

Billy tipped his head to the side and shrugged.

"I've had a lot of trigger time with it. And not just shooting melons, either. You and your engineers really did a fine job. That blaster can reach out and do some serious damage."

"You're disgusting," Peter said. "You sit here pretending to be a decent person, doing the right thing. How many people did you kill?"

"You have no right to judge me." Billy narrowed his eyes.

His countenance became cold and hard.

"You made that weapon. What did you think people would do with it?"

It was more an accusation than a question. And it cut to his marrow.

There was no doubt in Peter's mind as to his guilt. Kate was right. He was a merchant of death.

He lowered his gaze to his latte, hands cradling it reverently like it offered some power to heal his soul. Then an idea came to mind.

"How much do you want?"

"Depends. Two weeks ago, I would have said five million. But now—"

"You're insane," Peter blurted, a bit too loud, and the cashier looked at him.

He lowered his voice. "I'm not paying you five million dollars for my property."

Billy smiled. "And I'm not asking for five mil. But I gotta cover my expenses. Fifty grand."

Peter considered the proposal. Fifty thousand dollars was a lot of money. But if he could get the PEAP…

"Okay," he said. "I don't have that much cash just laying around. I'll need some time to get it from the bank."

"Take your time. You have all afternoon. Tomorrow, same

time. I'll be here enjoying a coffee. If you don't show with the money by the time I'm finished with my drink, the carbine will be on the auction block by the end of the day."

"I'll be here." Peter pushed his chair back.

"One last thing," Billy said. "No police. Got it? If I even suspect you've brought the law in on our exchange, the deal is off, and you'll never see me again."

"I'll have the money. Just make sure you deliver on your end of the bargain."

Peter rose from the table and walked out into the bright sunlight.

⊕

Billy waited five minutes and then left the café. He walked opposite from where he'd parked, and covered a mile before turning and looping back along a different route. He surreptitiously glanced back every now and then but didn't see anyone following him. Eventually, he returned to his Dodge truck, drove directly back to his hotel on the east side of Bend, packed up the remainder of the cash and his few possessions, and checked out.

This was the most dangerous phase of his plan. He didn't know where Cho and her team were. He didn't know if Peter was talking to the police, setting up a trap. For now, his best move was to change locations, and he knew the ideal place.

On a short bluff overlooking the Old Mill District, and of particular importance, EJ Enterprises, was a hotel. Once Billy was told they had several vacancies, he asked for a room overlooking the shops below. As before, he locked some of the cash in the room safe and carried the remainder in his daypack. The PEAP was still in the gun case, out of sight behind the seat of his truck. Carrying it with him was risky, as it was certain to draw attention .

He recalled walking past a music store. They had several guitars, electric and acoustic, on display in their window. It wasn't far away, an easy walk. The salesperson was helpful, and when Billy explained that he was just beginning to learn how to play, the salesperson showed two basic guitars. Billy bought the more expensive of the two because it came with a carrying case.

Next, he visited a sporting goods store that specialized in camping and backpacking equipment. He purchased a large duffle bag made of heavyweight black nylon. It had two carry straps that could also be looped over the shoulders and carried as a makeshift backpack. He also selected a pair of Nikon Monarch binoculars with a tripod, and paid cash for everything.

Back in his hotel room, Billy placed the guitar in the corner and tested the fit of the PEAP. The weapon was much smaller than the guitar. To prevent it from rattling as he carried the black case, Billy used a bath towel for padding.

The duffle bag was large enough to hold all the money he'd taken from Cho, so there was no need to keep the suitcase. He cut the handle with his knife, then took the bag down to the registration desk. He explained that since the handle had broke, he couldn't use the luggage any longer. The polite staff agreed to dispose of it for him.

From the window of his hotel room, he had a decent view of EJ Enterprises and the nearby shops. The tripod provided a solid rest for the twenty-power binoculars, affording a clear view of people shuffling by the stores.

⊕

"Who's your new friend?" Nancy said, as Peter passed through the lobby, on the way to his office.

"He's not my friend," Peter called back.

Two minutes later he strode past Nancy again.

"Cancel my appointments for the rest of the day. And

tomorrow morning." Then he was out the door.

"That's odd," she said to herself.

It wasn't like Peter to cancel his appointments, unless something more important had come up. It also wasn't like him to not offer a brief explanation.

Peter's behavior didn't feel right. She paged Todd Steed, the person at EJ Enterprises who knew Peter best.

A few minutes later, Todd was at the reception counter. He was still wearing safety glasses over his chestnut eyes, suggesting he had been working at one of the machining centers. He was wiping his hands on a blue bandana that normally rode in a back pocket of his canvas jeans. His short-cropped hair and goatee beard, both the color of milk chocolate, combined with an ever-present dour expression, gave many the impression he was former military. In fact, like Peter, he had never served.

"Hey, Nancy. What's up?"

"I was hoping you could tell me. Peter just left suddenly. He's not himself."

"Really?"

Nancy relayed the few details she had, and added her observations of the unannounced visitor, as well as Peter's behavior.

"I really don't know," Todd said. "I wouldn't worry about it, though. Trust me, Peter can take care of himself."

"Yeah, I'm sure you're right. Still, this guy's behavior was odd. Something just doesn't feel right."

"Well, if you're that concerned, why don't you call that detective with Bend Police who interviewed all of us a couple weeks back. Maybe this visitor is somehow related to that crime."

"Yeah. I think I will."

Nancy still had Detective Ruth Colson's business card in her desk drawer. She made the call while Todd stood by.

CHAPTER 19

FROM THE HOTEL ROOM, Billy watched as a dark-blue sedan parked in front of EJ Enterprises. The vehicle had cheap stock wheels and a license plate that indicated the car was registered to a government agency.

Shit. He's called the police.

A woman with short-cut gray hair and neon-green sneakers walked inside.

Billy moved the binoculars left and right, taking in the pedestrians and vehicular traffic within his field of view. He didn't expect to find any marked patrol cars, and he didn't see any. Still, he'd half-expected Peter to contact law enforcement. And he'd planned for it.

To Billy's thinking, the odds were fifty-fifty that Peter would show up with the money. Regardless, after the exchange was made, he'd force Peter to take a long walk with him, circling around the hotel before ending up at his pickup. If police were following them, Billy would have many opportunities to spot them. And if the police cornered him, he would have Peter's life to trade for his own freedom.

⊕

"Is Mr. Savage here now?" said Ruth Colson.

Her trademark bright-green University of Oregon Duck sneakers seemed to glow against her indigo jeans and gray sweater. Approaching retirement age, she was old-school to the core and insisted on writing her notes on the lined pages of a pocket-sized notepad.

Nancy shook her head. "No. Like I explained, he came back from the coffee shop, told me to cancel his appointments, and then left."

"And he didn't say where he was going or when he'd be back?"

"No. Nothing."

"This visitor he met with...did he give his name? Maybe a business card?"

"No, I'm sorry. I asked for his name and company, but he just said he had something he thought belonged to Peter, and that he wanted to return it."

"Can you describe him?"

Nancy rolled her eyes toward the ceiling, seeing the man's face in her mind.

"He was the same height as Peter. Probably similar weight. He was black, had a full beard, and his hair was cut short on the sides but much longer on the top of his head."

"Any obvious scars, birthmarks, tattoos?" Colson was scribbling, even as she asked questions.

"Nothing that I saw."

"What was he wearing?"

"Blue jeans and sneakers. He wore a dark gray, almost black, sweater that was untucked."

Detective Colson looked up from her notepad. "Anything else you can think of?"

Nancy frowned. "No."

"Well, nothing you've shared suggests a crime has been

committed. I have no justification to put out an APB for this guy, or for Mr. Savage. Still, I would like to talk with him once he returns."

"I understand. And I'll let him know you'd like him to call you."

"I'll just stop by tomorrow. He won't call me. We aren't exactly friends." Colson slipped the notepad in the back pocket of her jeans before turning to leave, but hesitated. "You know, life is never dull when it comes to your boss."

Nancy raised her eyebrows, considering the detective's words an understatement.

⊕

Fifteen minutes after she arrived, the gray-haired lady with the green shoes left EJ Enterprises. Now that the police were involved, Billy would modify his plan slightly, putting into play contingencies he'd already thought through.

He could deal with the police. They were nothing more than an inconvenience. But a greater threat still loomed.

Billy continued glassing, even through the twilight of sunset. Only when it was too dark to make out facial details did he stop for the night. He was famished, and ordered room service—cheeseburger with fries, and two beers. After devouring the meal, he reclined on the bed and fell into a restless slumber.

⊕

Cho was following the tracking signal using a proprietary app on her phone. The app had been developed by the Technology and Cyber Bureau of the RGB. She had used the app many times in training, but never before when an important objective was at stake.

Halfway between Boise and Bend, she noticed that the tracking icon was moving. She watched with trepidation, fearing that Billy was leaving Bend. They could certainly pursue him—the battery in the transmitter would last another two weeks—but what if he decided to travel across the country? Or worse, into Canada or Mexico? She and her team always carried their forged papers—passports and driver licenses—but a border crossing represented risk.

She exhaled a sigh of relief when the icon became fixed again. Billy was still in Bend.

Sung was behind the wheel of the minivan, driving with the flow of traffic, mindful of his speed. The nylon sports bag in the back of the van was filled with ammunition and weaponry they did not want to be discovered by a nosy police officer conducting a routine traffic stop.

"He's moved to a new location," Cho said. "How long until we're in Bend?"

Sung glanced at the odometer. He always made a mental note what the mileage reading would be when he reached a predetermined destination.

"Another two hours," he replied.

Cho sat lower in the passenger seat, staring at the tracking icon. She spread her thumb and index finger to zoom in the map.

"Looks like he's at a hotel. Let's hope he stays there."

The remainder of the drive was completed with hardly a word spoken. Sung remained focused on the road, while Ahn, Moon, and Hann—the muscle of the team—road stoically in the rear seat.

Arriving at the outskirts of Bend, Sung slowed and navigated to the location of the hotel that coincided with the tracking icon. He parked away from the front entrance and turned off the engine. From the minivan, the five pairs of eyes scanned the parking lot for Billy's truck. It didn't take long to spot it.

"That sure does look like his truck," Mr. Ahn said, from the back seat.

"Walk over there slowly and confirm it's the right one," Cho told Sung.

When he was next to the Dodge Power Wagon, Sung stopped and removed his wallet. While pretending to look for some item of importance, he glanced inside the locked cab, where he saw the blanket spread over the seat, and a smear of dried blood at the junction of the seat back and cushion. Still enacting the ruse, he frowned and pushed his wallet back into his pocket, then turned and walked back to where he'd come from.

After a quick scan of his surroundings, and determining that no one was watching, he entered the minivan.

"Yeah, it's Billy's truck, all right. A blanket is covering most of the seat, but I could see dried blood on the seat where Sung put the lady's head."

"Good," Cho replied. "So he is at the hotel. Why?"

No one dared to venture an answer.

She drew in a deep breath and exhaled. "Doesn't matter. He's here. That is all we need to know. Let's go inside. Moon—you stay here and watch the parking lot. If you see him, call me immediately. If he drives away before I get back to the van, forget about me and follow him. Understood?"

"Yes, ma'am," Moon replied.

After the others vacated the vehicle, he sat behind the wheel, keys in the ignition and ready to go.

Inside the hotel lobby, Sung and the other two Koreans found seats and pretended to focus on their phones while Cho walked up to the reception desk.

"Hello." The receptionist gave a warm smile. "I'm expecting to meet a business colleague here. His name is Reed. Billy Reed. Can you tell me if he's checked in yet?"

"Just a minute while I check." The young woman typed information into a computer hidden from view by the counter. A moment later, she said, "Yes. Mr. Reed checked in today. Would you like to leave a message?"

"No, thank you. I'll come back a little later."

Cho took the rear exit from the hotel and found herself on the bluff overlooking the stores of the Old Mill District. There was a narrow patch of lawn and a few benches. The sidewalk tracked back around the hotel to the front.

Cho strolled back to the minivan. After making a short call, she shared her plan.

"Okay. He's definitely here. I ordered a backup team to be here within eight hours. I'm not taking any chances this time."

The sun was almost touching the Cascade Mountains to the west.

She continued. "There's a restaurant and a bar inside the hotel, and several diners down the hill in the shopping district. Go two at a time and get something to eat. Use the facilities, because it's going to be a long night. There are some benches behind the hotel. We are going to watch the back entrance, the front entrance, and Billy's truck. When he shows himself, we follow him until I determine it's safe to take him. Does everyone understand?"

Naturally, they did.

CHAPTER 20

MAY 31

BILLY ROSE BEFORE FIRST LIGHT and ordered room service—scrambled eggs, biscuits and gravy, coffee. As the morning sky brightened, he was again scanning the streets and shops surrounding EJ Enterprises, through the Nikon binoculars.

Having observed the unmarked police car yesterday afternoon, he was wary of a trap. He figured the police would come in early so they could nab convenient parking slots that weren't too near the coffeehouse where he would meet Peter Savage in a few hours, but not too far away. Then they would station one or two plainclothes officers in the café, and most likely several more nearby. They wouldn't make a move on him until he displayed the PEAP carbine or delivered some other form of incriminating evidence.

Billy also assumed Peter would be wearing a wire, and that video would record his meeting. They might reposition the security cameras inside the coffee shop. Or maybe they would have high-def cameras placed across the street, filming through the front window of the café.

Whatever the plan might be, they would be on-site to

prepare well before the meeting time. And so he patiently watched.

After two hours, nothing out of the ordinary had appeared. No unmarked police sedans. No delivery vehicles came to the coffee shop. No people loitering. Nothing.

He was beginning to believe he'd overreacted and that there was no trap, no imminent police action. Then he recalled a local district attorney's interview he'd read in the Idaho Statesman. The DA had quipped, "If criminals were smart, we wouldn't catch as many."

Billy was determined to continue being a smart criminal. No—a brilliant criminal.

One hour before the appointed meeting time, Billy left his hotel room, sporting his dark sunglasses, guitar case in hand. The large nylon duffle bag he purchased the previous day, now filled with the money he'd taken from Cho, was resting on his shoulders. He wore a different shirt from the day before, just in case law enforcement had his description. His gray and white flannel shirt was buttoned but left untucked, so he had easy access to the Smith & Wesson Model 66 holstered high on his hip.

He avoided the elevator and took the stairway to the lobby. In the stairwell, he had freedom of movement not afforded in the confined elevator. On the ground floor, he passed two rooms being cleaned, their doors opened while housekeeping completed their tasks. He came to the main hallway. To the right was the lobby, and a few people were milling about. Indistinct chatter floated over the air.

Billy froze. Two Asian men were seated opposite each other. One was watching the people in the lobby, while the other seemed to be peering outside across the parking lot.

First one foot, then the other, and Billy eased back around the corner and out of sight. *Could they be working for Cho?*

Although he didn't recognize the faces, he was certain Cho had others on her team he'd not yet seen.

He reversed direction, seeking a rear exit. He approached one of the maids, who was at her cart in the hall, collecting an armload of folded towels.

"Is there another way out?" he asked the woman.

She pointed. "The lobby's that way."

"No. Is there another exit this way." He pointed down the hall.

"Just the employee entrance. But you have to have a key. It's not for guests."

"You can help me. I can't go out the front entrance."

"I'm sorry, sir. Those are the rules."

"Please," Billy pleaded.

He reached into his pocket and pulled out two twenty-dollar bills.

Offering the money, he said, "There are men in the lobby who want to hurt me."

She took the money, made certain no one was watching, then led Billy to a door marked by an overhead exit sign. A sign on the door said, Employees Only. She removed a key card from her pocket and swiped it past the lock. With a metallic click, the door opened.

"Go to your left," she said. "You'll see the exit door. It's not locked from the inside."

Billy nodded. "Thank you."

"You stay outta trouble, mister," she called, as Billy disappeared from view.

He swiftly followed the concrete walkway away from the hotel, past the employee parking, and down a triple flight of stairs to the upscale shopping district. It was midmorning, and already there was a lot of pedestrian traffic moving past the storefronts.

Billy slowed his pace, occasionally stopping to look at a window display, using the reflection in the plate glass to furtively observe activity on the far side of the street. He was looking for specifics: license plates indicating a publicly owned vehicle, strangers taking an undue interest in him, Asian men and women who might be agents for North Korea. Specific, but subjective.

His plan was to walk a large loop around EJ Enterprises so he could see what might have been missed from his hotel window. He took his time—just a visitor with his guitar, checking out this trendy part of Bend. At one point, he stopped and sat on a bench, the guitar case upright between his knees. He leaned back as far as he could with the duffle bag on his shoulders and stretched his arms out, turning his head side to side and stretching his neck.

Nothing. If someone had been following him, they might have stopped, feigning some innocent activity like Billy was. But he saw nothing to raise suspicion.

He continued his surveilling until he arrived at the coffee shop and found a seat in a far corner, as he had the previous day. He stood the guitar case against the wall, placed his duffle bag on a chair, then went to the cashier and ordered a large mocha. While the barista was preparing his beverage, he glanced around, trying to locate the security camera. He found two: one was pointed at the entrance, and the second was behind the counter and aimed so that any customers would be directly in the lens view.

He gathered his drink and returned to his table. The few patrons paid him no attention. It was still early. He didn't expect Peter for another thirty minutes. With time to kill, he sipped his mocha and watched people walking by the window.

⊕

"Some guy—maybe it's Billy—just left the hotel through the employee entrance," Moon said to Cho, on his phone.

"He's probably just one of the hotel staff. Why do you think it's Billy?" she said with vexation.

Although, with her backup team, she now had seven covert agents, she couldn't afford to have their numbers reduced by a wild goose chase.

"I thought about that," Moon replied. "But he was carrying a guitar case, and had a backpack on his shoulders. I didn't get a good look at his face. I was too far away. But he's the right height and build, and has a dark complexion."

Cho thought for a moment, trying to come up with a reason why one of the hotel staff would have a guitar and a backpack. She couldn't.

"Okay," she said. "Follow him. See where he's going, but keep your distance. If you need to, call for backup."

CHAPTER 21

"YOU'RE QUIET THIS MORNING," Kate said, as Peter poured a mug of coffee.

"Oh, sorry," he replied. "Just have a lot to do today."

"Don't forget, you promised to meet Abby and me for lunch."

Abby was Kate's coworker and best friend.

"I did?"

"Yes, you did. Pine Tavern at noon. Remember?"

"I'm sorry. It completely slipped my mind. Would you mind if I skipped? You can have a relaxing lunch with Abby. I've got a really full day, and with the wedding coming up, I need to be at work."

Kate turned her mouth down in a pretend frown.

"All right," she said. "I'll excuse you. But this time only. Anyway, I have a lot of errands to run so that everything will be perfect for the ceremony."

"Thank you." Peter leaned forward and kissed Kate on the lips. "Tell Abby I said hello."

Then he left out the front door.

⊕

Peter entered the coffeehouse, his hands empty, and strode directly to Billy.

"Have a seat," Billy said. "Glad you could make it."

Peter sat across from Billy.

"You're in a jovial mood today," Peter said.

"Well, don't do anything to change it."

"Do you have the PEAP?"

Billy tipped his head, indicating the black guitar case.

"Did you get the money?" he said.

"Took some doing, but I got it."

"Where is it?"

"You didn't expect me to bring fifty thousand dollars in here and just lay it on the table."

"Suppose not. Doing a weapons deal here in this lily-white neighborhood wouldn't be good, would it?"

"No, not if you want to avoid attention."

"Speaking of attention, what were the police doing at your business yesterday afternoon?" Billy said po-lice with a pronounced long O, like he was ordering a po'boy sandwich.

Peter was taken aback that Billy had the ability to surveil his company. Clearly he'd underestimated his adversary.

"It's nothing," Peter replied.

"Best if I make that determination," Billy said.

"Okay. My receptionist, Nancy—you met her yesterday—she thought something odd was happening. Thought you were suspicious. She called the Bend Police after I left for the bank to get your money."

"What did you say to the police? Are they here?"

"I didn't say anything. And no, they're not here. We made a deal. You give me the PEAP, and I give you fifty grand. I've got the money—in a safe location."

"And where's that?" Billy said.

"First, I want proof you actually have the PEAP."

Billy shrugged, then placed his phone on the table. It showed a photograph of the PEAP carbine laying inside the open guitar case. Peter studied the image, using his thumb and finger to enlarge the photograph. Yesterday's Bend Bulletin newspaper was laying next to the weapon.

"Satisfied?" Billy said.

"Yes."

"Where's the money?"

"Across the street. I live above EJ Enterprises."

Peter knew it was risky to bring Joshua Jones—or whatever his name really was—into his home. But he had backup.

"That's convenient," Billy said. "Alone?"

Peter hesitated before answering. Technically, he did live alone. Both his children were adults and living their own independent lives. Kate had a key, naturally, and she came and went as if it was her home. And soon it would be. But for now, it was only Peter and Diesel on a regular basis.

"Yeah. Just me and my dog."

"All right, let's go. I'll follow you."

As Billy walked across the street, a step behind Peter, he never noticed the Asian man watching from a half-block away.

⊕

As soon as the front door opened, Diesel was there to greet his master. But it wasn't right. There was a stranger present, and Diesel emitted a guttural growl that left no ambiguity as to his intentions.

"Easy boy," Peter reached down and rubbed the large head and thick neck. "He's with me. A… colleague. It's okay."

"Nice dog you have there," Billy quipped. "Where'd you find him? At the junkyard?"

"Just don't do anything aggressive or threatening, and you'll be fine."

Peter opened the door wider and entered first, followed by Billy. Diesel was locked onto the stranger, on edge, and showing it with raised hackles and occasional growls.

Inside Peter's home, Billy's gaze was immediately drawn to the mantle above the hearth. His head turned as he took it all in. Extending off the west-facing wall separating the fireplace from the bookcase was a rustic deck, built from wood and steel, the metal having taken on an orange patina. With access through two pairs of French doors, the deck offered breathtaking views of the Cascade Mountains.

"Nice digs you have here," Billy said, still exploring the interior décor. "Aren't you going to offer me coffee, or maybe a drink?"

"Let's be clear—this isn't a social visit. Set the case on the sofa. I want to see what you're selling."

Billy held his ground. "Where's the money?"

"Locked away in my safe. Let's stop playing games, all right? I'm pretty sure you're armed. So if you want to see the money, you better show me you're holding up your end of the bargain."

"You're a pretty smart dude, you know that?" Billy said.

"Flattery won't get you anywhere." Peter scowled.

"Okay, okay. I'll show you what I got."

Billy laid the guitar case across the leather cushions. He popped the clasps and tilted the cover back. When he removed the towel wrapped around the weapon, Peter felt his pulse quicken.

There, before his eyes, was a stocked weapon. About the size of a carbine, it had a large-diameter barrel machined from a billet of aluminum, with an oversized scope mounted above the barrel. On the bottom of the butt stock was the master power switch and a mini-LED light that indicated remaining battery power. Inside the pistol grip is where the battery should have been located, but there was just an empty space.

"Where's the battery pack?" Peter said.

"Used up all the juice. It's dead. I was looking for a replacement, but couldn't find anything. Not even online. So I came to the conclusion that *that* battery is unique to the military."

Peter nodded. The sight of the weapon resurfaced conflicting and powerful emotions. This fabricated chunk of metal and circuit boards had wrought much death recently, and Peter had come to realize it did not feel good to be the architect and inventor of such a device.

"Tell me something," Peter said, his gaze fixed on the PEAP carbine. "I have a pretty good idea what you did with this, although I could never prove it. Still, I deserve to know…" He faced Billy. "Why?"

Billy shrugged. "I'm not a big fan of the government. They haven't done me or my family any favors. Treated us pretty badly, in fact."

"Then why are you returning this to me? Why not simply continue on your murderous journey? Or sell the weapon to some terrorist group? Or maybe to Iran or Russia? You could make a lot of money."

"Thought about it. Came close to doing just that. They were supposed to pay me a million bucks."

"Supposed to? Let me guess, they lied to you. Imagine that. There really is no honor among criminals."

"Listen to you. You got it all figured out, living the life of Riley and all. I'll bet you have no idea what it's like to lose everything. To live on the street and fight everyday just to survive. To sit on the corner with a cardboard sign, begging for spare change. Maybe a buck or two if you're lucky. More often than not, nothing. Rain or shine, hot or cold, it don't matter, because you got nothing other than the filthy clothes you're wearing, and whatever money strangers give you. No one will give you a job because you stink of piss and sweat. There ain't no one from the government to help. Hell, the government sends the cops out after you. They say you can't sleep here, can't sleep there. You can't be here. There ain't no help. They just want you to go away."

Peter swallowed hard. Billy was right, he had no comprehension of how hard life was for many.

Billy continued. "The government doesn't care about people like me. They only care about people with money and power. I don't have any allegiance to this government, to this society. They took my mother and my father from me. Left me nothing. But I found a purpose."

"You still haven't answered my question," Peter said.

"The people who were going to buy the PEAP, they double-crossed me. They murdered my friends. So I took their money."

"But it wasn't the full amount they promised, is that right?"

Billy shook his head. "I told them the deal was off. But they wouldn't let it go. They told me to bring the weapon to a second meeting, and I refused. They cut off the head of a waitress I knew from Grangeville. Her name was Courtney. She was a nice kid. I liked her. Anyway, they killed her and put her head on the seat of my truck."

"Did you go to the police?"

"Are you serious?" Billy said, his voice elevated, his eyes red and moist.

Diesel took a step toward Billy and lowered his head. The canine's muscles were taut.

Peter said, "Easy, boy. Stay."

"The Law ain't gonna help me. Haven't you heard anything I've said? They would just throw my ass in jail and put me on trial for the murder of my friends. Then once I was convicted, they'd put a needle in my arm. Done and over."

"Okay, okay. Calm down," Peter said.

Billy sniffled and wiped the back of his hand across his nose.

"I'm good with a rifle," he said. "Figure after you give me my money, I'll go into the wilderness north of Boise. I know the area, and when Cho and her men come looking for me, I'll kill them. I'll kill them all."

"Cho? Is she the leader of the group you were doing the deal with?"

"That's right. Koreans."

Peter started to get a bad feeling.

"You mean North Koreans?"

"That's right. Now, I want my money."

Peter strode across the great room, eager to complete the transaction, and opened a hinged panel in the bookcase, swinging it aside to reveal a secret room—his gun room.

"My safe's in here," he said.

From the middle of the great room, Billy watched as Peter spun the combination dial on a large two-door safe. On the walls of the gun room were an assortment of antique weapons— muskets, pistols, and even a blunderbuss.

"You collect old guns or something?" he said.

"Yeah, something like that." Peter pulled open the heavy door.

Inside the safe were more firearms—rifles, shotguns, and pistols—but modern in design. He grabbed a small nylon briefcase and lifted it from the floor of the safe. He stepped back into the great room and set the briefcase on the floor, then stooped over and opened it. Inside were five bundles of hundred-dollar bills. Each bundle was one hundred notes, or ten thousand dollars.

"That's a lot of money," Billy said.

"You're telling me. It was hard to round up on short notice.

Seems not all banks routinely keep large amounts of cash on hand."

A knock at the door startled Peter. He exchanged a glance with Billy, who said, "Expecting someone?"

"No. Probably a delivery. I'll take care of it." Peter walked to the door and turned the knob.

The door flew open, narrowly missing his face.

While Peter was stumbling backward, a stout Asian man barreled through the opening, a pistol in his hand. But the man's forward progress halted when the seventy-pound red pit bull flew into his midsection and clamped down on his gun arm. Cries of pain melded with Diesel's throaty growl. As the canine's weight hung from the man's arm, furthering the ripping of muscle and tendons, he collapsed to his side. With four feet on the floor, Diesel pulled the man's arm until it was stretched straight and away from his torso, all the while shaking his head violently from side to side.

Peter picked up the pistol, a compact Walther PK380, and aimed it at the Asian man. His hand smothered the grip, and with the short barrel it felt comfortable.

"Diesel. Enough."

The pit bull released his grip on the man's bloodied arm and took two steps backward but never relaxed his focus on his prey. The dog's canines and premolars had lacerated large sections of flesh on the gunman's forearm. Blood was flowing from severed veins, and he was attempting to staunch the flow by pressing his hand against the wound.

"Who are you," Peter said.

The man glared back, his teeth gritted, a visage of malice.

Billy stepped forward. "You work for Cho, don't you?"

"You're a dead man!" the Asian shouted at Billy.

"Maybe. But not by your hand. How did you find me?"

"I need a doctor," the Asian said.

"You need to answer our questions," Peter said, "or I'll let my dog eat your arm for lunch."

The Asian man's eyes darted about the room, and finally settled on Diesel. The pit bull was giving his best menacing posture: lips pulled back in a permanent sneer, revealing ivory fangs and blood-covered gums. Tense shoulder muscles, a tight spring ready to launch, and blood-chilling snarls that seemed to originate deep within the creature's throat and reverberate until escaping his teeth.

With wide eyes , the Asian man looked at Peter.

"Okay. Moon. My name is Moon. Just keep your dog away from me."

"Did Cho send you?" Billy said. "Who else is here?"

"Yes. Cho placed a tracking beacon in the suitcase that you took with the money. She knew you would try to trick her and take the money without delivering the product."

Billy felt like he'd been punched in the gut. It never occurred to him to check the suitcase. The tracking beacon explained how the Koreans were able to find his trailer in the forest and then track him to Bend. They would've had plenty of time to organize and position a kill team.

He had one option, and that was to grab his cash and get out of Bend. Fast.

CHAPTER 22

"I'M OUT'A HERE," BILLY SAID.

"What do you mean?" Peter replied.

"You got your weapon back, and I got my payment. The deal is done."

Billy grabbed the handles of the satchel, repositioned the straps of the duffle bag across his shoulders, and headed for the door.

"Nice doin' business with you," he said. "Now I have to get out of here while I still can."

He figured he had a small window of opportunity. Since he'd ditched the suitcase at the hotel, once he left, Cho wouldn't have any means to track him. Or so he hoped. But what if she'd placed a GPS tracker on his truck?

He'd have to get rid of the truck after leaving Bend, and replace it with an inexpensive used vehicle. Then he'd head straight back to Idaho and vanish into the wilderness. There, he would wait and watch, like a spider. And if Cho or her men ever showed up, they'd get a .30-caliber hunting bullet delivered at more than twice the speed of sound.

Billy had only taken three strides when the front door flew open a second time. He brushed his shirt aside and wrapped his hand around the grip of the Smith & Wesson revolver. He drew, clearing his holster before the gunmen rushing in could raise their weapons.

Billy looked along the barrel, not really using the sights. He pulled the trigger, and the room was filled with a deafening explosion as the 125-grain hollow-point bullet sped toward the first man at fifteen hundred feet per second. It struck him in the upper left side of his chest, expanding rapidly and dumping energy into muscle and bone. The man spun as if his shoulder had been hit with a sledgehammer.

The bullet clipped the top of the Korean's lung, and blood was pumping into the internal void. His breathing was labored, and with each breath, he exhaled frothy bright-red blood. His body weakened rapidly, and he was soon unconscious.

The second man through the door had his pistol raised, and he wasted no time firing. A soft *pft* coincided with each shot from the suppressed pistol.

Diesel launched, his new target the gunman shooting at Billy. Peter was raising the Walther as the canine rushed forward.

Billy went down, a red mist shrouding his chest.

Peter fired the Walther—again, and again, and again. The bullets struck the man. Shaky, he was still able to stay on his feet and adjust his aim. *Pft, pft, pft.*

Bullets whistled past Peter. Diesel jumped and clamped down on the gunman's arm, yanking his pistol lower and to the side.

Peter kept firing. On the last shot before the magazine was empty, the Asian gunman slumped to his knees and released his weapon. The man fell forward, and Diesel released his grip on his arm.

Peter heard footfalls on the steps leading to his door. Anticipating the worst, he dropped the Walther and closed on Billy. The man was motionless, a pool of blood gathering beneath his chest and gradually expanding. Peter removed the revolver from his lifeless fingers.

Resting on one knee and holding the revolver with two hands in a classic shooting stance, Peter aimed the weapon at the doorway. He cocked the hammer and tickled the trigger with his index finger.

"Diesel. Stay."

The dog stood by his master. And like his master, his gaze was focused on the doorway. He growled an ominous warning to whoever was approaching.

Step by step, unseen persons grew closer. First, heads came into view. Black hair and dark complexion indicated their race and suggested their nationality. But there was an anomaly. And then Peter's heart skipped a beat. He was overcome with trepidation, and for a moment his arms fell limp.

Quickly, he recovered. Four men and two women filled the entry. He aimed the revolver at the largest of the men, but his hands were unsteady.

Kate was there, held in an iron grip, a suppressed pistol pressed to her temple.

"Let her go," Peter said.

The Asian woman stepped forward, taking in the scene before her, a submachine gun hanging across her chest. The gun barrel was pointed toward the floor. Her gaze tracked first to the three Korean men, and then to Billy. All four were laying prone in their own blood.

She said, "I see you overcame Mr. Sung and Mr. Ahn."

"They were amateurs," Peter said. "It wasn't hard to do."

"Mr. Moon is still alive?"

He was slouched against the wall, one hand covering the ragged wound on his arm.

"For now," Peter said.

Cho took another step toward him. If she felt any fear, it didn't show.

"Another cocky American. Just like Billy Reed." She made a point of casting her gaze toward his lifeless body. "I see he didn't fare well either."

Now it made sense to Peter. The stranger he knew as Joshua Jones looked familiar for a good reason. Billy Reed was the principal suspect in two murders that had been committed using the PEAP carbine stolen from EJ Enterprises. A photograph of him had aired on national news, but the face in that picture did not have a beard. The eyes were identical, though, and Peter had no doubt it was the same man.

Peter shifted his aim to the Korean woman. "What do you want?"

Diesel was still by his side, the dog's muscles rippling with anticipation, his amber eyes locked on the woman.

"I should think you would know that. I want the weapon."

"No. You can't have it."

"Really? What's to stop me from just taking it? You?"

Peter was staring into the muzzles of three guns, and his fiancée had a pistol to her head. Far from the best position for negotiation.

"Let Kate go, and we can work out a deal."

"Kate? Is that the woman's name? She must mean something to you. I thought she was just another nobody. Someone with the misfortune of being in the wrong place at the wrong time."

"Story of my life," Peter mumbled.

"I'm sorry, I didn't get what you just said."

Peter rolled his eyes. "Just that I always seem to be the one who is in the wrong place at the wrong time. Like now."

Cho smiled, convinced she had the upper hand.

"Indeed." She paused, continuing to smile. "Where is the weapon?"

It suddenly dawned on Peter that from her position in the entryway, she couldn't see the open guitar case resting on the sofa before the fireplace, or the contents within.

"Who are you?" he said.

"My name is not relevant. But if it makes you feel better, I am called Cho. My mission is at the direction of the Supreme Leader. I want the weapon."

"North Korea." Peter kept his revolver aimed at the close group of armed men.

"Yes," Cho replied smugly. "If you do not give me the laser weapon, I will instruct my men to gun you down."

Kate was struggling against her captors, and cried out, "No! Let us go!"

"Only when I get what I want, my dear," Cho said, obviously enjoying her moment of power.

"Let her go," Peter said. "Then I'll give you the PEAP."

"You have no leverage to dictate terms—"

The sound of distant sirens.

"Time is running out." Peter shifted his aim to the man holding Kate.

"Last time, Mr. Savage," said Cho. "Where is the—"

For the second time, the Model 66 roared and dispatched the man holding Kate with a hollow-point bullet to his head.

Peter yelled, "Kate, run!"

She did. But rather than fleeing for the safety of the street and the constant pedestrian traffic, she bolted toward Peter and Diesel, who charged for the closest gunman, protecting Kate as she fled. The pit bull leaped for the man's face but fell short, and instead bit down on his throat. Claws on all four legs were tearing at his chest and abdomen. Blood sprayed from the wound, his cry truncated to a gurgling plea. But the cry was to no affect as he collapsed, Diesel's jaws still clamped in a death grip.

Cho raised her weapon—a Type 79 submachine gun—and began firing. Bullets shot toward Kate and Peter. Cho moved the barrel and sprayed bullets toward Kate, striking her in the lower extremities. Kate fell to her face, her arms splayed out to the sides.

"No!" Peter shouted.

He adjusted his aim to Cho, but before he could fire, a bullet grazed his right shoulder. He fell to his right at the same time he squeezed the trigger. His shot just missed Cho. She heard as much as felt the sonic crack of the bullet, and ducked.

Peter snapped off another shot at Cho, but again narrowly missed. Still, it drew her attention and aim away from Kate.

He shouted to be heard above the din: "Diesel! Attack!"

Peter tried to rise to his feet, but instead dove to the side as Cho let rip another wicked volley from the Chinese-made submachine gun. Cutting through the ringing in his ears, he heard the predatorial snarls and growls from Diesel, followed quickly by cries of pain and terror. Unleashed from the verbal restraint Peter had imposed only minutes earlier, the canine was viciously lashing out at the strangers with a savage ferocity.

The red pit bull abandoned the dead man who's throat he'd just ripped open, and darted to the closest standing figure. With blood and saliva flying from his mouth, Diesel attacked from the side and bit down hard on the man's thigh. The long canine teeth punctured the fabric of his jeans and penetrated deep into muscle. As the man struggled to pull away, Diesel thrust his head side to side while pulling backward. When the man and dog separated, a large chunk of flesh was missing from the Korean's leg, and the femoral vein was severed. Blood poured from the hideous wound, and the gunman collapsed, writhing in agony.

Cho was sidestepping away from the enraged canine. She was also trying to get a new angle of attack on Peter.

Diesel charged head-on to the last of the Korean gunmen still on his feet. Wide-eyed, the Korean lowered his pistol and began firing at the blur of red fur, teeth, and claws. Bullets dug into the pine flooring on either side of Diesel, but miraculously none struck him.

Cho also swung her weapon at the charging dog and fired a volley of bullets, but Diesel remained a step ahead of the rounds. He lunged, a missile of muscle and claws and teeth. Upon contact, Diesel closed his jaws with hundreds of pounds of bite force, right on the man's gun hand and wrist. Another shot was fired, more out of reflex than intention, but the shot, like the others before, went wide. As gravity inevitably took hold, the pit bull fell to the floor, and with him came the wrist of the shooter. The rest of the Korean followed.

The suppressed pistol escaped his grip and skittered across the floor as the strong jaws and sharp teeth punctured flesh and crushed bone, accompanied by panicked screams of anguish. The man desperately tried to break free, using his good arm to slam punches into the dog's large head and shoulders. But the blows seemed to have no effect. Diesel was unfazed, and he carried out his genetically coded mode of attack, which now meant that he thrashed his head and upper body side to side. The effect being to open the wounds, increase the degree of lacerations, and push bone splinters into neighboring tissue.

Renewed screams of agony erupted from the Korean, and then his body shut down from the excruciating pain and torment as he fell unconscious.

Peter kept his focus on Cho. She was the prime threat—the leader whom the others followed. She seemed transfixed by the speed and ferocity of the attack. The canine had inflicted debilitating injuries on her team in short order.

Pft, pft, came the suppressed sound of a pair of shots fired from her submachine gun. But Diesel's rapid and unpredictable motion made it nearly impossible to hit him, and the bullets punched into the wood flooring instead.

Peter rose to his feet and fired off another round at Cho, and then dove for the nearest cover, which happened to be the sofa and leather chairs positioned in front of the hearth. He tumbled over the backrest of the sofa, knocking the guitar case within which the PEAP lay. The black case and futuristic weapon slid across the floor.

Cho's gaze locked on the prize. The sirens, no longer distant, announced the imminent arrival of police.

Diesel continued to savage Moon and the other conscious gunman, who did their best to retreat from the dog at every opportunity, only to discover that their movement invited renewed attacks.

Cho fired two shots at the sofa, hoping for a lucky hit. The 7.62-millimeter bullets went high—one passing over Peter's shoulder, and the other above his head.

"It's over," Peter shouted, from behind his cover. "The police will be here any second now. You can hear the sirens."

"Give me the weapon," Cho said.

Her gaze darted between Diesel, who was fully occupied with the two men, and the furniture she knew Peter to be hiding behind. Maybe if she charged forward, she could retrieve the weapon and escape.

"I'd rather give it to the police," Peter replied.

"You're out of bullets." She fired two rounds into the sofa to punctuate her point.

Peter was curled into a ball, hugging the floor. He peeked under the sofa and squeezed off a shot. The round creased Cho's calf, and she stifled a cry. Abandoning her hastily drawn plan, the hit convinced her to move, and hobbled back toward the front entrance.

With his face pressed against the floor, and peering under

the furniture, Peter watched her movements. He hoped she was fleeing.

He called Diesel to return, thereby denying Cho an opportunity to shoot the dog that had ravaged her team. Reluctantly, the red pit bull broke his attack and ran to Peter's side. More gunfire chased Diesel, but none of the shots connected.

Peter fired his last two bullets at Cho, and then she was gone.

CHAPTER 23

PETER DROPPED THE EMPTY REVOLVER and rushed to Kate. Kneeling beside her, he was consumed with dread. Her legs were soaked with blood, and she wasn't moving. With her face turned to the side, he pressed a finger against her neck and felt a pulse.

He sighed with relief. But only briefly.

Peter gently rolled her over onto her back, then recognized his error. Over and over, during first aid training classes he'd taken, it had been stressed to never to move a victim unless it was known with certainty that a back or neck injury had not transpired. He didn't know the degree or type of injuries she'd suffered, and it was reckless of him to move her. He silently cursed himself for his rash actions.

It was obvious she was gravely wounded, and he needed to get his act together. Time to think, not to feel sorrow or self-pity.

As he examined the apparent sources of the bleeding, he discovered one bullet hole in her thigh that was different. Blood was pulsing—arterial flow.

Now the sirens were just outside his home. The ringing in

his ears had subsided, and he heard the moans from the two mauled Koreans.

"Diesel. Guard."

The pit bull sat beside Kate's motionless form and locked his gaze on the wounded men near the entry. If either man attempted to grasp a weapon or rise and advance toward Kate, Diesel would rip him to shreds.

Peter was frozen with indecision. Kate had been out meeting with the photographer and caterer, busy completing the details for their wedding. *Will we even have a wedding?*

"Stop it," he said to himself. "Pull yourself together, man."

He had to stop thinking of Kate, the woman he loved, and instead think in the abstract. He had to view the body before him as a generic person, a stranger. He knew that people, like machines, needed certain requirements to be met in order to function. An engine needs oil, gasoline, and air to operate. Humans need blood, water, and oxygen. He also knew it was essential to identify the injuries and treat them in order of priority, just as he would organize his work to fix a broken machine.

In four strides, Peter was back at the PEAP and the guitar case. He grabbed the futuristic weapon and tossed it across the room, venting his anger in the process. That solid-state weapon had wrought so much death and pain. It crashed to the floor and slid into the safe room. He grabbed the towel that had padded the PEAP inside the case, and returned to Kate.

Next, he stripped off his shirt and wrapped it around the most severe wound on Kate's upper thigh. He pushed the sleeves beneath her leg. It was difficult with her unconscious, but the pool of blood bizarrely provided lubrication, allowing the fabric to slip between her leg and the wood floor. He wrapped the sleeves around the fabric and tied a tight knot to staunch the flow of blood. The jolt of pain nearly brought Kate around. She moaned, and her eyelids fluttered. Then she was still once again.

Outside, Peter heard car doors open and men shouting commands. Their voices sounded frantic, but he couldn't make out the words.

After removing a folding knife from a pocket, he slashed the towel into two smaller strips and wrapped these around other leg wounds. He thumbed his phone and dialed 9-1-1.

"What is the nature of your emergency?" the voice said.

It was unnervingly calm.

"I need an ambulance. My wife—fiancée—she's been shot. She's bleeding badly. Hurry!"

He gave his address and stayed on the line as he ran to the safe room and tossed the PEAP into the large gun safe. Next, he closed the doors and spun the dial. From this point on, he would be the sole caretaker of the PEAP. What he would do with it was an unanswered question.

With the secret door to the safe room closed, he darted back to Kate. Her face was ashen, and he feared she was in shock. He grabbed a leather seat cushion from the sofa and placed it under her legs to encourage more blood flow to her brain. Another bullet hole in her calf was still oozing blood, and Peter pressed his hand against it to stop the flow.

With the phone on speaker, he shouted, "Hurry! I need an ambulance, now!"

A pounding of feet on the steps outside announced a gathering, but he still couldn't see who was there.

An artificially amplified voice called out. "Put your guns down!"

"I'm not armed! There are wounded inside. I need an ambulance. Hurry! There's a woman with gunshot wounds. She's lost a lot of blood!"

"Come out and keep your hands up."

"I can't. She's bleeding. I need help, or she's going to die!"

A police officer slowly showed his head, steeling a glance around the doorframe.

"Hands in the air!"

Peter still had a hand pressed against Kate's leg. He raised the other.

"Both hands up! Now!"

"I can't! She's bleeding. If I remove my hand, she'll die."

The officer stepped into the entryway and was shocked at the scene. The two Koreans still alive were leaning against a wall, doing their best to reduce blood loss from their own wounds. Neither said a word, but both glared at the officer.

"Keep your hands where I can see them," he said to Peter.

Diesel snarled at the trespasser, viewing any intruder as a threat.

"Is that dog safe?"

"He's protecting Kate. As soon as the medics get here, I'll put him in another room. Hurry! Please!"

The policeman keyed his mic. "Send the medics in. All of them. This place is a charnel house. We've got at least three wounded. One appears to be critical."

Moments later, a pair of EMTs rushed to the door, then paused while Peter removed Diesel to a bedroom. When he returned to the great room, another pair of EMTs had just entered with a gurney, soon followed by a third team. They split up, and each began triage on the wounded.

A young woman completed a quick visual examination of Kate's injuries. Peter noticed her nametag—Asevedo—but nothing else. He was focused only on Kate. There was no point in asking how she was, or if she'd be all right. He knew the answers.

"What can I do to help?" he said.

"Stay out of the way," Asevedo said.

Her partner had already taken Kate's vitals and attached

a blood pressure cuff and oximeter to her finger. Asevedo removed the makeshift bandages and then quickly sliced through Kate's pant legs with surgical scissors. While she applied sterile bandages, her partner inserted an IV to replace the large amount of blood she'd lost, and to stabilize her blood pressure.

He said, "She's experiencing hypovolemic shock. BP is low, and pulse is weak. We need to get her to the ER stat."

Peter stood back, watching, but unable to help. It was as if the Fates had once again delivered a cruel blow.

While he watched, an alarm suddenly blared.

"She's arrested." Asevedo ripped open Kate's shirt and moved her bra so they could \ place the pads and electrodes of the portable defibrillator.

"What's happening?" Peter cried, and stepped forward.

"Stand back," Asevedo said. "Clear!"

The machine sent a jolt of electricity into Kate's chest, her muscles tensed, causing her torso to jerk. But it worked, and her pulse returned.

Asevedo said, "We have to move her now."

With the defibrillator and IV bag cradled on top of Kate, the two paramedics lifted her onto a gurney and rushed her out the door into a waiting ambulance.

Peter followed but was stopped at the door by a police officer, the man who was first to enter.

"Where are you going?" he said.

"That's my fiancée," Peter replied.

"This is a crime scene. And you aren't going anywhere until you've been cleared to do so."

"But—"

"Save it. The emergency doctors will take good care of her. Nothing you can do to help, anyway."

He gripped Peter's arm and led him into the dining room,

avoiding the bodies and shell casings on the way. The officer pulled out a chair and motioned for Peter to sit.

"Now, just settle down. Once the detectives arrive, they'll want a statement from you. In the meantime, I'll ask the medics to take a look at your shoulder."

CHAPTER 24

PETER SAT MOTIONLESS in the wooden chair, his hands clasped and resting on the dining table. His red eyes were focused on a nondescript point on the opposite wall. He'd lost track of how long he'd been sitting there. He hardly noticed the muffled voices of the paramedics as they treated the wounded Koreans, or the occasional comments from the police officers as they secured the crime scene.

His mind was focused on Kate. Images of Kate lying unconscious and bleeding flashed before his eyes. He knew the wedding would have to be postponed. It was only a few days away. So many years after Maggie had died, he'd finally been able to love again. And now this. Was he destined to live in solitude? Was that it?

More than anything, he wanted to be with Kate, to live the rest of his days with her by his side.

As another wave of despair washed over, Peter wept for the third time. He refused to believe he could lose Kate, and instead recalled their recent trip to Washington, DC. Her companionship, her laughter, their intimate moments together. Already he missed her gentle touch and warmth.

With a jolt, a voice cut through his reminiscing. It was a

voice he knew too well—from a person he'd rather not speak to.

"Mr. Savage."

Peter slowly turned his head, looking over his shoulder. As expected, it was a short woman with gray hair who'd called his name. She was wearing a green University of Oregon polo shirt and pale-blue jeans, the pant legs just breaking on a pair of neon-green athletic shoes. Her service weapon was holstered on her hip, and she was holding a pen and a small notepad.

"Detective Colson," Peter replied. "Can this wait? I need to get to the hospital."

Detective Ruth Colson was tough, in contrast to her disarming appearance. He'd had several encounters with her— few that he considered pleasant. In all those interactions, he'd never seen her hard veneer crack, even for a moment. Until now. Her glare softened, and both eyes glistened with moisture.

She said, "The patrol officers told me your fiancée was seriously injured. I already called the hospital to inquire on her status. I didn't get much. Just that she was expected to be in surgery for several hours. There's nothing you can do there. Not now."

Peter fought hard to maintain his composure. He swallowed the lump in his throat and nodded sharply.

Detective Colson sat at the table across from him.

"The State Police are sending over a forensics team from Salem. They'll be here in a couple hours, maybe sooner. I need you to tell me what happened."

Starting from his first meeting with Billy Reed, Peter retold the events just as they'd happened. Except for the PEAP. He had already decided that it would not be turned over to the government, even though DARPA funding had paid for the development. Kate was right, Peter had decided. The weapon should not be given to anyone. It had already caused too much death, too much sorrow.

Even as Peter rationalized these thoughts, he realized how hypocritical it was for him to deem one weapon of his many creations as immoral, and not all of them. After all, weapons were, by definition, designed to kill. Dead is dead. How could he feel remorse for inventing the PEAP, while being perfectly comfortable manufacturing and selling his magnetic impulse pistols, knowing they were prized by US Special Forces for covert missions where killing silently at close range was highly valued?

Maybe it's time for a different profession? Or maybe I should just get my head straight and concentrate on Kate's wellbeing.

Regardless how the debate unfolded in his psyche, he was determined that he alone would decide the fate of the pulsed-energy carbine.

"You never met Billy Reed before two days ago?" Colson said.

"No," Peter replied.

"How did he find you?"

"I already told you. He said the Idaho militia that stole the prototype carbine shared my name and the name of my company. It was easy enough for him to track me down."

The detective jotted notes furiously while Peter spoke, flipping page after page of her notepad.

"So let me get this straight. Mr. Reed wanted to sell the carbine back to you."

"Yes, that's what he said."

"And you agreed to the transaction?"

"I did."

"But," Colson read from her notes, "he didn't have the weapon, is that right? He showed up, expecting you to give him fifty thousand dollars for nothing? I mean, wouldn't he know you would refuse to pay if he couldn't produce the weapon?"

"I can't tell you what he was thinking. All I can say is that we met across the street at the coffee shop. He was carrying a guitar case—the one on the floor in the other room. He claimed the PEAP was inside the case, and I suggested we complete the transaction here, rather than in a public location. Maybe he was counting on that, and planned to rob me. I don't know. What I do know is that the guitar case was empty."

"And the money in the briefcase—five bundles of one-hundred-dollar notes—you're saying that's your money."

"Yes. I withdrew that cash from two accounts yesterday. You can check with my bank."

"We will." Colson held up a hand. "But let's not get ahead of ourselves. So Mr. Reed told you he had cheated a band of North Korean agents who were going to buy the PEAP from him. He took their money, but did not turn over the carbine. Is that right?"

"That's what he said."

"North Koreans. Really?"

Peter was too tired, and in no mood for her sarcasm. He just shrugged.

"Did Mr. Reed say how much money he took from the North Korean agents?"

"No."

"Did he say why he wanted fifty thousand dollars from you? I mean, if he just stole a sizeable sum, why would he want so much from you?"

"Look, Detective," Peter said, his temper rising, "I've indulged your questions and played your games. Maybe you fancy yourself being some sharp-witted detective in a film noir. I don't know. And I don't care. I've told you what happened. When the State Police complete their investigation, their results will corroborate what I've shared. You have two of the gunmen to question. Right now, I just want to go to the hospital and be there for Kate."

Colson scrutinized Peter's face for an uncomfortably long moment.

Failing to see any hint of deception, she said, "And how many gunmen escaped?"

"Only one. The woman named Cho."

"Do you know where she might have gone?"

"No. Forensics will find several bullets she fired from a submachine gun, embedded in the floor. They will also find her blood."

"How's that?"

"I nicked her leg, firing from under the sofa."

"You shot her in the leg, and she still managed to get away?"

Peter's eyes flared with anger. "Yes. She got away. Believe me, I would like nothing more than to put a bullet between her eyes."

Colson closed her pad and placed her pen on the table. She didn't jot down Peter's last words.

She lowered her voice. "Mr. Savage, I know you don't care for me. And I'm fine with that. It goes with the territory." She paused. "Contrary to what you must think, I do not believe you are a criminal. If my hunch is right, the evidence will back up your story—that you acted in self-defense. And I empathize with what you must be feeling right now. However, I strongly advise you to refrain from sharing statements, as you just have, that might be interpreted as *intent* to harm another. In this case, Miss Cho and her associates."

Peter leaned back in his chair and exhaled deeply. He slowly shook his head.

"I don't believe it. Now I'm the bad guy? Those bastards shot Kate." As the words left his lips, he broke down and tears streaked his face.

Detective Colson waited silently while Peter composed himself.

After he took a paper napkin from a holder on the table, and wiped his eyes and nose, Colson said, "I'm sorry, but I have one more question to ask. Then you may leave."

Peter nodded.

"How did Kate get involved in this? Why would you have brought Mr. Reed here and endangered Kate?"

"That was never the plan. Kate wasn't here. She was out, running errands, preparing for our wedding. She was supposed to meet a friend for lunch at the Pine Tavern. I didn't expect her back until the afternoon. For whatever reason—I don't know why—she came back early, and must have been grabbed by the North Koreans."

"Why did you have the meeting here? Why not at your office, or in a public location? How could you trust Billy Reed not to kill you and take your money?"

He answered with a half-truth. "Because I knew Diesel would watch my back."

The other half of his reasoning was that he couldn't risk co-workers asking questions about someone showing up for a meeting with a guitar case, or possibly catching a glimpse of the PEAP carbine.

"Okay," Colson replied. "It probably isn't important, but I had to ask."

Peter nodded and wiped his nose again.

Detective Colson rose from the table and crossed over to the open dining room door. Beyond, the crime scene lay undisturbed, waiting for the forensic team to arrive on site.

She stood at the door and faced Peter. "Mr. Savage. I understand what you must be feeling. Anger. Revenge." She paused to make certain Peter was listening, and when their eyes met, she said, "Don't go there. Let the law handle this. This is not the nineteenth century, and we will not tolerate vigilantism. My best advice is, go to the hospital and be there for Kate. She will need your strength as she recovers. Put this behind you and move on."

"May I leave now?" Peter said.

Colson nodded. "You won't be allowed back inside your home tonight. I don't know how long it will take for the forensics team to finish their work. It might be late. I'll need to talk to you tomorrow. I'm sure we'll have more questions."

"Yeah. Sure."

"If you check into a hotel, let me know where you are. I'll have a patrol car pick you up late morning."

"I'll be at the hospital. With Kate."

"Of course." The detective hesitated. "We'll handle this, Mr. Savage. Okay?"

Peter seemed to contemplate her words, and when he replied, his voice was clear and strong.

"You do your job. And I will do what has to be done."

CHAPTER 25

AFTER DETECTIVE COLSON RELEASED PETER with the usual admonishment to stay in town, he leashed up Diesel and descended the stairway from the great room to his company on the ground floor below. It was an access he seldom used, and its primary purpose was a second avenue of egress in case of emergency. But he wanted to avoid as much of the active crime scene as possible, and the stairway to EJ Enterprises allowed him to skirt the evidence.

With Diesel by his side, Peter emerged between the office cubicles and the machine shop. The space was vacant. The employees had forsaken their work and were clustered near the windows fronting the business, gawking at the assembled police cars. Although the gunfight had occurred on the floor above them, heavy soundproofing had severely muffled the gunshots, making it sound like the battle had happened farther away.

They'd witnessed four ambulances driving to the rear of the building. From their location, it was impossible to observe the medical teams. A police officer at the front door, armed with an AR-15, refused to allow anyone to leave. There was an active shooter in the area, she'd said without further explanation. Across the street at the coffee shop, the clothing store, and other businesses, armed police were likewise guarding the entrances, securing the patrons and employees inside.

Peter approached, his mind numb from the horror he'd experienced. His movements were stiff, and he appeared to be on autopilot as he walked to the front door.

At first, none of his employees spoke to him. But when he touched the door handle, Nancy said, "We can't leave. The police officer said there is a shooter nearby, and—"

As Peter faced her, she was stunned into silence by his blank expression. His eyes were still red and sunken.

"I know," he said.

Todd stepped to Peter's side. "Are you okay?"

Peter started to nod—a reflex—but then stopped. He faced his friend, trying hard to hold back his emotions. At any second, he felt like he'd burst forth in uncontrollable sobbing. He'd always prided himself on being strong, able to suppress his emotions. Maybe that was why he had found it so hard to tell Kate how he felt—that he loved her.

Now he was falling apart. Tears welled up in his eyes, and he bit his bottom lip.

"No," he managed to choke out.

"What's wrong?" Todd said. "What happened?"

"I have to go to Saint Charles. They shot Kate."

"What? Who shot Kate? What happened?"

"Not now. I don't have time. I have to go to the hospital."

"You're not in any shape to drive," Todd said. "I'll take you."

He pushed the door open and was immediately stopped by the officer.

"Sir," she said, her tone unyielding. "I already told you. You have to stay inside until the all-clear is announced. It's not safe outside."

"There hasn't been any gunfire for an hour. My friend here

needs to go to Saint Charles. His fiancée was one of the shooting victims."

"Sir. I'm just following my orders."

"Then call your sergeant," Todd said.

"Both of you. Step back inside, or you will be charged with failing to comply with a lawful order. This is for your safety."

Todd squared off with the officer. They were of the same height, and he looked directly into her eyes, only inches away.

"I don't think you understand. My friend says his fiancée is injured and at the hospital. Now I'm going to drive him there. And if you want, you can hop in your squad car and meet me at Saint Charles. You can arrest me there, and I won't resist. But if you try to stop me now…well, I will resist. And you won't like that much."

"Sir, please. Let's not make this worse. I understand what your friend is feeling. Let me make a call and explain the situation."

Todd nodded, and the officer spoke into her radio, asking for her sergeant.

Peter said, "Ask for Detective Colson. She knows me. My name is Peter Savage. Detective Colson said I was free to go to Saint Charles."

A minute later, the crisis was defused, and Todd led Peter and Diesel to the employee parking alongside the street. Todd insisted he drive his truck. Diesel sat in the middle, and Peter took the passenger seat.

Ten minutes later, the sergeant in charge of the scene announced all was clear, and the lockdown was lifted.

⊕

Fortunately, Todd found a parking space under the shade of a mature juniper tree. He left the windows cracked to provide Diesel with fresh air, and promised to return within an hour.

The lobby of St. Charles Hospital was light and airy, the benefit of a major remodel years earlier. Peter strode to the information desk, with Todd two steps behind him.

"I'm here to see Kate Simpson. Can you tell me what room she's in?"

The receptionist checked her records, then replied with a frown.

"Do you know when she was admitted?"

"Not long ago," Peter said. "Maybe an hour?"

"She would have been brought here by ambulance," Todd said. "Gunshot wounds."

"Oh. That explains why she's not in my system yet. She would have been admitted through the ER. Let me check. She may be in surgery."

The woman stepped away from the counter and made a phone call. Two minutes later, she returned.

"Yes, Miss Simpson is still in surgery. You're welcome to have a seat in the lobby. It might be a while before she's out of recovery and assigned a room."

Peter took a seat in the lobby. It was a comfortable chair—one of two grouped side by side with a small table in between. He looked across the waiting area and noticed that most of the chairs were grouped in pairs, or occasionally four together with a coffee table in between. Puzzles, in various stages of assembly, covered some of the tables. Magazines on others. Each seating area was separated from those nearby to afford a small measure of privacy. That suited Peter. Right now, he had zero interest in socializing.

Todd excused himself, promising to take care of Diesel until Peter could take him back. The forensics team would probably work into the night. When they were done, he would hire a crew to clean the blood stains from the floor and walls. It would be at least twenty-four hours before Peter could return home.

CHAPTER 26

PETER GLANCED AT THE STALE COFFEE half-filling the paper cup, then checked his watch. He had been waiting for more than two hours.

He grabbed the cup and disposed of it on the way to the information desk—his third visit since he'd arrived. The receptionist knew him by name.

"I'm sorry, Mr. Savage. I still don't have any new information. She's still in surgery. But I've asked the doctor to give you an update once she's in the recovery room."

Peter thanked her, then paced another lap around the large lobby. He stopped at the coffee shop and purchased another latte, then settled into his chair again.

The minutes passed slowly. He couldn't focus on even the simplest activity, like reading a magazine. He would thumb through the pages and look at the pictures, but his thoughts kept drifting to Kate. *Why is it taking so long? Shouldn't it be a simple matter to stitch together the severed veins and arteries, and then suture the wound closed?*

Peter looked up and saw a man approaching, wearing a white medical jacket with a black name plate above the breast pocket. As the separation shortened, Peter began to rise. But then the doctor stopped at another chair where a young man with a toddler had been seated. Peter couldn't hear what words were spoken, but shortly the doctor shook the man's hand and pointed across the room. The man, smiling now, carried his child off to the elevators.

Several more hours elapsed, and Peter found himself passing the time between catnaps by pacing laps around the lobby and people watching. He had long since thumbed through all the magazines and studied every piece of artwork decorating the space.

He approached the information desk yet again.

The receptionist said, "I'm sorry, Mr. Savage. I still don't have any information, other than the doctor has promised to come down here and meet with you once she's in recovery. I wish I had something more to share."

Peter nodded and turned.

"There's a restaurant on the second floor, in case you're hungry," she said.

Peter raised his hand as if he was waving, and returned to his chair. He just sat there and stared at a painting across the room. For how long, he didn't know. He wasn't looking at his watch anymore. He'd seen many doctors come and go, most dressed in a clean and pressed white medical coat. Occasionally, a surgeon wearing blue scrubs would make an appearance to meet with a family member.

Peter found himself playing through all his memories of Kate—from their first meeting until that very morning, when she had left to meet with the florist and the photographer, and Peter went to work. It wasn't the first time he realized how fragile life was. How quickly it could go from normal and safe to tragedy and loss.

His musings were interrupted by a masculine voice. Peter hadn't even noticed the man walk up.

"Excuse me. Mr. Savage?"

Peter raised his gaze and noticed the white medical coat. He pulled himself upright in the chair.

"Yes, I'm Peter Savage."

The doctor smiled and extended his hand, which Peter accepted.

"You probably don't remember me. I'm Dr. Scott Hale. We met a while ago. I recall you were investigating a viral outbreak on the Warm Springs Reservation."

"Oh, yes," Peter replied, his mouth downturned and his eyes drifted to the carpet.

"Am I interrupting?" Dr. Hale said.

"No, I'm sorry. I was just hoping you were someone else. My fiancée has been in surgery for hours. I thought maybe you were her doctor and could share with me how she's doing."

Dr. Hale read the meaning behind the dark shadows beneath Peter's sunken eyes, the deep creases on his forehead, and his unfocused gaze. He'd seen it many times in the expression of family members whose loved ones were fighting to recover from an injury or illness.

"The surgeons here are very good," he said. "I'm sure there is nothing to be overly concerned about. Is she here for a routine procedure?"

Peter shook his head. "No. She was shot."

"I'm sorry."

Peter had looked away, his mind back to Kate.

"If you'd like, I can check her records."

"Yes," Peter replied. "Anything would be helpful. This waiting and not knowing…"

"I understand. I'll need your fiancée's full name and date of birth."

Peter shared the information.

"Let me check and I'll be right back." Dr. Hale left in the

direction he'd arrived from, and disappeared down a wide hall with many closed doors on either side.

Peter collapsed into his chair again. He was emotionally exhausted, and he closed his eyes, expecting it might be ten or fifteen minutes before Dr. Hale returned. Hopefully, with good news.

It seemed like he'd only closed his eyes for a minute, when there was a gentle nudge at his shoulder.

"Mr. Savage?"

Peter opened his eyes and sat upright in the chair while Hale scooted a nearby chair closer.

"What did you find?" Peter said.

"Kate had a good surgeon. One of our best." Hale drew in a deep breath. "She went into cardiac arrest while the paramedics were getting ready to transport her to the ER. Fortunately, they revived her without complications."

"I was there and saw them shock her chest."

"The cardiac arrest was most likely due to loss of blood."

Peter nodded, recalling the blood pulsing from her leg before he bandaged it off.

Hale continued. "She suffered four bullet wounds, including one that fractured her femur, and another that pierced her pelvis. Those were the worst of the injuries. Bone fragments from the shattered femur pierced her femoral artery. Fortunately, someone had enough presence of mind to apply a tourniquet and stop the arterial bleeding before she bled out."

Listening to the extent of Kate's injuries strained Peter's composure. He removed a tissue from his pocket and dried his eyes. He cleared his throat and waited for more, but Dr. Hale didn't offer anything further.

Peter said, "Where is she? Can I see her now?"

Dr. Hale explained that she was just moved to the recovery room.

"There's more you need to know. The combination of her injuries and low blood oxygen levels in her lower extremities… they were unable to save the leg."

Peter felt like he'd been sucker punched. The color drained from his face, and his vision narrowed. Tears streaked his cheeks as he was overcome with a profound sense of loss. A sensation he hadn't felt since Maggie had died years earlier in an automobile accident.

"I'm sorry," Dr. Hale said. "Honestly, it's a miracle she survived."

Peter didn't feel any divine miracle was at play. Instead, he felt cursed. *Why Kate? It should have been me.*

Kate was innocent, whereas Peter was guilty of a long list of sins. Not the least of which was making the pulsed-energy carbine, and the death it wrought.

Overcome with sorrow, Peter closed his eyes and slumped in his chair. As he drifted into a restless sleep, he never heard Dr. Hale leave the lobby.

⊕

Some hours later, Peter awoke to a masculine voice.

"Mr. Savage?"

At first, it was just another figure in Peter's dream. But the voice persisted, and eventually pulled Peter from his semiconscious state.

As Peter opened his eyes, the voice said, "Excuse me. Are you Peter Savage?"

The words came from a middle-aged man dressed in blue surgical scrubs. The creases on his forehead were deep, and there were obvious bags under his eyes.

"Yeah. That's me." Peter stood and greeted the surgeon with an outstretched hand.

"I'm Dr. Alexander." He clasped Peter's hand with a firm

grip. "I'm sorry I didn't have time to speak with you sooner. The ER has been busy today. First, the shooting victims. Then there was a multicar accident between Powell Butte and Prineville."

Peter nodded. He wondered what Dr. Alexander had to share that he hadn't already heard from Dr. Hale.

"Kate is recovering from rather extensive surgery. We had to—"

"Yes, I know." Peter wasn't ready to hear the surgical report for a second time. "A few hours ago…" Peter searched the walls of the lobby for a clock, but failed to find one. "What time is it?"

"Late," Dr. Alexander replied.

"Another doctor already briefed me on the injuries Kate suffered. And the surgery."

"I'm sorry. The damage was too extensive. There wasn't another option."

Peter absorbed the words in silence, still numb to this new reality.

"I served in the Army," Dr. Alexander said. "Afghanistan. I saved the lives of a lot of soldiers with far more severe injuries than Kate's. She'll be heavily sedated for a while. Given her age and good health, I want to get her into therapy as soon as possible."

"Of course," Peter said. "Whatever it takes."

"I'm glad to hear that. Kate is going to need your support. This is a difficult adjustment for any person. For some, even more so."

Peter nodded.

Dr. Alexander said, "Maybe you can help me. Do you know how to reach her parents? Or maybe her siblings?"

"No. Her father left when Kate was just a child. And her mother passed a couple years ago. She doesn't have any brothers or sisters."

"I see."

"When can I see her?" Peter said.

"She's sleeping now. Her body has a lot of healing to do, and the pain from her injuries is very severe. The road to full recovery is long, requiring physical and mental therapy. You'll need to be patient and supportive."

Peter nodded in silence.

CHAPTER 27

WITH HIS LOWER BACK PROTESTING from slouching all night in the chair, Peter rose to his feet and stretched. The hospital lobby was far too familiar by now. He yawned and then shuffled to the coffee shop, checking his phone for messages along the way. There was only one, and it was from Todd. It wasn't long, just asking Peter to call when he could.

Peter returned the call.

"Good morning," Todd said.

"Good morning. I got your message. I'm still at Saint Charles."

"How is Kate? I've been worried all night. So is everyone at work."

Peter shared the medical reports and prognosis. He had to work down the lump in his throat before he could say that Kate's leg had been amputated. But he managed to do so, and without shedding any more tears.

"Oh, man," Todd said. "I am so sorry. You know I'm here for both of you. Anything. Anytime. You just say the word, okay?"

"Yeah, I know. Thank you."

They talked a bit more. Todd updated Peter on business at

EJ Enterprises, trying to give his friend something else to think about. He also shared that Peter's home had been cleaned, and that he could come back. Todd didn't bother to mention that he'd paid double time to get the cleaning crew in after hours.

"I don't know how I can ever thank you," Peter said.

"You already have. Diesel can stay with me as long as you like. But to tell you the truth, I think he misses you."

It was a gentle nudge. Todd knew how important pets could be in helping people overcome trauma. And in the case of Peter and Diesel, there had never been a human-canine companionship as close as theirs.

"I miss him, too," Peter said.

He promised to get Diesel later in the day. He wanted to check once more on Kate. Then he needed to call Detective Colson and check in.

There was no new information on Kate's condition. Her vital signs were still strong. And with heavy doses of antibiotics running thorough her body, there had not been any sign of an infection beginning to take hold. Good news.

Not surprising, Peter's call to Detective Colson was put right through to her office. The detective said she wanted to speak with Peter in person, at the station. She instructed dispatch to send a patrol car to St. Charles. Ten minutes after the call ended, a uniformed police officer entered the lobby and approached Peter.

The ride to the police station was only five minutes, and Peter was buzzed through the security door, where he met Detective Colson. She led him to a small meeting room and offered him coffee. Peter declined, preferring to get this over so he could collect Diesel and go home. It had been more than twenty-four hours since he'd had a shower or slept in a bed.

Detective Colson got right to the point.

"The preliminary forensics report supports your statement.

The number of shooters and their locations around the great room are all consistent with what you told me. Although the two wounded men aren't talking, their fingerprints, photographs, and blood samples are all being shared with the FBI. We need your permission to draw a blood sample and sequence your DNA." She slid a paper across the table and Peter read it and then signed his name.

"Forensics needs to be able to identify your blood at the crime scene."

Peter nodded. "Any word on Cho?"

"Nothing definitive. Several of the security cameras at neighboring stores captured video of a person appearing to match her description leaving the general area of your home just before the first patrol cars arrived on scene yesterday. She was heading east on foot, maybe toward the hotel. Another detective questioned the reception staff at the hotel earlier this morning. They confirmed that several Asians, including one female, had checked in two days ago—the same day Billy Reed also checked in. They all presented Idaho drivers licenses."

Peter said. "Was Cho one of them?"

"Don't know. The female did not use that name. But then again, if they are agents of a foreign country—"

"North Korea."

"Like I was saying. If they are foreign agents, I would expect them to use well-developed aliases to cover their tracks."

"What now?" Peter said.

"The forensics team gathered blood samples from every location around the room, including where you said Cho was when you grazed her leg with a bullet. We'll have DNA soon. It will all be part of the package we share with the FBI. The Idaho State Police has also been notified. They'll be searching for her. But I'll be honest. Without a picture of Cho, it's going to be hard. Maybe we can pull something from the security cameras.

But my guess is the images will be too pixelated to by useful for ID purposes."

Peter had nothing else to offer, and since Colson had no more questions, Peter was allowed to go home. The detective offered to have a patrol officer take him home, but he declined, choosing to hail an Uber instead. He needed to be away from the police presence. It was simply too strong a reminder of what had happened.

⊕

Although the driver tried her best to engage Peter in casual conversation, after his third one-syllable answer, she gave up. With the sedan idling in front of EJ Enterprises, Peter used the app on his phone to give the driver a five-star review—it wasn't her fault that he was in no mood to banter about trivial things.

He entered and nodded to Nancy as he crossed the lobby. She seemed surprised to see him, and issued a pleasant greeting. Peter glanced at her with a half-smile and kept walking.

In his office, he found Diesel stretched out on a plush dog bed. In a deep slumber, the dog didn't hear him enter. Peter gazed upon his friend with envy, knowing that deep, restful sleep would not be coming anytime soon.

"Hey, buddy," Peter said to gently wake Diesel.

The red pit bull opened his eyes and then lazily rose to his feet. As if he had no cares, which was largely true, he stretched and then sauntered to Peter, tail wagging.

Todd knocked on the doorframe and stood at the opening with a leash in one hand.

"I was just about to take Diesel out for a walk."

"Thank you for taking care of him."

"It was no trouble at all. He's been curled up on the dog bed. Hasn't made a sound all morning."

"How are we doing on the current order?" Peter said.

As chief engineer, Todd managed the daily workflow. He also worked collaboratively with Peter when it came to developing new prototypes, which had included the PEAP carbine.

"Everything is on schedule," Todd replied. "No problems at all. Look, why don't you take some time off? A few days of rest would do you good. I can manage the business in your absence."

Peter sighed. He felt bone tired.

"Yeah, you're probably right." He looked down at Diesel. "Want to go for a walk?"

Diesel's eyes brightened, and he cocked his head to the side, as he often did when Peter was speaking to him.

With the leash clipped to his collar, the pair exited EJ Enterprises and turned right. Soon, they would be at a paved trail that paralleled the Deschutes River.

Todd hung back in the lobby, still gazing through the glass door and windows.

It wasn't long before Nancy said, "Think he'll be all right?"

"He's tough," Todd said. "And that's the problem. It's his greatest weakness. He's never learned how to process his emotions. Right now, he's hurting really bad. But he can't deal with the pain. He doesn't know how to process what he's feeling and then let it go. Instead, it remains bottled up inside him— raw energy seeking a pathway out."

"I wish there was something we could do," Nancy said.

"There isn't. Even if there was, Peter wouldn't let you. He won't let anyone help him. It's like he's punishing himself."

"That doesn't make any sense at all. He didn't do anything wrong. Peter would never hurt anyone."

Todd looked at Nancy. She'd been employed by EJ Enterprises almost as long as he had. He thought he knew her reasonably well. At least, in a professional setting, since they didn't socialize much other than the year-end holiday party and summer barbeque. She had a friendly, outgoing personality, and she was generous in her trust, even with complete strangers. So it came as no surprise to hear her proclamation on Peter.

"That's the Peter we all know," Todd said. "But there's another side of him that you haven't seen. And you never want to."

"What do you mean?"

"He holds himself to a high personal code of conduct."

"I agree. He's always treated me fairly and honestly."

"The problem is, he expects everyone to behave the same way. To be honorable and respectful. And when they're not… well, Peter can be rather unforgiving."

CHAPTER 28

AFTER A THIRTY-MINUTE WALK along the riverbank, stopping often to allow Diesel to stick his nose in clumps of grass and under sage and rabbit brush, Peter returned home. He'd decided to follow Todd's advice and take some time off so he could be at St. Charles most of each day to be with Kate. Even though, in her state of unconsciousness, she wouldn't know of his presence, he needed to be there. As much for himself as for Kate.

He paused at the transition from the entry to the great room. Although the floor and walls had been expertly cleaned, the gouged wood planks and holes in the wallboard provided ample evidence of the gun battle. The images were still fresh and vivid in his mind. He drew in a breath, and the scents became real, as if he were reliving that horrible ordeal—the pungent smell of burnt gunpowder, the sweet metallic fragrance of blood, the fetid odor of death.

Despite the warm surroundings created by the patinaed wood floor and bookcases, brick walls, vaulted ceiling, and rich leather-upholstered furniture, the space felt cold to Peter, and he involuntarily shivered.

He'd moved into this space shortly after Maggie had died,

to escape the constant haunting of her memories. Now, he wondered if he could ever again feel at peace in his present surroundings.

The buzz of his phone interrupted his melancholic mood. He didn't recognize the number.

"Yes?" he said.

"Hello, Peter Savage."

His pulse jumped, and he felt a prickly sensation down the back of his neck. It was a voice he would never forget.

For a moment, he wondered how she got his phone number. Then he realized she must have called EJ Enterprises and asked to be put through to his office, and the call was automatically routed to his cell phone.

"What do you want?" he said.

"Don't play games. You've seen what that has already cost you."

"Now you listen to me. You will never—"

"You know exactly what I want. And you will give it to me."

"Come and get it." Peter hung up.

He remembered tossing the PEAP carbine into his gun safe before tending to Kate's injuries. Since he'd had no time to inspect the condition of the weapon when Billy had presented it, other than noticing the battery was missing, he decided it was time for a closer examination.

He crossed the room to the bookcase, opened the secret panel and unlocked the safe. He placed the unique pulsed-energy weapon on the reloading bench next to the gun safe. On its side, Peter scrutinized the polymer butt stock and pistol grip, and finally the shroud which surrounded the lasing matrix. This feature resembled the barrel of a conventional firearm, although the function was completely different.

He turned the carbine over to complete his inspection, and saw the small hole above the pistol grip where the receiver would have been located if it fired bullets. The plastic had mostly returned to its original shape, which may be why he hadn't noticed it the previous day.

Using a screwdriver, he removed the butt stock and pistol grip to access the internal electronics and solid-state ceramic matrix that formed the laser pulse. The matrix was cracked, and a large piece dropped onto the bench top, along with copper-jacketed bullet fragments. A magnetic oscillator was also shot through, and a critical circuit board was ruined.

He didn't have the components to repair the weapon, even if he had wanted to.

Peter removed other circuit boards from the butt stock and carried them into the kitchen. He placed all the boards into the microwave and pressed the popcorn button. Tiny blue arcs flashed between diodes, resistors, and microprocessor chips on the boards. The high-voltage potentials generated by the microwave energy scrambled the on-chip programs and shorted microscale insulating layers between conductors. In seconds, the circuit boards were ruined beyond repair, but Peter allowed them to be nuked for the full two minutes, ensuring there was nothing that could be salvaged.

Later in the evening, when his employees were all gone for the day, he'd go down to the shop and smash the boards into tiny pieces, mix the fragments in a single bag, and then scatter the fragments in the outdoor garbage dumpster.

For now, he locked all the various components back into the gun safe. The knowledge that no one could use the PEAP carbine again was comforting. There was still the question of the design documentation residing on the company server. Naturally, he had the ability to delete those files and erase the blueprint for manufacturing the weapon. The rub was, that information was owned by DARPA since they had put forward the funding. Since the development program was not formally concluded yet, the weapon design had not been turned over to the government. Peter would be breaking the law if he deleted the files.

Was his moral principle worth a possible felony conviction?

He left his gun room and secured the hinged panel in the bookcase. Then he stretched out on the leather sofa and drifted off to much-needed sleep.

⊕

Two hours later, Peter woke feeling rested. He called St. Charles and was told that Kate's condition hadn't changed.

The short nap helped to clear his mind, and he'd decided to move the PEAP files from the company server to a cloud account under his name. By moving the files, it would not be possible for one or more of Cho's team members to hack into the computer system and steal the information. It was a blocking move, aimed to slow the cyberattack he assumed was coming, if not already underway. But it would buy time for him to decide on a permanent course of action.

Many times, he considered delivering the files to Commander James Nicolaou, head of the Strategic Global Intervention Team in Sacramento. Peter knew he could trust Jim to protect the information from foreign theft. But he wasn't ready to release ownership. Not just yet.

With Diesel riding shotgun, Peter drove to St. Charles. He stayed by Kate's side, although she never woke. At 7:00 p.m., a nurse told Peter that visiting hours were over, and that he'd have to leave. She promised to call if Kate's condition changed.

Instead of going home, Peter drove to a big-box electronic store, where he purchased a laptop and a high-capacity thumb drive. Once back at his condo, he installed a new software subscription that included access to cloud storage.

Everything was in place.

CHAPTER 29

IT WAS LATE, AND PETER LED Diesel down the front steps of his condo. He would use this regular dog walk to view the cars parked in front of EJ Enterprises. All of his employees should have left work hours ago, and he was relieved to see that no vehicles were found in the employee parking slots.

The evening walk typically lasted about thirty minutes, and Peter kept to the routine. Given the phone call from Cho earlier in the day, he decided to take the extra precaution of packing his Kimber .45 Ultra Carry subcompact pistol. He found solace in the simplicity and reliability of the pistol design that originated with John Moses Browning in 1911. This small handgun fit in a hip holster, easily hidden with casual clothing.

Having completed their normal routine without any issues, Diesel lay down on his dog bed near the stone hearth in the great room and Peter returned the small pistol to his gun safe. Carrying the new computer, plus the thumb drive, he descended the stairs from his condo to the shop on the ground floor below. The space was dimly illuminated from a couple overhead lights that were always left on. At the base of the stairs, he entered a code into the alarm system to disarm it. Then he went straight to his office.

After powering up the PC at his desk, Peter proceeded to transfer the complete pulse-energy weapons system folder to the thumb drive. The electronic file included the hardware design files with both 3D models and 2D prints, PCBA layout files, source code for the microprocessor that controlled the PEAP, material specifications for the ceramic lasing matrix, bill of materials, and massive data files. All told, it was gigabytes of data—far too large to email. Besides, he didn't want a digital trail showing where the data had been moved.

Next, he turned his attention to the company server. Given the classified nature of much of the work conducted by EJ Enterprises, the Department of Defense did not allow the use of cloud storage. Instead, Peter had been instructed to use a dual hard drive server maintained in a locked room. Data was written simultaneously to both hard drives. One drive was designated as the primary, and the other the backup drive. The server room was built to withstand a fire for one hour. In theory, this construction also made the room resistant to conventional burglars. Although, fortunately, that theory had never been tested.

As one of two company administrators, Peter had direct access to the server. Authentication was easy but effective. After he entered his sixteen-digit password, a code was sent to his cell phone, which he then entered. With the two-factor authentication completed, he went to work deleting the folder on the primary drive and the backup drive.

Over a few days of general use of the internal network by the company employees, the majority of the digital bits of information would be wiped from the hard drives. Any residual bits would be scrambled, making partial data recovery difficult, and complete recovery impossible. Eventually, after maybe a couple weeks of normal use, recovering even fragments of the PEAP carbine data would be inconceivable.

With this task completed, Peter thoroughly smashed the fried printed circuit board assemblies. With the bag of fragments in one hand, he left through a side entrance located near the industrial dumpster. His eye caught a glimpse of movement—a shadow scurrying away from the bricked enclosure where the garbage and cardboard were stored in large metal bins for weekly pickup.

"Who's there?" he called out.

Nothing.

He called again, "Who's there?"

His hand instinctively edged to his side, where his .45 would normally rest, and he cursed his lack of preparedness.

Frozen in place with the door at his back and overhead light shining down on his figure like a spotlight, Peter suddenly felt vulnerable. He presented an easy target if a North Korean assassin was gunning for him.

No, they wouldn't kill me. Not yet.

Getting on with his task, he opened the gate to gain access to the dumpster. Then he tossed the ruined pieces of the circuit boards—the remnants of the electronic brain that made the PEAP function—into the large bin. There, they fell into gaps between other rubbish. It would be difficult for any foreign agent to find all the pieces, even if they were so inclined.

Peter banked on playing a different game than what Cho expected. *In all likelihood, she's betting on me to preserve the weapon, not destroy it.*

Nevertheless, he couldn't shake the feeling that someone was sneaking around the side entrance, intending to force their way inside to conduct industrial espionage.

He entered the building again and ensured the side door was locked. As added measure, he found a four-foot length of steel bar stock and wedged one end underneath the door handle. Then he double-checked that the front entry door was also locked. Just before he ascended the stairs to his condo, he engaged the alarm system. All the windows and doors were wired, so if anyone did attempt to break in, the system would automatically call the police and ring Peter's phone.

Between his worry over Kate, and his uneasiness about the North Koreans, he doubted he would get much sleep tonight.

CHAPTER 30

JUNE 2

AT SUNRISE, PETER WAS AWAKE. He showered and dressed, then took Diesel for a quick walk—he was anxious to visit Kate, hoping she might be awake.

As he approached Kate's room, a nurse exited. He stopped her and introduced himself, then asked about Kate's condition.

"She's doing well," the nurse replied. "In fact, she's awake now, if you want to say hello."

Peter entered quietly. Kate lay motionless, her eyes closed. An IV bag hung next to the bed, the thin plastic tube connected to her arm. Next to the bed was a large bouquet of fresh flowers in shades of pink and lavender. He stood next to her side, gazing upon her face, and gently curled his hand around hers. Her eyelids fluttered and then opened partly. Her face remained expressionless.

"Hey, it's me." Peter beamed.

Kate's eyes opened wider, and she nodded weakly.

"What…what day is it?" she rasped. "How long have I been here?"

"Not long. A couple days. How are you feeling?"

She swallowed before answering, as if she needed time to

think before formulating a response.

"I hurt everywhere."

"I'll get the nurse." Peter relaxed his grip and prepared to turn, but Kate stopped him.

"No, it's okay. I'm tired."

"Just rest. The doctor says you're doing well. He thinks you'll be able to leave before long."

"What happened? Why am I here?"

"Do you remember anything that happened at my home two days ago?"

Kate closed her eyes. After many seconds, Peter thought she had fallen asleep, but then she said, "No. I remember talking to the florist, picking out flowers for the wedding. And then..."

It seemed to Peter that she was drifting in and out of consciousness.

"Abby called to say she couldn't make it for lunch. So I thought I would surprise you. I was walking up the steps," she said, her eyes still closed, "and two men grabbed me. I was frightened."

"It's okay, Kate. You're safe now."

"I don't remember anything after that."

"There was a fight," Peter said. "And you were injured."

"Oh." She nodded again.

"How are you doing? Are you tired? Should I let you get some rest?"

She shook her head. "Stay with me. I like having you near."

Peter pulled a chair next to the side of the bed. For the next twenty minutes, he monologued about everything and nothing. He was fairly certain Kate had fallen asleep almost immediately, but it didn't matter. He would do whatever she wanted. Anything to help her recover sooner and to make her more comfortable.

For the next two hours, he just sat there, her hand cradled

in his. He was concerned that she wasn't aware of the extent of her injuries, or even that she'd had major surgery. How would she react to knowing that her leg had been amputated? He buried that question for now.

Leaving Kate in a deep sleep, he checked in with the nursing station on his way out. He made certain they had his cell number, and left instructions to call anytime if Kate's condition worsened. He asked when meals were served, but was told Kate would not be given food just yet.

After leaving the hospital, Peter stopped at the florist who was supposed to do the flowers for their wedding. Without going into detail, he explained that the ceremony was delayed because of an injury Kate had suffered. Then he ordered a large floral arrangement for delivery to Kate's room later that day.

Peter still had to contact the wedding guests and let them know that the ceremony was postponed. As he ascended the steps to his condo, he noticed a large cardboard box sitting near the front door. Logos printed on the packaging tape and the side of the box indicated it was an Amazon shipment. Curious. He hadn't placed any mail orders for more than a month. Maybe it was something Kate had ordered?

After unlocking the door and greeting Diesel, he gathered the box with both hands and set it on the dining table to read the label. It had Peter's name on it, not Kate's, and the return address was for a fulfillment center operated by the global mail-order behemoth. Diesel was standing next to Peter, his nose lifted, nostrils flexing rhythmically as he scented the air.

Still believing it was something Kate had ordered, Peter walked to the kitchen to retrieve a box cutter. When he returned, he was surprised to see Diesel standing with his head lowered and facing the package. The hackles along his spine were raised, and his entire body was tense. A nearly inaudible growl reverberated through his clenched teeth.

"What is it, boy?"

But the words did nothing to distract the canine. He ran a hand along Diesel's head and back, long soothing strokes. Eventually, Diesel relaxed and sat, but he remained fixated on the box.

"It's just a box."

While Diesel watched every movement, Peter used the box cutter to slice the tape sealing the top closed. As he opened the cardboard flaps, Diesel began barking furiously.

"Enough."

Diesel quieted, but remained fixated with the package. Looking inside the box, Peter saw it was filled with crumpled kraft paper, the same brown color as the cardboard. He placed a hand inside and pulled out the wad of packing material. Just as the padding material cleared the box, there was a blur of motion followed by a thud of something heavy striking the side of the box.

Peter jumped back and the box crashed at his feet, coming to rest upside down. Out from beneath the box slithered a five-foot rattlesnake.

Diesel growled and barked ferociously, then lunged at the snake but pulled up short and air snapped. The snake coiled, readying to strike. Peter rushed Diesel, sweeping him out of harm's way, and pushed him from the dining room before closing the door.

The rattler struck just as Peter jumped again, trying to gain distance from the reptile. He saw the pink mouth and white fangs flash through empty space, missing his legs by inches.

On the other side of the door, Diesel was pawing and barking. Thankfully, with Diesel outside, Peter didn't have to worry about the pit bull trying to kill the snake. That was not a conflict he wanted to see, in part because he wasn't convinced Diesel was fast enough to avoid the fangs.

The rattlesnake slithered toward Peter, and he retreated into the kitchen, where he pulled a large chef knife from the block. Although, he wasn't sure what good it would do him. He'd have to get dangerously close to use the knife.

He reasoned that the pantry held his best option. On the tiled kitchen floor, the snake slowed. It's tongue was darting up and down, gathering scent molecules. Peter dashed for the pantry door, opened it, and snatched a folded linen tablecloth. It took less than three seconds, and when he turned back to the kitchen, the snake was two feet away. It had coiled and was vigorously shaking its tail. But the rattle was silent.

With a firm hold on the hemmed edge of the tablecloth, Peter allowed the bulk of the fabric to fall. A moment later, the triangular viper head struck. Peter dodged, and again just barely missed having the fangs sink into his leg. Instead, the snake's bite landed on the linen sheet.

With the body of the reptile extended, it began drawing the rear half forward so it could coil and attack again. Peter threw the tablecloth forward and it fell over the serpent, slowing its movement and partly entangling its body. He picked up an oven mitt and slid it on, then stepped onto the linen laid open on the floor.

The snake was still squirming, trying to find a way out. Peter studied the motion and identified a lump he thought to be the head. Pushing aside the instinctive fear that was threatening to petrify him, he placed the mitted hand on the head and pressed down. If he guessed wrong, the thick quilted layers of the mitt might protect him from the fangs. If not, the snake would inject him with enough poison to kill.

With the oven mitt in place, ripples moved violently through the tablecloth—the snake's body thrashing, fighting for freedom. Peter lowered the chef knife until it was right next to the oven mitt. Then he pressed down firmly. The sharp steel blade felt like it was cutting through a muscular rope until it came to rest against the stone tile. Blood soaked into the linen, and the rippling motion separated from the object under his mitted hand.

Peter stood and stepped away from the tablecloth, then whisked it aside. The decapitated head lay motionless, while the body of the snake continued a macabre writhing, the result of random neurons firing.

He carefully picked up the snake body and then the head, and placed both on the tablecloth. Then he gathered up the corners of the sheet and tied them together, containing the dead reptile within the linen sack, and tossed the sack into the pantry. He breathed deeply and wiped the sweat from his brow, then strode through the dining room and opened the door. Diesel ceased barking when he saw his master.

Peter crossed through the great room and opened the doors to the veranda. For several minutes, he just stood there, the gentle breeze and fresh air helping to ride down the adrenalin rush.

⊕

After cleaning the spot on the tile floor where the rattlesnake had been dispatched, including using bleach to sanitize the area, Peter went to his office and found Detective Colson's business card. She didn't pick up when Peter phoned, so he left a short voice message asking that she call him.

Ten minutes later, she did.

"Mr. Savage, I'm sorry I missed your call,"

"Hello, Detective. I think you should send someone over."

"I can do that. But you'll have to tell me why."

Peter spent the next five minutes explaining what had happened.

He concluded with, "The snake is in my pantry, and the box

it was delivered in is on my dining table."

"You're certain the rattlesnake is dead?"

"Very."

"And the box. You handled it?"

"Of course."

"Anyone else?"

"No one is staying with me, if that's what you're asking."

"Very well. I'll be right there. Refrain from handling the box any further. It could be important evidence."

Peter didn't wait long before there was a knock at his door, and he let Detective Colson in. Diesel growled at her but kept his distance.

"Your dog still doesn't like me."

"He's a good judge of character. It will take more than your sunny disposition to win him over."

With Peter's help, Colson placed the snake—still tied within the linen tablecloth—inside a large garbage bag. With gloved hands, she put the shipping box into a second garbage bag.

"Sometimes we can lift fingerprints from paper, but not always. Maybe there's something unusual about the tape used to close the box. If so, the lab will find it."

"There's something more I want to tell you. Last night, I got a glimpse of someone by the garbage dumpster next to the side entry door."

"You mean, to your company?"

Peter nodded.

"Did you recognize who it was?"

"No. I didn't get a clear look before they took off running."

"Were they trying to break in?"

"I don't know. I don't think so. But Cho also called me yesterday. She told me to turn over the PEAP carbine."

"I thought you didn't have the weapon. That's what you told me two days ago."

"That's right. I don't."

"I find it hard to believe that Cho would insist you have the weapon if, as you say, it's not in your possession. Wouldn't Cho know that by now?"

Peter was finding it hard to keep his story straight and logical. He decided it was best to continue to play ignorant.

"How can I say what the North Koreans know, think they know, or don't know at all. All I can say is she demanded I surrender the PEAP."

"Or what? Did she threaten you? And why didn't you report this yesterday?"

Peter shrugged. "I didn't think it was important. She must have called my work number. Since I wasn't in my office, the call automatically forwarded to me. And no, she didn't threaten me in so many words."

"Meaning, you understood her words as an implied threat?"

Peter nodded. "Yes. That's how I took it."

"And you didn't think this was important to share with me?"

"No, I didn't. Not until I saw whoever it was lurking by the side entrance."

Colson rolled her eyes and then held her hand out.

"May I have your phone?"

"Why?"

"I want to know what number Cho called from."

Peter opened his call history screen and handed the phone to Colson.

"Is this the number?" She pointed to the only out-of-area call received the day before.

"Yes," Peter replied.

Colson copied the number onto a page of her ever-present notepad.

While she was writing, Peter said, "The phone number is

no good. You get a recording saying the number is no longer in service."

"I'm not surprised. Cho is too cagy to use a number we can easily trace to her. Still, we should be able to get the phone company to tell us who the last registered user was for this number."

"You're grasping for straws. You just said so yourself—Cho is too smart. You think she's using burner phones registered in her name? Of course not."

"Look, I know it's a long shot. But I have six homicides to solve. That means any lead and every lead is important."

"Cho and her people are still here," Peter said. "The anonymous delivery of the snake-in-a-box proves it."

Colson sighed and pulled her lips back in a frown.

"I'll request a patrol unit drive by a couple times every night for the next week. If someone is thinking about breaking in, maybe the extra police presence will discourage them."

Peter nodded. "Thank you."

"I'll take a look around the trash dumpster and your side door on my way out. And if you get any more phone calls from Cho, let me know right away. Understand?"

The detective placed her pen and notepad in a pocket of her blue jeans, then grabbed the two garbage bags, one in each hand. Peter led the way and held open the front door. After Colson stepped through the entry, she turned back and faced Peter.

"You'd be wise to take extra precautions until this mess is resolved. The rattlesnake was probably a warning. A message to frighten you."

"I don't frighten easily."

"Figured as much. Still, do me a favor and be careful. I don't need another homicide added to my case load."

CHAPTER 31

AFTER DETECTIVE COLSON LEFT, Peter took Diesel for a long walk. The fresh air and exercise helped to calm Peter's nerves, and it gave him time to think.

What's the reason for threatening me with a poisonous snake? Although serious, he knew that a bite from a rattlesnake was seldom fatal. And if he had been bitten, medical care would have been rendered quickly. So as nasty as the idea was, it really wasn't a threat to his life. No, there had to be another reason.

Upon returning to his condo, Diesel immediately went to the kitchen and dining room. He could still smell the snake. He paced and occasionally whined, always going back to the trail left by the slithering serpent from the dining room to the pantry. Peter decided it best to mop the floor again with a bleach and detergent solution. Once the chore was done and the floor had dried, Diesel seemed unable to find the scent, and he returned to his normal relaxed behavior.

Peter checked the time. It was late afternoon. He drove to St. Charles, hoping to visit Kate again.

Before entering Kate's room, he checked in at the nursing station, where he was informed that she had been asleep since he'd last seen her earlier that morning.

The drapes were closed, making the room dark, save for a few ceiling lamps that were on. Peter sat in the chair next to Kate. Her eyes were closed, and she looked to be completely normal and well. But he knew the truth. He'd seen the extent of the injuries to her legs and hip, and he knew of the surgery to remove her leg below the knee.

He turned his gaze to the light blanket covering the lower half of her body. From the outline of her left leg, it was clear where the amputation had been made. *Does she know?*

The IV drip metered out a steady addition of fluids and drugs to her damaged body, each drip marking the passage of time at a steady beat. He placed his hand on hers. Upon his touch, she stirred and turned her head to the side, facing Peter.

"Hey there, handsome," she said, her eyelids only half-open.

"Hey there. Can I get you anything? Maybe some water?"

"That's okay. I'm fine."

"The nurse says you're doing well."

Kate gave a weak chuckle. "I'm asleep most of the time. They said it's the pain medication."

"I spoke with the doctor, and he said the same thing. They need to keep you on this for a few more days. If all looks good, then they will start to reduce the medication and try you out on solid food."

She closed her eyes, and Peter thought she was falling asleep again. But she was still conscious.

"Food sounds good. Maybe a steak?"

Peter smiled. "I'll put in the request." He hesitated, but he had to ask, "Do you know what time of day it is?"

With her eyes still closed, she whispered, "I'm not sure. I remember you came to see me already."

"Yes. That was earlier today. It's late afternoon. Would you like me to open the drapes and let the light in?"

"No. I'll just go to sleep again after you leave."

"Has anyone talked to you about physical therapy once you get a little better?"

Her eyes fluttered and then opened.

"Therapy? No. Why do I need physical therapy?"

Peter felt the lump growing in his throat, and he worked to force it down. He recalled the advice from the surgeon, that Peter would need to be supportive while Kate underwent physical and emotional therapy.

"Kate...you were shot. Don't you remember?"

She shook her head. "No. What happened?"

"Two days ago, after you returned from the florist, some men grabbed you just outside my home."

"I...I remember leaving the florist. I was walking up the steps to the front door. But...I can't remember anything else. Not until I woke up here, at the hospital."

Peter cleared his throat and gazed into Kate's eyes.

"I'm so sorry. You were shot in the legs." His voice cracked, forcing him to stop.

He swallowed and used the back of his hand to wipe away the tears.

Kate smiled and squeezed his hand. "It's okay. I'll recover and be fine."

Peter nodded and snuffled his nose. "Yes. You're going to recover, but it will take some time. They..." The lump returned to his throat, and he took a moment to work it down and gain his composure. "You'll be fine. We will be fine. But there's something you should know."

Kate's eyes narrowed. "What?"

"The damage to your leg was severe. And there was a lot of blood loss. When you arrived here..." Peter paused again to wipe away the tears, "...they...they had to remove your leg."

Kate's eyes widened. "No. I would know."

She looked toward her feet, but because she was reclined,

she couldn't see them. She tried to push her shoulders and head up, only to receive a stab of pain that caused her to collapse onto her back.

Peter reached out and cradled Kate's face. As she looked into his eyes, reddened and teary, she knew she had heard correctly.

She didn't know what to do. How would she be forced to live the rest of her life? What did it mean for the plans she and Peter had made?

She felt a sudden sense of emptiness, and that all purpose had vanished.

Kate closed her eyes and cried herself to sleep.

⊕

Peter sat by Kate's side for another hour. He had wept until there were no more tears to shed.

Eventually, a nurse entered to check Kate's vitals.

She glanced at Peter. "Were you able to get in a little visiting time?"

"She didn't know," Peter replied, his voice flat.

"Sorry?"

"Kate didn't know the extent of her injuries. Or the amputation."

"She's still on a heavy-duty painkiller. She's been unconscious most of the time. Her periods of waking have been short. And even then, she wasn't totally aware of her surroundings. Provided the stump continues to heal correctly, and we see no signs of infection, the doctor will ease back on the medication in a few days."

"How long until she can come home?"

"It's hard to say. In addition to the amputation, there was also a wound to her pelvis."

"Will she be able…" Peter cleared his throat, "…to walk again?"

"I know you're worried. And it's a big adjustment you both are facing. But we have excellent staff here to help with everything from physical therapy to mental therapy. It takes time, though. You have to be patient."

"You haven't answered my question."

"Mr. Savage, I understand this is difficult, and made worse by uncertainty. Maybe you want to consult with the doctor? I can make a note in the chart, if you'd like."

"Do that."

Peter walked away with slumped shoulders. He knew it would be another sleepless night.

CHAPTER 32

PETER FIXED A SMALL CHEF SALAD and sat on the veranda as the sun was setting. With Diesel by his side, he mostly picked at his meal, losing what little appetite he had after a few bites.

Once the sun dipped behind the Cascade Mountains, the temperature dropped, and soon it became chilly. Peter went inside and put on a winter vest and poured a double shot of Oban single-malt Scotch whiskey. He returned to his chair on the deck, with the tumbler warming in the curl of his palm.

A little more than two weeks ago, at this very spot, he proposed to Kate and she accepted. His heart was filled with boundless joy, and their future together seemed without limits. How quickly that had changed.

Kate was right. He never should have invented that infernal laser weapon. Like Alfred Nobel, inventor of dynamite, and Hiram Maxim, father of the machine gun—who both believed their inventions would make warfare so terrible that large-scale conflicts would cease—Peter had fallen prey to his own hubris. In hindsight, it was painfully obvious that the PEAP carbine would be used for assassinations. It was the perfect weapon for that purpose, so how could it be otherwise?

He had allowed himself to be blinded by his misplaced

faith that the knowledge he embodied in the first prototype could be limited to only those that *he* chose to share it with. His arrogance gave him confidence in ignoring human nature. The PEAP carbine was the opening move in a new arms race. As long as the weapon existed, the opposition would stop at nothing to acquire its secrets.

Only now could Peter admit to himself that the heady cocktail of egotism and naiveté that had clouded his judgement, had also allowed him to conveniently forget historical precedents: atomic weapons, advanced missiles and aircraft, stealth technology.

He also knew that knowledge, once gained, could not be erased.

Or could it?

If he acted quickly, decisively, maybe there was still a chance.

Peter finished the last of his Scotch and then entered the great room, hope beginning to displace despair. He opened the hidden panel in the bookcase, and then the gun safe. The remaining components of the PEAP carbine where right where he'd stashed them.

The circuit boards were already destroyed. That left the ceramic laser matrix, magnetic oscillators, ultraviolet flash diodes, and their control circuitry. The machined aluminum shroud and stock held nothing of significance, but the rest would have to be destroyed.

He gathered up the assorted components and placed them in a paper bag. None of his employees should be working, which gave him free access to use his company's shop and tools to destroy the sensitive parts.

Still worried that one of Cho's men might try to break into the shop, Peter decided to arm himself and bring Diesel along. He knew the dog's keen senses would alert to an unwelcome presence long before Peter gained awareness on his own.

The compact Kimber .45 pistol was on a shelf in the safe, snugged in a leather holster. He picked a loaded magazine from the adjacent shelf and inserted it into the grip before pushing the holster in place inside his waistband.

After closing the safe and the hidden door, he said, "Come on, Diesel. We've got some work to do."

The pair descended the staircase from the great room to EJ Enterprises. After deactivating the alarm system, Peter emptied the contents of the paper bag on a steel work bench. It was a sturdy and durable surface, but also conductive—a necessary attribute for arc welding.

Opting to begin with the ceramic lasing matrix, he found two plastic bags used to ship small parts. The brittle ceramic tube had been fractured by a bullet during the gunfight, leaving him two pieces. But the longer of the two was too big to fit inside the bags, so he used a hammer to break it in two. Three taps did the job. He placed all the pieces inside the bag, and then inserted that into the second bag. Again, using gentle blows from the hammer, he reduced the novel ceramic tube to powder in a matter of minutes.

He decided to torch the magnetic oscillators. An arc welding machine was next to the workbench, and he powered it up and turned on the argon shielding gas. After placing a welding helmet on and covering his face, Peter struck the arc against the magnetic oscillators. The intense heat soon reduced the sensitive electronic components to worthless slag.

The ultraviolet flash diodes and their control circuit did not possess sufficient conductive metal to strike an arc against them, so Peter placed these final parts in the microwave oven in the breakroom. After three minutes on high power, he was confident the diodes and microprocessor chips were unusable. Finally, he smashed these components with the hammer, as he had the lasing matrix tube.

After placing all the rubbish back into the paper bag, he turned the alarm system on again. And with Diesel by his side, he ascended to his condo.

Rather than discarding these fragments in the company trash dumpster, he decided to randomly select a garbage dumpster behind one of the many restaurants in downtown Bend. Still packing his .45 pistol, and with Diesel riding shotgun, Peter drove south on Wall Street until he found a parking spot.

On the west side of Wall Street were many popular restaurants, and behind those establishments was a service alley. With Diesel on a leash, Peter sauntered along the alley—just a guy walking his dog. Ahead, light appeared at the back of Taj Palace, and a man exited the Indian restaurant, carrying two bags of garbage that he tossed into a dumpster.

Peter moved closer, looking both directions for the presence of others. He was alone.

He instructed Diesel to sit and stay. Then he dropped the leash and raised the dumpster lid with one hand. The rank odor of rotting food assaulted his nose. He turned his head to the side and fought back the urge to vomit.

Checking again to see if he'd been followed, and failing to see anyone, he tossed the bag in with the rancid food scraps and closed the lid.

"Come on, Diesel. Let's go." He picked up the leash.

Peter continued on for another block and turned the corner so he was out of sight from the alley. After waiting five minutes, he meandered back the way he'd come. Holding Diesel's leash in one hand, he brushed his hand against the pistol at his side, hidden by the vest he was wearing. If he was being followed, he expected to meet the tail in the alley.

Peter took his time—a full ten minutes to stroll the two-block length of the alley. Not once did he meet another person.

Satisfied, he returned to his Hummer pickup truck, loaded Diesel, and drove home.

CHAPTER 33

PETER AWOKE AS THE FIRST RAYS of the morning sun penetrated his bedroom windows. He felt rested for the first time in days, although his heart still ached. The clear sense of purpose he'd come to realize the previous night helped to occupy his mind, rather than dwelling on Kate's uncertain recovery.

How long could he continue the ruse that the whereabouts of the PEAP carbine was unknown? That the weapon had not been transferred by Billy Reed, back into his custody? Both questions were imponderable. But he was convinced that the longer he kept any investigation at bay, the better were his odds of perpetuating the lies.

The next step was to eliminate the digital records. The files on the EJ Enterprises server had already been deleted with the previous backup, and within a week, two at the most, the routine of writing and deleting files to the server would wipe clean the digital record. Still, that left the information on the new laptop he'd recently purchased, plus the USB memory stick.

After retrieving the thumb drive from his desk, Peter placed it in the microwave. Several minutes later, the drive was destroyed, and he tossed it in with the kitchen garbage. Next, he accessed his cloud account and deleted every file he'd uploaded. Then he closed the account.

Peter was at the point of no return, and beginning to second-guess his decision. Everything needed to recreate the PEAP carbine was in the files uniquely residing on that laptop. It was all that was left, other than the knowledge in his own brain. His training in science told him to preserve the knowledge. *It can be protected.*

Peter was still wrestling with his conscience when his phone buzzed. The caller ID was blocked.

"Hello," he said.

"Good morning, Mr. Savage."

The voice was familiar. Cho.

Peter remained silent.

"What? No greeting?"

"I have nothing to say to you."

"That's okay. I'll do the talking. Did you like my present?"

"What do you want?"

"I want my merchandise. I want the PEAP carbine."

"I destroyed it."

A long pause.

"Then I will take the plans. All of the documentation."

"Deleted from the company server. Was that your man I saw hanging around at the side entrance to my company? You're wasting your time. The primary disc drive and backup are both clean. And before you ask, there is nothing in the cloud. Department of Defense security protocols forbid it."

Peter hoped to discourage Cho from ordering a break-in.

She said, "It would be unfortunate for you if you are telling the truth."

"You lost. Get used to it. I only made one prototype, and the documentation was not yet transferred to DARPA. It's over."

"I don't think so. There is still a source of the information. It would have been easier, and painless to you, if you'd simply given me what I want."

"Well, that's the thing about a one-off prototype. When it's gone, it's gone. So—"

"Tell me, how is Kate doing? Did she like the flowers?"

Peter recalled the bouquet in Kate's hospital room. He'd never checked the card, and never asked the nursing staff who sent them.

"Leave Kate out of this. She has nothing—"

"On the contrary," Cho said, her voice elevated, "she has *everything* to do with this."

"Anyone you send to harm Kate will have to get through me. And I can promise you, they won't."

"Oh, Mr. Savage. How gallant. I understand she lost a portion of her leg. How is she dealing with that?"

"I should have killed you before."

"Maybe next time she will lose another limb."

"You stay away from her!" Peter shouted into the phone, spittle spraying from his lips. "Or by God, I'll—"

"You'll give me what I want. And if you don't, everyone you love—Kate, your children Ethan and Joanna—they will all pay the price for your stubbornness."

Peter was pacing the great room, trying to gather his thoughts. He had to stall.

"All right," he said. "What do you want?"

"That should be obvious. I want you."

"Me?"

"You said it yourself. The prototype is destroyed, and the plans have been deleted. So if there is no record of the design, then it must come from your brain. As I said before, this would have been so much easier for you if you had simply surrendered the prototype. However, I am confident the Supreme Leader will be pleased when I deliver you to the RGB. Who knows what secrets they'll pry from your mind."

Peter was trapped. His gamble had backfired, and now he was left with little choice in dealing with Cho.

"What if I don't agree? What if I tell you to go to hell?"

Cho chuckled. "I think you know the answer. However, I will make you this promise. If you refuse me, you will never rest. You will spend the rest of your life looking over your shoulder, never knowing who will strike, or when. You will spend every waking moment in fear for your family. You can't protect them. And I assure you, I will get revenge."

After several moments of silence, Peter finally said, "Give me two days. I need to take care of certain things."

"Out of the question. I will send—"

"My demand is *not* negotiable. Give me a number where I can reach you. You either accept my terms, and I'll surrender myself to your men. Or you take your chances with me."

Now it was Cho's turn to think over the offer.

After a long pause, she said, "Very well. Two days."

She gave Peter a number to call to arrange the meeting location, and the call ended.

Peter wiped his shirt sleeve across his forehead. Any second thoughts he'd had about destroying all the documents was now gone.

He went to his study. The new laptop was resting on his desk. While it was booting up, he phoned his good friend Gary Porter, who ran a cyber security firm in California.

"Hey, buddy. What's up?" Gary greeted.

"I need your help," Peter said.

"Of course you do. Silly me, thinking you just wanted to have a friendly chat. You know, like most people do when they call a long-time friend."

"I'm sorry. But I have a big problem."

Peter proceeded to fill Gary in on the gunfight, Kate's injuries, and the demand from the North Korean operator named Cho.

"Why don't you just give her the plans? That's the only scenario where she and her team go away and leave you alone."

"No, I can't do that. This weapon, the PEAP carbine, is a game changer. The weapon can't fall into North Korean hands. I think there's another way. I've decided I have to eliminate all record of it. I've already destroyed the prototype and deleted the records from the company server. Now I just have to delete the data from my laptop."

"And that's why you called me?" Gary said.

"Yes."

"Well, you called the right guy. Sounds like you know that simply deleting a file really does nothing to remove the data from the hard drive. Only the file marker is removed. But with the right software, the data is still there to be retrieved. Even reformatting the hard drive may not ensure complete removal. No, what we need to do is wipe your drive."

"I've heard of that," Peter said.

"Yeah. Politicians like doing this to remove incriminating evidence from their computers and cell phones. The process takes time, but—"

"How much time?"

"Depends on how much storage you have on the drive. The program will rewrite every bit in every file on the hard drive. My guess is a half-hour, maybe longer. When done, there won't be anything to recover."

"Okay," Peter said. "Can you install the software and set it up so I can initiate the wiping process with a click of the mouse? And once it starts, no one can stop the program?"

"Really?" Gary said. "After all I've done in the past, you still question my skills."

Peter was given instructions to go to the website for Gary's security company and click on an icon that allowed Gary to access Peter's laptop. Once in, Gary did his magic. And in minutes, he installed a program that, when initiated, would flip every bit on the hard drive. He finished by placing the program icon on the tool bar.

"Just click on that icon," Gary said, "and the program will commence. It can't be stopped. Even if someone tries to power off the laptop or place it in sleep mode, the program will keep the PC running until every bit has been flipped. At that point, the operating system will also have been wiped, and no one will be able to start up the computer."

"In case this laptop is confiscated," Peter said, "will anyone be able to trace it back to you?"

"Nope. They'll know—or at least suspect—the hard drive has been cleaned. But who did it will remain a mystery. Still, unless you have a fond connection to this laptop, I'd suggest you destroy it once the program has completed the operation."

"That's a good suggestion," Peter said.

"Look, I know it's silly of me to ask, but have you told the police what's going on?"

"They've been involved since the gunfight. And before you ask—no. They have no idea who Cho is, or the other men who were shot. They can't protect my family. You know how it works. The police investigate *after* a crime has been committed."

"Okay," Gary said. "What are you going to do? You can't give yourself up to North Korea."

"I don't plan to."

"All right, you lost me."

"I told Cho I would call her in two days."

"And?"

"And tell her where she can come and get me."

Gary sighed. "Sounds to me like you're going to have another Rambo moment."

"I didn't start this."

"What can I do?"

"You've already done it."

After the call, Peter stared at the screen. This laptop was the last remaining tangible link to the pulsed-energy carbine. He'd have preferred to destroy it now, but decided it could still be used. It may even be crucial to luring Cho and her team into a face-to-face meeting at the time and place of *his* choosing.

To be prepared, he still had much work to do. Top of the list was to contact a powerful ally.

CHAPTER 34

MORE THAN A YEAR EARLIER, Peter had stumbled upon a short article called, "Yellowstone Zone of Death." Intrigued by the title, at first he thought it was about the Yellowstone super volcano. But as he read the first paragraph, it was clear the story had nothing to do with geology. Rather, it was about an obscure loophole in the law. Peter had committed the trivial fact to memory, never expecting it to have any greater importance than an amusing curiosity to share at a cocktail party.

Now, it was the cornerstone of a plan coalescing in his mind.

Peter opened his contacts list and called Jade. Although he believed she was still in California, she traveled a lot, and Peter didn't expect her to pick up. But she did.

"Hello, Jade. It's Peter."

After exchanging greetings, Jade said she planned to attend the wedding, scheduled to be in a few days.

Peter said, "I'm sorry to tell you that the wedding is postponed. Kate was injured, and she's still in the hospital."

"I'm so sorry," Jade said. "What happened?"

Peter shared the gunfight, and the degree of Kate's wounds.

"Oh my gosh. If there is anything my family can do—

anything I can do—please don't hesitate to let me know."

"Thank you, Jade. Your uncle has been very generous. In fact, there is something. A favor. Please understand that I would not ask for this help if it wasn't important."

"Of course. I understand. You have never taken advantage of my uncle or his wealth. Please. What is it you need?"

"A helicopter with range of at least six hundred miles. Plus a pilot. Also, a sat phone with extra batteries. And I need to leave within twenty-four hours."

"I don't understand. You're going somewhere?"

"I have to leave Bend. It's the only way to get the North Koreans away from my family."

"Yeah, I suppose that makes sense. I'll contact my uncle right away. Right now, it is late night in Brunei, but he tends to be a night owl. In the meantime, I'll call some air charter services and see what I can arrange."

"No," Peter said. "I need this to be off the record. That's why I'm calling you."

Jade pondered this for a minute, then said, "You want to be smuggled to your destination, is that right?"

"Yeah, I guess it is."

"Let me see what I can do. I'll call you as soon as I have some news. Oh, and give Kate my best wishes. I was looking forward to meeting her. I guess that will have to wait."

"Thank you. Please convey my gratitude to His Majesty. I wouldn't ask for his help if there was another option."

With that item checked off his list, Peter moved to the next time-sensitive task.

Hanging on the wall in his secret gun room, along with reproduction 18th century and early 19th century historic weapons, was an old double-barrel twelve-gauge shotgun. Manufactured by A.H. Fox, the shotgun had been purchased from a pawn shop by Peter's father when he turned twenty-one.

Since his father no longer hunted, nor did he have any interest in shooting sporting clays, the gun had been handed down to Peter.

Although not an expensive firearm in its day, it had held up well over years of use, and was still in excellent condition. Peter had shot it on several occasions, hunting pheasant and chukar. Now, he had an altogether different use in mind.

He placed the shotgun in a soft-sided case. Leaving Diesel behind, he left his condo, carrying the gun case, and walked around to the main entrance to EJ Enterprises. Nancy raised an eyebrow when Peter entered the lobby.

"How is Kate doing?" she said.

"Okay. She awoke enough that I could visit with her a bit yesterday."

"Promise me you won't spend too much time here. You need to be at the hospital with Kate."

Peter nodded and walked into his office. He laid the gun case on his desk, then called Todd.

"I need to speak with you. It's a new high-priority project."

"Sure," Todd replied. "Be right there."

Peter had unzipped the case and was removing the shotgun when Todd entered his office.

"What do you have there?" Todd said.

Peter pressed the lever to the side and opened the breach, proving the gun was not loaded. Then he handed it to Todd.

"My father gave this to me many years ago. It shoots well."

"It's a dandy." Todd examined the simple lines of the old gun.

"I need for you to remove the butt stock and build a replacement. Make it a pistol grip machined from aluminum."

"Are you sure? That's gonna kick like a mule."

"Yes, I'm sure."

"Okay. I can draw something up on the computer, and then

have the CNC mill turn it out. All three machines are loaded at the moment, manufacturing parts for the next DoD order. Should be able to get some machine time tomorrow. The next day for sure."

"No." Peter shook his head. "This is top priority. As soon as you have the design ready to go, interrupt the workflow on one of the mills and manufacture this new piece. I need it by the end of business today."

Todd narrowed his eyes, accentuating the lines just above the bridge of his nose.

"You know I'll do whatever you want," he said, "and I can get this done today. But there's something more going on. Something you're not saying."

The two men went back nearly two decades. Peter trusted Todd with his life. They'd been in a tough situation a few years ago in the Sudan, fighting shoulder-to-shoulder to rescue Peter's son from Janjaweed rebels. They made it out, just barely, and the incident served to strengthen Peter's trust in his friend.

What Peter was about to do now was different. He had to do it alone, to cross that line between right and wrong. To protect his family, he would risk everything—his freedom, even his life. But he couldn't ask Todd to do that again.

Peter knew, without a doubt, that Todd would be by his side if asked. And that just wouldn't be right. Instead, Peter compartmentalized his information, sharing with Todd and Gary only what they needed to know. Never the big picture, or Peter's true intentions. By doing this, he was giving his friends plausible deniability—shelter against criminal prosecution. At least, he hoped it would work that way.

Todd knew the conversation was over. With pursed lips, he nodded and left with the shotgun.

CHAPTER 35

AFTER GIVING TODD HIS NEW ASSIGNMENT, Peter visited Kate at St. Charles. She was awake when he arrived. Her eyes were puffy and red.

"Do you remember my visit yesterday?" Peter said.

"Yes. I think so, anyway."

After the usual questions of how she was feeling and if there was anything he could get for her, Kate's eyes teared up.

"It's okay," Peter said, trying to make his voice soothing, but not pulling off. "You're going to be fine. We're going to be fine." He wrapped his hands around hers.

"I'm not a whole person anymore. I don't know if I'll even be able to walk again."

Tears streaked from the corners of her eyes, to her earlobes.

"No, that's not true." Peter's voice cracked. "And of course you'll walk again. It is just going to take some time."

She forced a smile. "You're always the gallant gentleman. But..."

She snuffled her nose, and Peter handed her a tissue.

After she dabbed her eyes and wiped her nose, she continued, "...but I won't hold you to your proposal. I'm not the same woman you asked to marry. I'm disfigured, and I don't want to be a burden."

Peter leaned over and gently kissed her forehead.

"I love you, Kate. Don't you know that? You could never be a burden. Never. I just want to be with you. And no, this injury doesn't change anything."

"Are you sure?"

Peter smiled. "Yes. More certain than I've ever been."

She wept again, but this time with tears of joy.

After several minutes of silence, just enjoying each other's company, Peter said, "I won't see you tomorrow, or for a few days. There's something I have to do."

"Why? Where are you going?"

"Not far. It's just something I need to do."

Kate nodded slowly, but Peter had a nagging suspicion that she knew better.

He spent the next two hours there, by her side. Long after she'd fallen asleep, he kissed her cheek and slipped away.

⊕

After leaving St. Charles, Peter stopped by a hobby and craft store. There, he purchased one square foot of suede leather. It was dyed emerald, but the color was immaterial. He also purchased a large piece of thick cow hide—the type that could be used for belts.

Back at his condo, Peter entered his gun room and inventoried his shotshell ammunition. He wouldn't be taking any rifled weapons, due to the potential to yield forensic evidence in the form of unique rifling marks left on fired bullets. On the other hand, shotguns did not have rifled barrels, and thus were not subject to this downside.

The shelves above the reloading bench held a reasonable supply of twelve-gauge loads, both 00 buckshot and slugs. But he wanted another load—a round-ball shell—that he would have to prepare himself.

He opened a box of sixty-nine-caliber lead balls that he occasionally fired from his Brown Bess musket. Weighing in at one ounce, they would make for a deadly close-range load.

After loading twenty shells, Peter plugged them into the loops of a shotshell belt. There were some leftover, and those, he placed into a small shell box. Next, he grabbed two bandoliers and loaded them up with a mix of buckshot and slugs. He loaded the ammunition into his daypack, and to this he added a traditional Ka-Bar USMC knife, and his combat tomahawk. Finally, he placed his laser-ranging binoculars, spotting scope, and night-vision goggles into a pack. Later, he would add spare batteries, first aid supplies, and a variety of dried foods—hard salami, fruit, nuts, and cheese sticks.

Prior to handing the double-barrel shotgun over to Todd, Peter had measured the circumference around the breach—the widest portion of the gun. With that information, he set to making a thigh holster from the thick cow hide he'd purchased. The un-died leather was stiff and difficult to work, but after tracing an outline of the desired shape, it cut easily with a razor knife. Stitching was accomplished by first punching holes in the leather using an awl, and then sewing with waxed heavy-duty thread, also purchased at the hobby store.

A length of two-inch-wide nylon webbing served to suspend the holster from his belt to mid-thigh, and two lengths of narrower webbing would form the tie around his leg. It was ugly and crude, but he deemed it to be serviceable.

It had taken most of the day, but Peter was satisfied with his accomplishments. He texted Todd to inquire on the status of the priority machining task.

Another half-hour, Todd had replied, so Peter decided to pass that time by uploading topographic maps of Eastern Idaho, into his handheld GPS unit. Then, from his laptop, using Google Earth, he surveyed a narrow strip of extreme western

Yellowstone National Park that overlapped with Eastern Idaho. After studying the terrain, he jotted down the coordinates of his destination: 44°14'32" N by 111°03'21" W.

He had just finished when Jade called.

"I have good news," she said. "I was able to hire a helicopter from a small company that hauls logs and other freight in and out of the forest. Sometimes they even contract out for firefighting. The guy is pretty much a one-man show, mostly working in Oregon and Washington. Anyway, he said if the payment was right, he didn't care who you are or where you want to go."

"No names?" Peter said.

"No names. The pilot said, as far as he's concerned, you're just cargo."

"I've been called far worse."

"The sat phone was a bit more difficult," Jade said. "No problem buying one. But getting it to you by tomorrow morning is the challenge. I think I found a solution, though. Since the pilot flies out of McMinnville, Oregon, not far from Portland, I was able to buy an iridium phone from a store in Portland, and then hire an Uber driver to deliver it to the pilot in McMinnville. Within two hours, I should have confirmation that the delivery was made."

"Thank you, Jade. I mean it."

"Don't be silly. After all you did for me and my family, not to mention the government of Brunei, I think I still owe you. Besides, my uncle said I am to do whatever I can to get you what you need. He also offered to send a plane immediately, with a diplomatic pouch. I don't know exactly what he was talking about. Do you?"

Peter strongly suspected it was a thinly veiled offer of military equipment—most likely, communications gear and weapons. Probably even included light machine guns with abundant ammunition. Tempting as the offer was, he doubted the flight would arrive in time, even if he agreed. He figured the odds of mission success were slim, at best. And any weaponry that might be provided by the sultan's palace guard, if traced to the source, could prove to be an unwelcome embarrassment.

Peter said, "Please tell His Majesty how much I appreciate the offer, but that I respectfully decline. I suspect he'll understand my reasoning."

"Men. You are always so mysterious."

"Trust me, Jade. The less you know, the better. The same for your uncle."

"Now you're really beginning to freak me out. What are you planning to do?"

"Only what has to be done."

⊕

After concluding his phone call with Jade, Peter met Todd in his office at EJ Enterprises. The old Fox double-barrel shotgun was on Peter's desk. The original wood butt stock had been removed, and in its placed was a gleaming machined aluminum pistol grip. Peter hefted the gun—front heavy. No way could a man hold it by the pistol grip alone.

"Is that what you had in mind?" Todd said.

"Yes, exactly. Thank you. I know you had plenty of other work."

Todd folded his arms across his chest. "You and I both know how impractical that new grip is. And I also know you always have a good reason when you do something. I see the makings of a powerful weapon here, but one that is also illegal, if I'm not mistaken."

In silence, Peter returned Todd's stare.

"If you need something, anything," Todd said, "all you have to do is ask."

"I can't. You have to believe me. And trust me."

CHAPTER 36

LATE IN THE EVENING, PETER DESCENDED the stairs from his condo to EJ Enterprises. He was carrying the Fox double-barrel shotgun. After turning off the alarm, he clamped the gun to the worktable of a power band saw capable of cutting through thick steel bar stock in minutes. He turned on the blade and lowered the saw, cutting off most of the side-by-side barrels. All that was left was about nine inches from the breach to the cut end.

After carefully removing the burr left by the saw blade, Peter fixed the sawed-off gun barrels to one of the milling tables. Rather than programming the CNC mill, he chose to operate it manually, and proceeded to drill a series of small holes within a half-inch of the muzzle. The holes were only placed on the top side of the barrels so that when the gun was fired, some of the propellent gases would escape upward through the pattern of holes. The effect was to reduce muzzle jump.

He had finished, and was sweeping up the metal chips when a familiar voice said, "I suspected you would do that."

It was Todd.

Peter turned and faced his friend. "It's late. What are you doing here?"

"I was going to ask you the same question. But I can see plainly enough."

"I'm going to ask you, as a friend, to forget this."

"A pistol-gripped sawed-off shotgun is serious stuff. What have you gotten yourself into?"

Peter pulled up a stool and sat, his shoulders slumped. He hadn't shared many of the gunfight details with Todd.

"Those people from my condo. The shootout."

Todd crinkled his brow and narrowed his eyes as he stared back at Peter.

"Is that what this is about?" he said.

Peter nodded. "Yes. They claim to be agents of North Korea."

"Whoa. North Korea? For real?"

"That's what they say. Their leader, anyway. A woman named Cho. She wants the PEAP carbine."

"But you don't have it." Todd paused for a moment. "Do you?"

"No." Peter wore a smug smile. "No one has it."

"So just tell her that."

"I did. Now she wants the plans."

Todd pulled up a stool. "Okay. We could alter the design. Leave out critical specifications or components."

"No can do."

"Why?"

Peter rubbed a hand across his eyes. "Because...I deleted the files."

"All of them?"

Peter nodded.

Todd let out a soft whistle. "DARPA is gonna be pissed when they learn that piece of news."

"I know." Peter looked his friend in the eye. "Look, I didn't what you to be involved. And now it looks like you are. But as my friend, give me one favor. Don't go to the police. Not yet, anyway. Give me three days."

Todd pinched his eyebrows. "Three days? What the hell are you planning to do?"

"Cho has threatened my family. The police can't protect them. I can't either. Not twenty-four hours, every day." Peter drew in a deep breath and slowly exhaled.

"Go on," Todd said.

"So I agreed to turn over the only remaining record of the design."

"But that's…that's in your head."

"I have one copy of the files on my personal laptop. I transferred the data prior to deleting the information from the company server."

"You think they'll let you go after you give them what they want?"

Peter shook his head. "Doubtful. I could ID Cho."

"You can't surrender to North Korean agents. That's a death sentence."

"I don't plan to go quietly."

"If you go gunning for them, the police will arrest you."

"I know. The priority is to get Cho and her men out of Bend. If they are far away and occupied with me, they can't hurt Kate."

"I don't like the sound of this," Todd said. "Let's say you draw them away. Then what? If you kill them, law enforcement will be all over you. And you know it."

Peter nodded. "Ordinarily, I'd agree. Except there is one place I can go to hunt the North Korean agents. One place where I can kill them and be immune from prosecution. In theory."

"I know you too well to say you're crazy." Todd shook his head. "Still, there's no way that what you say can be true. It's just not possible."

Peter raised his eyebrows, then stood. "In a few days, we'll know."

He picked up the shotgun and started climbing the stairs to his condo.

Before he reached the top, he called back, "Activate the alarm before you leave."

⊕

Peter worked late into the night, finishing his preparations. He was interrupted only by a call from Jade confirming the sat phone had been delivered.

The aluminum pistol grip Todd had machined needed texture for improved grip, so he glued a layer of the green suede he'd purchased earlier to the metal. Then he wrapped parachute cord over the green leather. Satisfied, he slipped the double-barrel shotgun—or double-barrel smooth-bore pistol, as he preferred to think of it—into the leather thigh holster.

Between his daypack and a small duffle bag, he packed everything he and Diesel would need for three days in the wilderness. If it went much longer than that, he'd have to forage or hunt for food. Water wasn't expected to be a problem, as satellite imagery showed several creeks running through his target area. Fortunately, the forecast was for mild temperatures, and no precipitation was expected. There would be no sleeping bag and no tent. Peter would have to maintain a sharp vigil until the end.

Once everything was packed and ready, a last-minute thought came to Peter. He returned to the gun room and fabricated four paper tubes by rolling strips of newsprint around a thick pen. He glued the layers of the wrap with five-minute epoxy. After waiting until the glue was fully set, he carefully crimped one end, layer by layer, then filled the tube with a generous amount of black powder, inserted a length of waterproof canon fuse, and crimped the end to secure the fuse. He applied a generous amount of epoxy to the end crimps to finish the chore. Each explosive device was about the size and shape of an M80 firecracker. He expected they would pack about the same punch.

Peter tried to sleep but couldn't get his mind to turn off. He kept thinking through the plan, trying to find weaknesses and devise contingencies.

After an hour of tossing and turning, he gave up. Poured a shot of Oban and reclined on the leather sofa before the stone fireplace. Diesel seemed to sense his master's anxiety, and curled on the floor next to the sofa.

Eventually, fatigue won out and Peter fell into a light sleep, only to be awakened a couple hours later by his internal alarm.

5:00 a.m. Almost time to leave for the airport.

CHAPTER 37

JUNE 3

BEFORE LEAVING HIS CONDO, Peter dialed the number Cho had given him, hoping to wake her up. She picked up on the second ring.

"I've been waiting for your call," she said, her voice crisp.

"You agreed to two days," Peter said. "It's been one. I'm calling because I have something for you."

"Pray tell. You do have my attention."

"Give me your email address. I have a file to send to you."

"The design documentation for the weapon?"

"It's not a greeting card."

"You told me that you deleted the files. Why should I believe you?"

"I said I deleted the files from the company server. And I did. You didn't ask about my laptop, and I didn't volunteer to share that I had another copy."

"Why are you telling me this now? Why shouldn't I send my men to kill you and take the laptop."

"Because if you do, you will lose more of your team, and I will destroy the hard disc. You'll get nothing. I'm prepared to offer a deal."

After careful consideration, Cho decided she had nothing to lose, and everything to gain. Maybe her mission could be salvaged, after all.

She gave Peter a secure email address.

"The file is coming now," he said. "Let me know when you receive it."

He muted his microphone while he was on hold, knowing it would take a minute or two for the email to be received. He called Diesel, hoisted the duffle bag, daypack, and soft gun case holding his long gun, and exited his condo for his Hummer truck. He was still holding when he put the truck in gear and drove away.

After two minutes, Cho said, "I have the email, and I opened the file."

A three-dimensional image of the PEAP carbine appeared on her monitor. Using the mouse, she could rotate the image. It looked complete, based on her glimpse of the weapon several days earlier.

"Good," Peter replied. "Then you also know that this is just a sample. I didn't send the complete documentation package."

"Why not? It would make your life easier if we could just be done with this."

"The file size is too large to email."

"I'm happy to set up a secure file transfer site, and you can easily upload the files."

"I have a different proposal. I'll give you the laptop. All the information—designs, material and component specifications, circuit board layout, complete bill of materials with vendor list, everything—is on the hard drive. About four gigabytes in total."

"Perfect," Cho said. "I'll have one member of my team pick it up from you."

Peter chuckled. "I don't think so. I'm not at my home or

work. Shortly, I'll call back with the meeting location."

He ended the call, and prayed she'd take the bait.

⊕

Peter stopped at a fast-food joint on the way to Bend Municipal Airport. Diesel enjoyed four hamburger patties. He would have happily wolfed down the buns and condiments as well, but too much salt and vinegar would not be healthy for him.

The helicopter was being fueled when Peter arrived. It had the familiar lines of the Huey troop transports made famous during the Vietnam War. But unlike that vintage aircraft, this one had a four-blade rotor. The tail assembly was painted red, while the rest of the helicopter was white. The company name—Heller Airlift—was displayed in black lettering along the side of the cabin.

With Diesel by his side, Peter strode toward the parked aircraft with the daypack strapped to his back and the duffle bag in hand. He also had the soft gun case hanging from his shoulder.

When he was twenty yards or so away, a tall man with blond hair cut close, walked from around the far side of the helicopter. He seemed to be conducting a pre-flight inspection. When he looked away from the aircraft, he spotted Peter and Diesel.

"You must be my cargo," he called.

He wore a red flight suit and had a pair of sunglasses hanging from a breast pocket. He was taller than Peter, but lean.

"I am," Peter replied. "I assume you're Mr. Heller?"

He nodded. "Just call me Matt. Come on. Let's get your gear stowed. Has your dog ever flown before?"

"He has. He'll settle right down once you lift off."

The pilot slid the side door open, and Peter loaded his gear before lifting Diesel inside. The cabin interior was spartan, equipped with two canvas jump seats that spanned the width of the cabin. One was folded up to make room for three barrels labeled JET A. All three drums were strapped to D-rings set in the floor. Peter climbed in and sat on the bench seat facing the fuel containers.

The pilot handed him a communication headset. "It'll be real noisy once the engine is turning. We can talk over the intercom."

Having finished fueling, Matt climbed behind the controls and called over his shoulder to Peter.

"Just want to confirm I have the proper coordinates."

He rattled them off while Peter checked the latitude and longitude against the values stored on his GPS.

"Confirmed," Peter replied. "You have the correct coordinates."

Matt said, "If we fly a straight course and conserve fuel, we should make it okay."

"Should? That doesn't instill confidence."

"Nothing to worry about. I'll get you there. Coming back is the question. That's why you're riding with my reserve fuel. There's a hundred sixty gallons there. After I drop you off, I'll top up the tank. That should easily get me to Twin Falls, maybe as far as Boise, before I have to gas up for the final leg home."

"Why not just top up the tank on the way there?" Peter said.

"Well, ordinarily that would be sound advice. But a certain lady impressed upon me the need to keep this flight under wraps. So I figure it's better not to stop at any airport along the way. Flight operations centers have a way of keeping records and all."

"Hadn't thought about that," Peter said.

"Your friend is paying top dollar—more than I take in during a normal month of hauling timber. Just sit back and relax."

While Matt worked through his preflight checklist, Peter made a video call to Cho. The cabin of the Bell helicopter showed clearly behind Peter's image. He gave her the same coordinates he'd given the pilot.

"And I am to believe you? This sounds like what you Americans call a wild goose chase."

"I'm not playing games, Cho. I delivered proof that I have the files. Now, do want them or not?"

"Why this location? It's not in any city on the map."

"Because I don't trust you. Last time we met, your men shot up my home and injured an innocent woman. Any location I might select in Bend, your trigger-happy comrades are likely to start shooting again. I don't want any more innocents to be harmed."

Cho was silent for a long moment, and Peter feared she might reject the bait.

He continued, "What difference does it make where we meet? All you should care about is that I have the laptop and the files."

Peter felt his heart beating faster. Would she agree?

Another pause.

Finally, she said, "Very well. We will do this your way. But mark my words—if you attempt to trick me, I will make it my life's mission to kill everyone you hold dear. Have I made myself clear?"

"Abundantly," Peter replied, satisfied that the hook was set.

The image on his phone disappeared as Cho terminated the call. He was counting on the North Koreans needing several hours to organize people, gear, and a helicopter, and then a few more hours to fly to the rendezvous point.

He had to get there first. That would be his only advantage over what he knew would be a superior force—both in numbers and firepower.

Matt had overheard Peter speaking, and refrained from firing up the turbine until his call was concluded.

"We good to go?" he said.

"Yes," Peter replied. "Let's get the hell out of here."

Matt flipped a couple switches, and a high-pitched whine filled the cabin, the sound building in intensity as the twin Pratt & Whitney turbine engines fired.

Over the intercom, Matt said, "Sorry I don't have any peanuts, and there won't be a drink service."

"What's the flight time?" Peter said.

"We'll be cruising at about a hundred forty miles per hour. So figure three hours to get there. I'm not familiar with the patch of wilderness these coordinates match. I'm assuming there's a clearing nearby where I can put this bird down?"

"That's what the satellite image shows," Peter said. "Thin trees with scattered meadows."

Just as the skids of the Bell 412 lifted, Diesel hopped onto the canvas bench seat next to Peter and laid his head on his thigh. Soon, the drone of the engine lulled Peter to sleep.

CHAPTER 38

THE LANDSCAPE BELOW WAS AN EMERALD CARPET undulating up and down. Matt addressed Peter for the first time since they'd departed Bend.

"In a few minutes, we'll be at your landing coordinates."

"Roger that," Peter replied.

Diesel was still on the jump seat, where he'd been the entire flight.

Before long, the helicopter banked and circled in a tight turn.

"Look out the side window," Matt called over the intercom." I'm going to put us down in that meadow, unless you have any objections."

"Nope," Peter said. "Looks fine to me."

The Bell descended, and then the skids bumped on the grass and gravel. Peter waited while the engines wound down. After a minute, Matt unbuckled and stepped back into the cabin. He slid the door back and Diesel jumped out, seemingly happy to be on solid ground with new scents to take in. Matt jumped out next, and Peter handed him his gear, which Matt placed in a pile twenty feet away from the skids.

Peter stepped out and faced Matt. "Thank you."

"Don't mention it. Like I said before, your friend is paying me well. There's no reason anyone would ask. But if they do, I was just hauling cargo. What type of cargo, I can't say, because I didn't look in the crates. Just some scientific equipment, I suppose."

Peter nodded, and then Matt began the process of using a portable electric pump to transfer jet-A fuel from the drums into the helicopter fuel tank. It took him thirty minutes to complete his task. By then, Peter and Diesel were long gone.

⊕

Peter climbed a ridge five hundred yards from the helicopter. The face of the ridge was comprised of crumbling stone—gravel and small rocks punctuated with occasional boulders. With every step, he slipped backwards several inches, and maintaining his balance, especially with his load, made it slow climbing. Although Peter found it difficult, Diesel had no such trouble and was at the crest, waiting for his master to arrive.

The sound of a turbine engine drew Peter's attention west, and he watched as the red and white helicopter lifted into the air and departed.

A quick check of his handheld GPS showed that the Idaho-Wyoming border was two hundred yards east, behind his present location. He set his gear down and removed the binoculars from his daypack. His hunting territory was to the west—a thin strip of Yellowstone National Park, barely two miles wide, and extending north to the Montana state line.

He checked his cell phone. As expected, no connection. The nearest cell tower was probably miles away. He proceeded to methodically scan the terrain. The ridge he was on offered a reasonable vantage, and after he had a good understanding of the topography, he returned the binoculars to the daypack.

It was midmorning, and the air temperature was still cool. But in the sun, it was comfortable with only shirt sleeves. For now, he would leave his vest and jacket in the duffle bag. He buckled the shotshell belt around his waist, then strapped the large holster to his thigh. After loading two of the ball shells into the breach of the sawed-off shotgun, he slid it into the holster. It was a snug fit, which he preferred to help keep the heavy gun in place.

Next, he slipped one of the bandoliers over his head, allowing it to hang from his shoulder, diagonally across his chest and back. The other bandolier was placed within the daypack. Inside the soft gun case was his Benelli M4 shotgun. The semiauto M4 was devastating in close combat. Although, with the wide vistas, Peter would have preferred his Weatherby hunting rifle. However, he chose the handicap of smoothbore guns and their relatively short range so that there would be no forensic evidence left behind in the form of spent bullets with telltale rifling marks.

He slipped each arm through the grips of the duffle bag, and adjusted the weight so it carried easily on his back. The daypack hung over his chest. Lastly, he suspended the Benelli from its sling with the gun at hip level.

"Let's go, buddy," he said to Diesel.

Heavily loaded, Peter descended from the ridge into the meadow below, careful of his foot placement. A creek flowed through the meadow. It wasn't wide or deep, and he figured there would only be stagnant pools here and there by late summer. At least for now, it offered a ready supply of water. Later, when his two canteens were empty, he would filter water from the stream to replenish his supply. The water-purification filter would serve to remove single-cell pathogens. Diesel had no concerns about the water quality, and he paused at the edge of the flowing stream to lap up the cold liquid.

They continued following the creek southwest, and entered a thin forest marked by thick deadfall. For more than a century, since March of 1872, when Yellowstone became the first National Park, the land had been left to be shaped by the forces of Nature, without the influence of logging, ranching, or mining. No roads, no clear cuts. Trees remained where they fell, to slowly rot.

On either side of the creek, the terrain rose to low ridgelines, suggesting that perhaps the shallow ravine was carved by flowing water eons ago. Eventually, the sloped ridges gave way to a flat verdant meadow, and the flowing water split into three tributaries.

It was a decent landing zone, and he reasoned that Cho might put her team in here. To the west, he could see the land rose and was covered with thick forest, although undergrowth was virtually nonexistent.

He checked his GPS unit. It was configured with software that would display either a topographic map, or the most recent satellite imagery. The high-resolution aerial image showed only forest extending from his present position, west to the boundary of Yellowstone. About seven hundred yards to the north was another ridge that offered a good view of the meadow

"Diesel. Let's go check out that ridge."

The red pit bull cocked his head in silent reply, and then they were off. Walking at a steady pace so as not to overheat or waste calories, Peter skirted the edge of the grassy plain bordering the timber. The deadfall made it impossible to travel more than two dozen yards without having to detour around a fallen tree. He reasoned it would make good cover from which to defend, or possibly even spring an ambush.

Atop the escarpment, Peter found more fallen trees and an outcropping of man-sized boulders. Farther back from the rim, the timber began again—a dense growth of stunted trees, most not more than a foot in diameter.

He returned to the rim. Many of the dead trees appeared to have broken off close to the ground, and most showed weathered evidence of having been burned, perhaps decades earlier.

Peter moved closer to the edge and nestled into the outcropping. After finding a comfortable sitting position, he dug the binoculars out of the daypack and glassed the meadow below.

He whispered, "I think this will do, Diesel. They'll have to come in by helicopter, just as we did. With the rough terrain and fallen timber everywhere, no way they can get here by ATV."

Diesel sat with his tongue hanging out, panting lightly. Peter removed the folding water dish from an outer pocket of the daypack, and filled it half-full of water from a canteen. While Diesel lapped the dish dry, Peter took two long swigs, then capped the canteen.

They sat there for an hour, glassing every square foot of the landscape below, charting the preferred and secondary landing zones. Peter also used this time to plan his avenues of egress—directions to flee expeditiously if being fired upon, as well as pathways to slink away without the enemy detecting his movement.

Satisfied, he returned to the timber again to find a good location to construct a primitive lean-to shelter. Using the tomahawk, he felled and limbed several small evergreens, the largest no bigger than a couple inches in diameter. The sturdiest of the lot, he lashed between two trees only six feet apart. Next, he clipped dozens of branches from surrounding evergreens. Layered these into a thatched covering that sloped away from the rim of the escarpment, and also covered the sides. He even carpeted the ground within the lean-to with young bows to provide insulation from the cool earth. Although rain wasn't in the forecast, and the sky was clear, the shelter would help to retain warmth once the night descended and temperatures dropped. Plus, the shelter would camouflage his presence from every direction other than to the front.

Peter removed an assortment of food from his daypack. It had been more than ten hours since he'd last eaten, and his stomach was beginning to rumble. He scarfed down his ration and added a small amount of dry salami to Diesel's kibble. Then he refilled Diesel's water dish before finishing off the contents of the first canteen. The second canteen would be enough water until tomorrow, and when the opportunity presented itself, he'd fill them both.

His thoughts inevitably settled to Kate. His concern for her returned to being foremost in his mind, now that his preparations were as complete as possible. He wished he could be there at her bedside. She needed him, and he needed her.

Does she think I've abandoned her? God, how I want to be by her side, to give her encouragement and support, to show her I love her no matter what.

He blinked twice and then wiped his tears with the palm of his hand. He had to push these thoughts aside, for they made him vulnerable. He had to keep his head in the game. Had to be sharp and alert.

He had to be ruthless.

Once more, Peter checked his weapons. He was as ready as possible.

Since Diesel would hear sounds seconds, maybe even minutes, before Peter, the dog would be his advance warning system. With that knowledge, Peter made himself as comfortable as possible, and waited.

CHAPTER 39

TODD'S CONCERN OVER HIS FRIEND amplified overnight, and by morning, he was in a state of panic. But it wasn't just Peter he feared for. He also feared for Kate.

Todd drove to St. Charles early in the morning. He lied to the nursing staff, claiming he was Kate's brother and had just arrived in town. It took all his powers of persuasion, but he was able to convince them to let him visit Kate.

She was sleeping when he entered her room, and he sat quietly in a chair near the window. The draperies were still closed, and the room was dark. He opened the drapes a bit to let in a small amount of natural light. If anyone other than hospital staff entered, they'd have to get through him to reach Kate.

Todd knew he couldn't provide round-the-clock protection, and he planned to enlist help from his colleagues at EJ Enterprises. He figured that if he could get six or seven other men to share the duty, they could do a good job of providing security. At the moment, he wasn't sure how he would sell that to the nursing staff.

One step at a time.

After phoning Nancy to let her know he'd be in later, Todd called the Bend Police Department non-emergency number and asked to be connected with Detective Colson. At first, he was getting nowhere, until he mentioned Peter Savage and North Korean agents. After holding for five minutes, the detective picked up the line.

"This is Detective Colson."

"Detective, this is Todd Steed. I work with Peter Savage. There's something I need to share with you."

"I'm listening."

"I assume you know about the North Korean agents."

"I do."

"Peter told me yesterday that he believes they will try to harm Kate or his children."

"Why are you telling me this?" Colson said. "Where is Mr. Savage?"

"I don't know. I knocked on his door this morning, but he didn't answer. He's not at work either, and I have no messages from him."

"He's probably at Saint Charles."

"Nope. That's where I am, in Kate's room."

"If you expect me to initiate a missing person report—"

"Detective, that's not why I'm calling. Peter's worried about Kate's safety. I am, too. Can you have a police officer posted outside her hospital room for a few days?"

"Based on what reason? I'm sorry, but the department does not have the budget or manpower to assign a uniformed officer as personal bodyguard to every citizen who thinks they might be in danger."

"I know Peter. He doesn't spook easily."

"Look, I understand your concern. Mr. Savage is fortunate to have friends such as yourself. If you see any suspicious persons, call me." Colson gave Todd her cell number. "If I don't pick up, call nine-one-one."

"Right. I'll do that, and I'm sure help will arrive in time to tag the bodies."

Although Todd was disappointed, he knew Peter had been correct when he said the police couldn't provide protection. Still, he had to try.

Todd had one other card to play, and he dialed Commander James Nicolaou. Todd and Jim were acquaintances, not close friends, even though they'd known each other for several years. Todd had recently worked with Jim on the DARPA project.

Jim didn't pick up, and the call went to voicemail.

"Hello, Jim, it's Todd Steed. Look, there's a problem developing here, and I think you need to be briefed. It involves both Peter and Kate. Please call me as soon as you get this message."

Todd called Peter again but was immediately connected to his mailbox. He left a short message to call at the earliest opportunity.

For the next hour, he passed the time reading his email, which was mostly work related. Kate was still asleep, so he took a break. A nurse directed him to the cafeteria, and he bought a cup of coffee. While he was walking back to Kate's room, his phone buzzed.

"Todd, this is Jim. I just got your message. Sorry I couldn't reply sooner. Been in meetings all morning."

"Thank you for calling back." Todd found a quiet corner and spent the next five minutes bringing Jim up to speed, including Kate's gunshot wounds.

"I had no idea," Jim said. "Peter sent an email saying the wedding had been postponed, but he didn't share any details. How is Kate?"

Todd relayed what information he had, including that her leg had been amputated below the knee.

"I'm very sorry," Jim said. "I've got to tie up some strings here, but I'll be there late tomorrow."

"If you're coming to see Peter, don't. He's not here."

"What? Where is he?"

"I don't know. I think he left early this morning."

"Left for where?"

"Wish I knew. That's why I'm calling. I'm afraid he's gotten into deep trouble."

Todd repeated the essence of his conversation last night with Peter, leaving out the part about the sawed-off shotgun.

"North Korean agents?" Jim said. "In Bend?"

"I know. Hard to believe, right? But I spoke with a Bend Police detective earlier this morning. She confirmed that the people involved in the gunfight are thought to be North Koreans."

Jim whistled. "Listen, I need to get a couple of my analysts together and debrief you. Are you at a place where you can talk freely?"

"Not really. I'm in a hallway at the hospital. The police don't have the resources to post an officer outside Kate's room. So for now, anyway, it's me."

"I understand," Jim said. "However, this is important. I need to get my team up to speed. The PEAP weapon system cannot fall into the hands of foreign agents. Least of all, North Korean agents."

Todd agreed to call Jim back in thirty minutes. That would give him time to call one of the machinists to leave work and come in to cover for him while he made the call from his truck in the hospital parking lot.

While Peter was away, Todd had overall managerial responsibility. And although calling a few of the employees away to watch over Kate might slow productivity, Todd would gladly accept a dressing down from Peter when he returned.

If he returned.

⊕

At the Strategic Global Intervention Team HQ—unofficially known as The Office—Commander Nicolaou had gathered Lieutenant Ellen Lacey in his office. Lacey was a veteran of SGIT, with direct oversight of a team comprising some of the most intelligent and capable analysts to be found anywhere. Jim had already briefed Lacey, sharing the limited information he'd gleaned from the phone call with Todd.

Exactly on schedule, Todd called Jim's cell number.

Jim said, "I have my top analyst, Lieutenant Lacey, with me. I have you on speaker. Are you in a private location?"

"I'm in my truck, in a parking lot. The windows are up, and no one is nearby."

"Very good. Let's begin with these foreign agents. You said they're from North Korea?"

"That's what Peter told me. And the detective didn't deny it."

"The Bend Police detective?" Lacey said.

"That's right. Detective Colson."

Lacey told Jim, "I can call the Bend Police Department and find out if they've read in the FBI."

Jim nodded. "I'd imagine they have, but best to confirm. Then see if you can find out who's running the investigation for the Bureau."

"Will do. I'll also try to confirm they still have the PEAP carbine locked away in their evidence room."

The mention brought back painful memories for Jim. It had only been a month since the prototype PEAP had been stollen from EJ Enterprises in a daring robbery-murder that left Jim as the prime suspect for several days. Peter had eventually cleared his name.

"Just to be clear," Jim said, "there isn't another PEAP prototype at EJ Enterprises. Is that correct?"

"You got that right," Todd said. "Peter deleted the files

from the company computer system, but he still has a complete record on his laptop. Cho has demanded Peter surrender the files, or else she will harm Peter's family."

"You believe her threat is credible?" Lacey said.

"Two days ago, someone left a cardboard box on Peter's front porch. Inside the box was a five-foot rattlesnake. The next day, Cho phoned Peter and said it was a message. Said that if Peter didn't give her what she wanted, Kate, Ethan, and Joanna would all be harmed."

"Where is Peter now?" Lacey said.

"I don't know. He didn't say. Not exactly."

"What did he say?" Jim replied.

"You know Peter. He doesn't take to being threatened. Even worse if it's his family who's being threatened. Anyway, I warned him that if he went gunning for Cho or any of her team, he'd be on the wrong side of the law."

Jim cocked an eyebrowed. "That's sound advice. But I doubt Peter liked hearing it."

"No, I don't think he did. But then he said something odd. He said that there is one place where he could hunt the North Koreans and not be prosecuted for any crimes. That still doesn't make any sense to me."

Lacey leaned back in her chair, tapping a finger on the armrest.

Jim looked at her. "Does that mean something to you, Lieutenant?"

"Maybe. I recall reading something like that in a novel a few years ago. I can't recall the details though. Let me do a little research."

"Okay," Jim said. "Anything else, Todd?"

"No, nothing. There must be something you can do? I'm concerned Peter is going to get into trouble, if not killed."

"Since we don't know where he is, there isn't much I can do.

Lacey will check in with the FBI. This should be a high priority for them. In the meantime, if you learn anything else, or if Peter contacts you, let me know without delay. Understood?"

"I hear you. It just feels like we're letting him down. He needs our help."

"Listen," Jim said. "Peter is one of the most resourceful people I know. Whatever his plan is, you have to have confidence that he's thought it through, and he knows what he's doing."

"He's alone."

"How do you know that?" Lacey said. "Maybe he's cooperating with the FBI."

Todd thought of the sawed-off shotgun. "No, he's not working with law enforcement."

"How can you be sure?" Jim said. "You already said you don't know where he is."

"It's something…I'm sorry. I gave Peter my word."

Jim exchanged a knowing glance with Lacey, then leaned closer to the phone resting on the middle of his desk.

He said, "If you really think this is a matter of life and death, then you owe it to Peter to tell us everything you know."

Todd paused to let the words sink in. It went against his moral fiber to go back on his word. But he genuinely feared for Peter's safety.

"He had me make a pistol grip for a…"

Jim gave Todd several moments to complete his sentence.

When he didn't, Jim said, "What did you make the pistol grip for?"

"A sawed-off shotgun. Peter cut the barrel off an old side-by-side twelve-gauge down to eight or nine inches. I didn't measure it. But I saw it briefly."

"Why would he do that?" Lacey said.

"I don't know." Jim's mind was racing to come up with

possibilities. "But I agree with Todd. He wouldn't carry an illegal weapon if he was working with law enforcement."

Lacey said, "Then who's he working with?"

"I don't think he's working with anyone. I think Todd's right. Peter is out there alone. And if he really is going up against trained agents from North Korea, God help him."

CHAPTER 40

IT TOOK LACEY AN HOUR to work through the bureaucracy at the FBI, until she was finally speaking with an agent familiar with the shootout in Bend, on May 31st. The agent offered few details but did confirm they were working under the theory that it was North Koreans trying to acquire a classified military article.

Lacey was frustrated by the agent's refusal to confirm if the classified article was the prototype pulsed-energy carbine.

"I'm sorry, ma'am. I can't comment on that," he'd said.

"That prototype is supposed be secured in an FBI evidence room. Will you confirm that is the case?"

"Again, I'm sorry. I can't help you with that."

"Fine. I'll take it higher up the chain."

She fared better on researching the cryptic reference Peter had shared about a location where he could be immune from criminal prosecution. While Lacey was scrolling through her Kindle library, a particular book cover sparked her memory. The title was *Free Fire* by C.J. Box. As she read the back-cover blurb, her pulse quickened. It didn't take long to complete a cursory search, and soon she found the lead she was hoping for.

She gathered her tablet and hurried to Commander Nicolaou's office. His door was open, and he was sitting at his desk, concentrating on his computer monitor. She knocked on the doorframe.

Jim raised his head. "Come in, Lieutenant. What did you find?"

"Not much from the FBI. However, they did confirm that intelligence operatives of North Korea are alleged to be directly involved. Apparently, there's a lot of physical evidence—fingerprints, blood samples, six deceased, two wounded and in custody. This is something the Defense Intelligence Agency should be involved in. Maybe Colonel Pierson can apply some pressure and get the feds to share what they have."

"Maybe," Jim said. "I'll reach out to him. What else?"

"Remember I said that I read a novel a few years back that referenced a portion of the US where criminal law doesn't apply?"

"Yeah. Sounds totally unbelievable."

"Well, here's the book." She passed her tablet across the desk.

Jim read the description silently, then repeated portions aloud.

"...a backcountry corner of Yellowstone National Park, a free-fire zone with no residents or government regulation. In this remote fifty-square-mile stretch, a man can literally get away with murder." He passed the tablet back. "Tell me more. Is this for real?"

"Well, I did a quick search and found a dozen hits—mostly short articles, even one published by *Atlas Obscura*, referencing the Yellowstone Zone of Death."

"Who comes up with these names?"

Lacey shrugged. "Beats me. Although it sounds like a poorly conceived conspiracy theory, there's more to it. Much more."

"Go on."

"This idea, or theory, first came to light in a legal paper published in 2005, by an associate professor of law at Michigan State University. The title of the paper is 'The Perfect Crime.'"

"Sounds fitting," Jim said.

"Yeah. Well, the crux of his argument is that, due to reasons of vicinage, a person could commit a serious offense in this geography—the so-called Zone of Death—and not be subject to a jury trial. No trial, no conviction. That simple."

Jim sat upright in his chair, arching his back and stretching the muscles in his neck.

"Are you okay, sir?"

"I'm fine. Just feeling a whopper of a headache about to come on." He crossed his arms. "What geography? Where is this crime-free zone located?"

"Right here." Lacey turned her tablet and pointed to a map of Yellowstone National Park. "This narrow strip of land that is both within the park boundaries and part of the State of Idaho."

Jim squinted and leaned closer to the tablet.

"I thought Yellowstone was totally within Wyoming."

"No, sir. Small slivers are in both Idaho and Montana. Yellowstone was the first national park to be formed. Not only in the United States, but in any country. When the park boundaries were drawn up and approved by Congress in 1872, Idaho and Montana were not states. That came almost twenty years later."

Jim shrugged. "So what?"

"Actually, that's the reason this problem exists. At least, as it's argued in this paper. You see, when Idaho and Montana were admitted into the Union, each state ceded exclusive jurisdiction of its portion of Yellowstone to the federal government. This allowed all of Yellowstone to be exclusively within the judicial district of Wyoming, rather than having the park split among multiple judicial districts."

"Sounds reasonable." Jim nodded. "Go on."

"So let's say that someone commits a crime in the narrow strip of Idaho that's within the park boundary. If the offense is serious enough, the defendant has the constitutional right to a jury trial. Only, there's a problem. The Constitution—specifically, Article III, Section 2—requires that the trial be held in the state within which the crime was committed. No problem so far, until we read the Sixth Amendment."

Jim frowned. "Forgive me. You'll have to refresh my memory of the Sixth Amendment."

The corners of Lacey's mouth drew back in a half-grin.

"I couldn't recall the wording either, so I looked it up." She looked down at her tablet. "It reads, and I quote, 'In all criminal prosecutions, the accused shall enjoy the right to a speedy and public trial, by an impartial jury of the State and district wherein the crime shall have been committed.' End quote."

Jim pinched his eyebrows. "Let me get this straight. This law professor publishes a scholarly paper arguing that constitutional rights apply equally across the United States. Seems like a no-brainer to me. Tell me what I'm missing? And what does any of this have to do with Peter Savage, where he might be, and what he might be up to?"

"Simple," Lacey said. "The problem is that no one lives in that portion of Idaho that is also within Yellowstone National Park. No residents to make up a jury pool."

Jim opened a desk drawer and removed a small bottle of ibuprofen. He popped two tablets and swallowed them.

"Great," he said. "Leave it to a law professor to come up with an argument for how to legally commit a crime. Entertaining, I'm sure. But this can't possibly be the case. Surely, if this hypothetical scenario ever really existed, the laws would have been changed to remove any possible ambiguity."

Lacey raised her eyebrows. "I thought so, too. But that doesn't seem to be the case. In fact, three years after the professor published the first paper, he published a follow-up in which he described his efforts to get Congress to fix the problem. Although he seemed to have the attention of one senator, nothing materialized. And there hasn't yet been a criminal proceeding that would test how the courts would handle this."

Jim sighed and rubbed his temples. "All right. So Peter is going to the Zone of Death."

"This is only one theory, sir. I haven't had time to consider other possibilities."

"I understand. But if you were able to find this information quickly, then so could Peter. Tell me, is this geography unique?"

"Yes, sir. The Montana portion of Yellowstone is inhabited, albeit sparsely. Maybe a couple dozen full-time residents. And there is no other location I've been able to find where state borders and judicial districts are in conflict. I've tasked one of my analysts to thoroughly research this. Should have a conclusive answer within an hour."

Jim nodded and returned to rubbing his temples.

Lacey said, "If that is where Mr. Savage is headed, what could he hope to accomplish there?"

Jim stared back at Lacey through cold, hard eyes.

"Retribution."

"For the attack at his home on May thirty-first?" she said. "Why? The police and the FBI are all over this case. If he inserts himself into the investigation, he will also be charged and prosecuted."

"He knows that. He said as much."

Lacey thought for a minute. "Smoothbore weapon."

"That's right. Sawed-off shotgun, to be precise. Why? Because a pistol barrel is rifled. He gave up the superior firepower of a semiauto, magazine-fed pistol for a substitute that would not leave ballistic forensic evidence."

Lacey's mind was in overdrive. "If that's true, then he wouldn't have a rifle either."

"Correct. But you can bet he's still heavily armed. If it were me, I'd pack a full-size shotgun, preferably semiauto. Good for close-quarter combat, but no capability for long-distance sniping."

Lacey said, "If North Korean agents confront him, and if they're armed with military weapons, Mr. Savage will be outgunned."

"Outmanned and outgunned," Jim said.

"He must know that. Why would he do this?"

Jim pondered the question for a moment. Lacey was right, and Jim knew that Peter would never act rashly. He could only arrive at one answer.

"When they shot Kate, she nearly died. She lost part of her leg. I've had friends go through amputations after narrowly surviving IED blasts, and I can tell you it's hard. To have part of your body cut off...that's difficult for even the strongest person to accept."

"And then they threatened his children," Lacey said, in a low voice.

"Cho has no idea the firestorm she and her team are about to enter. She's unleashed a beast. And in the zone of death, if Peter truly believes he's immune from prosecution, then he's unfettered from the rule of law. He'll answer only to his personal morals. He won't back down or offer quarter."

"Even so, I don't see how Mr. Savage can prevail."

Jim's eyes were downcast. "You may be right. But I promise you this—it will be bloody, and the North Koreans will know they've been in a hell of a fight."

CHAPTER 41

THE FULL MOON SHONE BRIGHTLY against a black sky studded with countless pinpoints of light. Occasionally, a coyote would howl mournfully. Otherwise, it was silent. Without a campfire, the hours passed slowly as Peter fought to ward off the chill. He was wrapped inside a warm winter jacket, with Diesel pressed against his legs. Sometime after midnight, he found himself nodding off, only to suddenly awake minutes later.

The darkness and cold passed slowly, but eventually the eastern horizon began to lighten. Almost imperceptibly at first, then passing through shades of gray—dark to light. Peter rose to his feet and stretched, wishing he had a steaming mug of coffee. Instead, he made do with cold water from his canteen. After drinking his fill, he topped up Diesel's bowl with the last of the water.

"Stay here, boy."

With the sawed-off shotgun in his thigh holster, and the Benelli M4 slung from his shoulder, Peter gathered both canteens and walked off the ridge. He was headed for the creek several hundred yards away.

Each boot placement was silent—a skill he'd honed to perfection over decades hunting in the Cascade Mountains.

His mind returned to Kate. How was she feeling? Was the pain from her wounds subsiding? Again, he was awash in guilt for not being at her side. The only solace he found was that by drawing Cho here, Kate would be safe.

At the edge of the creek, he pumped water through an ultrafilter, into each of the two canteens. The filter was a tool used by backpackers to remove common pathogens from water, rendering it safe to drink without the need to boil the water or use a chemical sterilizer. The latter imparted an unpleasant taste to the water, and although Peter could drink it, he'd learned that Diesel would refuse.

With both canteens full, he retraced his route back to the top of the rim. Diesel watched him climb the last ten yards, his tail wagging. Peter reached down and rubbed the pit bull's blocky head.

"What do you say we have a bite to eat?"

Since the water bowl was almost empty, Peter discarded the remaining ounce of water and placed dry kibble, plus some diced salami, in the bowl. The salami, although salty, had a high fat content and would contribute to the calories the dog would require. Diesel attacked the food like he hadn't eaten in a week, earning a broad smile from Peter.

For his part, Peter decided a granola bar and a few pieces of dried apricot would suffice. He took his time eating, and washed the dried grain down with more water.

With the meal completed, Peter assessed supplies, making certain the ammunition and medical kit were within easy reach in outer pockets of the daypack, or cargo pockets of his trousers. He planned to be back at the lean-to by nightfall, so he loaded the daypack with only enough supplies for one day. Although it was still chilly, he knew the temperature would rise quickly as the sun moved higher in the morning sky, so he shed the winter coat and stuffed it back into the duffle bag. The fleece vest he was still wearing would be fine for the next couple hours, maybe even all day if he wasn't very active.

Leaving the duffle bag at the lean-to, Peter grabbed the daypack and moved to the edge of the escarpment. He found the same spot within the outcropping of man-sized boulders from which he previously glassed the meadows below. This would have been a good sniper's hide, with a commanding view of the open terrain below. Without his rifle, it could only serve as an observation post.

Gripping his binoculars, he scrutinized the grassy openings again. A flash of movement caught his attention, but it was only a solitary doe browsing beyond some bush willows at the edge of the creek.

All he could do now was to review and refine his plan. It had been twenty-four hours since Cho had seemingly taken the bait—enough time to organize and equip a team. He figured they were already en route, probably having boarded a helicopter at sunrise.

His entire plan was thin. Very thin. Observe where the North Koreans land, draw them to the laptop, and then pick them off one by one.

He knew the enemy would have the advantage in numbers and weaponry. In all likelihood, training too, although Peter had been in enough gunfights to know what he would likely face.

The first warning of Cho's imminent arrival would be the sound of helicopter blades slicing through the still air.

He didn't have to wait long.

⊕

It was midmorning, and from his vantage, Peter watched as

squirrels and rock marmots scurried about, in search of food. Diesel paid no attention to the little critters, preferring instead to sit next to Peter, swiveling his head from side to side, taking in the vista.

Suddenly, Diesel turned toward the northwest. His eyes were sharp and his ears angled forward, his head tilted up toward the horizon. His body was motionless, save for the slight movement of his chest with each breath.

"What is it, boy?" Peter cupped a hand behind his ear.

Nothing.

He waited, and five seconds later heard the faint *whump, whump* of rotors. Over the next half-minute, it grew louder, and then he spotted the aircraft while it was still a bright spot against the cerulean sky.

He pulled in tight against the boulders, hoping his gray vest and camouflage trousers would blend in well enough with the surrounding stone. Through his binoculars, the helicopter took shape—a large aircraft with two rotors, one forward and one aft. Peter had seen photographs of similar helicopters delivering troops into the mountains of Afghanistan. It was a Boeing CH-47 Chinook heavy-lift. The fuselage was painted white, with yellow and orange stripes on the side running the length of the airframe, so Peter knew it wasn't military.

It continued flying eastward, and for a moment Peter thought it would continue on. Then it banked to the south and circled back toward his location. As he watched, the aircraft closed the distance until the image occupied the entire field of view in his binoculars. Then it slowed to a stationary hover only a couple dozen feet above a clearing.

While he continued to watch, two ropes were tossed out the open door at the rear of the helicopter. Five figures, each wearing a pack and carrying a weapon from a sling, slid down the ropes. With its cargo of combatants disgorged and safely on the ground, the helicopter accelerated forward and soon disappeared over the northern horizon.

The group of five assembled in a circle. They were all wearing identical dress—military-style camouflage fatigues, black tactical vests, and green knitted caps. Peter identified Cho as the one giving orders. They spread out and moved north toward the coordinates he'd previously supplied.

"Diesel, we have to go."

In a crouch, Peter moved away from the rim, back to the lean-to. There, he locked eyes with Diesel.

"Go! Hide. Follow me."

The pit bull melted into the forest as Peter took off north. From his scouting the day before, he knew the ridgeline he was on paralleled the creek below for several hundred yards. A thousand yards to the east was the Wyoming border. As long as he stayed in the meadows bordering the creek, or on the ridges rising up on either side of the creek, he was still within the zone of death.

After covering about two hundred yards, dodging around deadfalls, he checked his handheld GPS. The meeting coordinates were just east of his location. He inched to a cluster of fallen tree trunks until he had a good view into the drainage below. As he'd hoped, Cho and her team were still moving, not yet having reached the meeting point.

Through his binoculars, he counted Cho and three others. *Where's the fourth one?* He continued glassing for a full minute, but still couldn't find the missing fighter.

Fearing Cho had sent a man up onto the ridge that Peter was on, he decided he needed to take control.

Peering over the top of a large horizontal log, he called out, "Cho!"

A second later, Cho raised her hand and the team halted. Peter's voiced echoed off the opposite wall, and he saw the enemy heads turn back and forth, uncertain from where the call had originated.

He yelled again and stood, raising an arm and waving. He held the binoculars to his eyes with his other hand. Cho pointed toward Peter, and her team all raised their weapons in response.

"I thought we agreed to meet," Cho yelled back.

"Isn't that what we're doing?" Peter replied.

"Do you have the laptop?"

"I do."

"Show me. I don't believe you."

Peter dropped his daypack and removed the laptop, which he then held up for Cho to see.

"Bring it to me," she called.

"Where's the other man?" Peter lowered the laptop back into the daypack.

His nerves were fraying, and he began turning his head to search his surroundings.

"It's just the four of us," she said. "There isn't another man."

"You're lying, Cho. I watched your team fast-rope out of the helicopter. I know there are five."

"You can't count, Mr. Savage. Now bring me the laptop."

"No deal until I see all your men in the open, standing by your side."

The three fighters standing near Cho all had their weapons pointed at Peter. He couldn't tell what they were exactly. They clearly weren't pistols, but were they brandishing rifles, or submachine guns? At this distance, submachine guns didn't represent much of a threat, but rifles did.

Peter's attention was drawn to his rear by the sound of nylon fabric rubbing against a hard surface. He spun and then dove to the side, expecting a bullet to slam into his body. But it never happened. The next sound he heard was a guttural growl followed by a scream of pain. Then a gunshot, but the scream became more intense. A cry of terror, as much as pain.

Peter drew the sawed-off shotgun from his holster and advanced toward the commotion. Pinned to the ground was the missing North Korean fighter. Diesel had his gun hand pulled to the side, teeth locked onto the man's wrist. The gun, a QCW-05 Chinese-made submachine gun, was still gripped in his hand.

From ten yards away, Peter ordered Diesel to stop the attack, and the canine trotted to the side of his master.

"Who are you?" Peter said.

The man rolled to his side and then slowly rose to one knee. He was still holding his weapon with the barrel angled toward the ground, blood streaming over his hand.

"It's over," Peter said. "Drop your gun."

"Keep your dog away," the gunman said.

"The dog is under my control. Drop your gun. Now."

Diesel emitted a throaty growl, as if to backup Peter's command.

The gunman relented and lowered the barrel even more. Peter felt his shoulders relax as the tension subsided a notch. Then the submachine gun was jerked up and fired. Bullets dug into the gravel between Peter's feet and Diesel, but neither was hit.

Peter pulled the shotgun trigger. *Boom!* The short firearm bucked high but remained firmly in Peter's grasp. He pulled the barrel down and had it aimed at the North Korean for a follow-up shot. But it wasn't needed.

The gunman was sprawled on his back, arms splayed out to the side. The large-caliber lead ball had struck high in his chest, near the base of his neck.

Peter approached with caution. With his gun still aimed at the prone figure, he felt the gunman's neck for a pulse. Nothing.

Peter returned to the vantage point where he'd left his daypack. Through his binoculars, he saw Cho and the other three hadn't moved. They were still looking up at his position, with guns raised.

"Cho," Peter called, barely looking over the edge of a large deadfall.

He had just finished reloading the sawed-off shotgun when she replied.

"I see you are still alive."

"Very much so. And I found the missing man."

"Is he still alive?"

Peter's mind recalled the instant he'd pulled the trigger—the recoil pushing the gun upward, the reaction of the gunman to being hit, how his eyes widened and his jaw dropped a fraction of a second before the life left his body.

Cho had no concern for the lives of her team. They were merely tools to be used for her advantage.

"What do you think?" Peter yelled.

"I just want the computer. Bring it to me, and you may leave."

"You're lying, Cho. We all know it."

Peter was studying her face through the magnification of the binoculars. She appeared to be smiling.

"What choice do you have?" she said. "If you do not deliver the laptop, my men will hunt you down and kill you."

She was right, and Peter knew it. He could either face Cho and her team now, or they would disperse. And if that happened, he would lose the only advantage he had.

"All right, I'm coming down with the computer. Make sure your men don't shoot, lest they put a bullet through the hard drive."

Peter faced Diesel and rubbed his ears and the loose folds on his neck. He leaned forward and touched his forehead to the dog's moist, cold nose. Then he stood and gave the command again.

"Go! Hide. Follow me."

Diesel hesitated, and Peter repeated the command, this time with his arm outstretched, pointing away from the slope down to the creek.

Diesel walked away, then looked back over his shoulder before trotting off.

Peter watched his companion slip into the tangle of deadfalls and stunted evergreens, wondering if they would see each other again.

He hoisted the daypack onto his chest. Then, with the Benelli still slung across his shoulder and hanging before his hips in the low-ready position, he descended the ridge.

CHAPTER 42

PETER TREKKED DOWN the slope, mindful of his foot placement in the loose talus. There were few fallen trees on the steep slope, but more at the base and extending to the perimeter of the grassy clearing where the North Koreans were assembled. To their rear, the creek meandered across the gently sloped ground.

After he picked a path through the tangle of logs, Cho called out, "That's far enough."

Peter stopped. At this close distance, he could clearly see the submachine guns carried by Cho's fighters.

"Drop the gun," she said.

Peter shook his head. "Not gonna happen. If I give up my guns, you'll just shoot me anyway. If I'm gonna die, I'll go down fighting."

"Then I will order my men to shoot you dead where you stand."

Peter tapped the daypack covering his chest.

"The computer is here. If you open fire, the bullets will destroy the hard drive. You'll lose everything you've promised to deliver to your Supreme Leader. The data will be lost, and you will have killed me. I don't think the little man will be too happy about that. Do you?"

Cho contemplated Peter's words for a full minute. It seemed an excruciatingly long pause to him.

This was perhaps the riskiest part of his plan—the moment when Cho would either call his hand, or concede and allow Peter to advance.

His heart was pounding, and he drew in several deep breaths to calm his nerves.

Finally, Cho said, "Very well. You may come forward. But I warn you—if you make any attempt to use those guns, you'll be dead before your head hits the ground. Am I clear?"

"Pretty hard to miss the meaning of your threat."

"Good."

Peter moved forward, paralleling a partly rotted log. It had broken off in a windstorm long ago. When he reached the stump, he stopped and shed his daypack, but still held it before his torso. Cho and her team were only five paces away.

He reached inside and removed the laptop, then dropped the pack.

"I'm going to power it up now," he told Cho. "To show you I honored my part of the bargain."

"No tricks, Mr. Savage."

The computer screen lit up with the three-dimensional model of the PEAP carbine. Peter opened a second window that listed all the files supporting the model, plus additional documentation. He turned the screen so Cho could see it.

She squinted, trying to read the file names, but the distance was too great. Still, she recognized the realistic rendering of the weapon.

Victory was almost within her grasp. Her mind drifted to the honors that the Supreme Leader would bestow upon her. She would be awarded a small fortune, and given her choice of assignments. Maybe even the entire US intelligence operation would be placed under her command. Her lips drew back in a thin smile.

She nodded to one of her associates, and he strode forward to retrieve the prize.

He stopped in front of Peter. "Give it to me."

He still had his submachine gun pointed at Peter's belly, and held out his other hand.

Peter looked down at the screen. The cursor was still positioned on the tool bar, over the icon Gary had installed. Peter tapped the touchscreen, then handed the device to the gunman, who smiled as if to express his gratitude, but it was a cruel grin.

"Before you thank me," Peter said, "I think you should look at the display."

With eyebrows pinched together, the gunman averted his gaze to the monitor. The three-dimensional model of the PEAP had vanished. In its place, a list of files showed. An icon that read, Deleting, flashed next to the top file on the list. The file names vanished one after the other.

The gunman released his hold on the submachine gun, allowing it to hang from its sling. He tapped furiously at the keyboard, trying in vain to stop the file deletion.

"What did you do?" he screamed, still working to stop the electronic destruction.

When he looked up, Peter's sawed-off shotgun was pressed against his gut.

"A small security program a friend installed for me. I activated it just before I handed the computer over to you. You can't stop it. It has already disabled the operating system, and now it is systematically wiping every file on the hard drive."

"What's going on?" Cho said.

With her fighter immediately in front of Peter, she couldn't see what was unfolding.

"He double-crossed us!" the gunman screamed, then dropped the laptop and moved his hand back to his weapon, but he never made it.

Peter pulled the trigger. *Boom!* The North Korean rocketed backward and slammed to the ground.

Cho and the other two fighters fired from the hip, but Peter was already in motion, diving behind the tree stump. Bullets chewed into the dead wood but failed to pass through the old-growth stump.

Peter shoved the short-barreled weapon back into his holster and unlimbered the Benelli. Holding the shotgun in one hand, he crawled forward three body lengths, using the horizontal tree trunk for cover. Then he rolled onto his back and popped up with the shotgun already shouldered. As he'd hoped, the North Koreans were still focused on the stump.

Peter snapped off two shots. One missed, but the second landed a load of 00 buckshot into the thigh of the man closest to Cho. She sprinted to the side, aiming for concealment behind a dense copse of small evergreens. The other gunman adjusted his aim.

Bullets ripped into the half-rotted log. Many passed through the pithy wood, but missed Peter. He squeezed the trigger and sent a packet of shot into his enemy's chest.

The North Korean's tactical vest stopped many of the pellets, but not all. The impact knocked him back, and his heel caught on a clump a grass. Wounded and off balance, he fell onto his back. The gunman tried to reacquire Peter in his sights, but that ended with a second shot that entered his pelvis and gut before shredding his aorta.

Peter swept the Benelli back and forth, searching for Cho. She was gone. He took advantage of the lull to reload, pulling shells from the bandolier beneath his vest. Next, he scurried back and grabbed his daypack. He took a moment to fire two rounds of buckshot through the laptop, ensuring its demise. Then he ran to the slope, keeping close to the deadfalls.

To his surprise, there were no gunshots. He scrambled up the scree. When he reached the top, he was breathing hard, and he found cover at the edge of the tree line.

After resting for a minute, he crawled closer to the rim so he could scan the terrain below, searching for Cho. If she'd seen him scramble up the ridge, certainly she'd follow him.

The lenses of the binoculars were covered with dust from his short crawl. He wiped them and then glassed for movement along the creek and the base of the ridgeline. But with the optics shaking in rhythm with his deep breaths, it was difficult to make out much detail.

After several minutes, he thought he saw it. Only brief, but some brush willows along the edge of the creek moved back and forth. No other vegetation was moving, so it had to be Cho or an animal. He doubted the latter, given the gunfire that had echoed over the meadow.

As he continued to watch, his breathing returned to normal and he was able to hold the binoculars steady again. He focused on the willows, and was rewarded with the image of Cho slinking from the brush to a pocket of trees. Even in the shadows, he was able to follow her progress toward the slope. She was at the end of the ridgeline and she followed the contours of the terrain to the west and out of his view.

Safe for the moment, Peter took a long drink of water. Then he worked to clear his thoughts and come up with a new plan. The time-proven cliché that no plan ever survives first contact with the enemy came to mind. *Ain't that the truth.*

He recalled the lay of the land from his previous scouting, and assumed that Cho had skirted around the end of the ridge to avoid being seen. And she'd almost succeeded. Now, he figured she would stay in the relative cover of the forest and fallen trees atop the escarpment, and hunt Peter. It's the tactic he would follow if their roles were reversed.

To counter, he had to move away from the rim, where his figure would show easily against the bright sky.

With the daypack on his back now, he entered the timber.

Where is Diesel?

CHAPTER 43

SILENTLY, PETER ENTERED THE FOREST. Although the jumble of fallen trees provided decent cover, it also made progress slow, as he had to constantly maneuver over, under, and around the dead fall.

After he covered a couple hundred yards, the skyline beyond the rim was no longer visible. He squatted onto his haunches where two tree trunks intersected, one laying atop the other at close to a ninety-degree angle.

"Diesel," he whispered.

Peter dared not make much noise, for fear of drawing Cho's attention.

He waited a half-minute, listening carefully and searching the forest for a patch of red fur.

Nothing.

Disheartened, he called again, "Diesel."

As he waited, he began to feel vulnerable. Not only had he called out, but he was also stationary. And while hunkered down in the jumble of dead trees, his vision into the surrounding timber was severely limited. For all he knew, Cho could be approaching from behind, and he wouldn't know until she was on top of his location.

He was just about to give up, when his peripheral vision picked up movement to his right. Resisting the urge to swing his head in that direction—a swift movement that could draw his adversary's attention—he turned his eyes in their sockets as far as he could. A moment later, the pit bull emerged through a tight thicket of stunted fir and pine trees.

Diesel trotted up to Peter, his tail wagging and tongue hanging low as he panted. Peter rubbed his companion's head and neck, then slowly poured water from his canteen into a cupped hand. The canine lapped it up until the canteen was empty.

"Good boy," Peter mumbled, barely audible, but Diesel heard clearly and looked up into Peter's eyes.

Rising slowly to his feet, Peter scanned his surroundings. After a couple minutes, not seeing Cho or any movement, he continued deeper into the trees, staying on a path away from the rim. The terrain undulated gradually, and Peter found a low rise—a hillock only ten-feet high. The ground in front and to the sides of the rise were free of trees, instead being a mix of bunch grass interspersed with gravel and stones.

He climbed to the top and into a dense knot of fir trees only a dozen feet tall. The trees were disrupted by a boulder about two-feet high and just as wide, and a scattering of smaller stones surrounding it. He decided to make this his hide. The combination of rock and evergreens would break up his form, and provided he was still, he reasoned it would be hard for Cho to see him before he saw her.

He settled in, stretching out prone and finding a comfortable position. Diesel did the same, laying on the duff covering the ground. It was a thick mat of dried needles, and being somewhat spongy, it gave a little under Peter's weight.

While he visually searched the opening in front of his position, he relied on Diesel to be his ears. For now, the pit bull was resting, his eyelids half-closed. A good sign.

The minutes passed slowly, and Peter was beginning to think he'd misjudged Cho. *What if she went a different direction?* The thought caused his pulse to quicken.

Then an idea came to mind.

With slow movements, he slipped the backpack off and opened a side pocket while stifling the sound of the zipper. Inside the pocket were the homemade M80 firecrackers, along with a disposable lighter. He held two in one hand, pinching the fuse on one so it was slightly shorter than the other.

The idea was to lure her toward him by lighting the fuses and throwing the two pyrotechnic devices forward. He was gambling that the report from their detonation would sound like gunfire and draw Cho in to investigate. But what if she was already nearby, and saw his rapid arm movement? She could pinpoint his location and circle around, coming in from behind.

He studied Diesel again. The dog was relaxed, and showed curiosity in what Peter was doing, rather than being alert to something out of the ordinary. *Trust the dog.*

Peter lit the fuses and tossed the two explosives out into the clearing. As expected, they exploded about a half-second apart. A good imitation of two rapid shots from his Benelli shotgun.

Diesel, startled by the reports, faced forward, his muscles tense.

Peter didn't bother putting the daypack on again. The movement would have been an unnecessary risk. Instead, he tucked it under the fore end of the Benelli, elevating the gun off the ground and achieving a steady shooting position.

The waiting continued. Something Peter was accustomed to from his years of hunting, when he'd often wait motionless for hours while glassing for game. It was close to the same thing, but not exactly. Bull elk didn't shoot back.

The shadows inexorably moved eastward, and Peter

considered repeating the tactic. He had two more of the large firecrackers left, and weighed the option. Using them here, if Cho was already out of the area, would be without effect. And he didn't have anymore.

Just as he decided to save them, his vision caught a shadow moving between the upright trees directly to his front and close to a hundred yards away.

It was Cho.

Diesel's keen vision also caught the motion. He emitted a guttural growl, barely loud enough for Peter to hear it.

He raised the binoculars. The image of Cho was clear. She was cautiously tracking toward the clearing. Every few paces, she'd stop and survey the surrounding area. Since she was in the deep shadows, and wearing camouflage clothing and a black tactical vest, it was difficult to see her when she was motionless.

As he watched, Cho looked directly at Peter. His instinctive response was to slink farther back from the boulder, melt into the dense tree cover. But he dared not move.

Abruptly, she turned away, continuing a methodical search for his whereabouts.

After five minutes, she advanced several more paces, carefully placing each footstep to avoid the snap of twigs. Again, she stopped and slowly scanned the opening in front of the hillock.

Peter was grateful that she was not using binoculars. He recalled that he hadn't seen her carrying field glasses after they'd fast-roped from the Chinook helicopter. Maybe it was an oversight on her part. Whatever the reason, it definitely gave Peter an advantage, and the realization buoyed his mood.

That's right. Keep coming forward.

She had closed the separation by a couple dozen yards, and Peter mentally urged her on. Her present heading would soon deliver her to the edge of the grassy opening, and a clear shot for Peter.

She turned and began paralleling the clearing. *Damn it.*

Peter understood why. He would have done the same thing. She'd wisely chosen to circumnavigate the open area while searching for Peter. Within the trees, her silhouette was masked by the evergreens and shadows.

Peter waited until she stopped. He then studied the terrain she was moving toward. The land sloped away into a ditch. If she didn't alter her course, she'd drop down into the depression.

That gave him an idea.

Slowly and silently, he crawled backward, away from the boulder and out of her sight. In a crouch, and with Diesel by his side, he descended the back side of the hillock and swept in a great arc toward the ditch. He had to get there before Cho did, but he also had to arrive undetected.

He was well-practiced in stalking, but his motion, and that of Diesel's, was a risk.

Hunched over to minimize his size, Peter advanced through the trees. Moving with grace, and in absolute silence, he stopped when he saw the terrain fall off in the distance. It was the draw.

He dropped to his knees next to a stump, and searched for Cho. He moved the optics slowly, taking time to scan every detail, looking for anything that was out of the ordinary—an unnatural bulge at the side of a tree, a color that didn't fit with the surrounding forest. A skill he'd learned years ago.

Nothing.

He kept searching, but finally concluded she wasn't there.

He knew it was possible she'd changed direction, but he thought that unlikely. Shortly, he would know if his gamble was going to pay off.

CHAPTER 44

PETER FELT HIS HEART RACING, and he rhythmically drew in deep breaths to steady his nerves. He placed his arms against the stump in order to hold the binoculars steady.

Still nothing.

Could he have miscalculated?

A crow cawed and then flew from its perch on an evergreen branch. Peter adjusted the field glasses.

Bingo! It was Cho, still methodically advancing, with her submachine gun gripped in both hands. Had she frozen upon startling the crow, Peter might have missed her. Her movement had triggered his attention.

She slowed as she neared the edge of the draw. Only fifty yards away, she was within range of the Benelli twelve-gauge. But she could also retreat back into the timber if Peter missed. Better to allow her to enter the drainage.

Perspiration dappled his forehead as she drew ever-nearer. Through the magnification of his optics, her facial features came clearly into view. She was looking across the draw, but had so far failed to spot Peter.

Finally, his patience was rewarded as she took a step down the bank, toward the dry creek bed. In the open now, Cho picked up her pace. As she reached the bottom, Peter lost sight of her, which meant she couldn't see him either.

He let go of the binoculars and shouldered the Benelli. Shifted his footing so he could rise to his feet quickly, and then waited for Cho to climb the near side of the draw. He counted off the seconds in his mind, imagining the North Korean agent closing the distance, step by step.

As if on queue, the black knitted cap covering her head appeared first, soon followed by the rest of her body.

She halted. Her hands gripped the submachine gun tighter, although it was still at her hip, hanging from the sling.

"Don't do it, Cho." Peter rose into full view. "Drop the gun."

Cho shook her head. "It is you who must drop your weapon, or I'll kill you where you stand. I should have ordered my team to shoot you in the meadow. That was a mistake. But one that can still be corrected."

"You need me alive."

"What one needs is subject to change with time. You've outlived your usefulness."

"Then I should just kill you now."

"You're not a murderer." Cho drew her lips back in a smug smile. "That's why you hesitated to pull the trigger before, and why you hesitate now."

"Don't press your luck. I've killed before. And after what you did, I won't lose a wink of sleep if I just drop you here and now."

"Oh, that's right. I had forgotten that the woman I shot is someone you have feelings for. A pity I didn't aim higher and kill her."

Peter's thoughts turned to Kate, and he wondered how she was doing. Did she believe Peter had abandoned her?

Cho said, "Well, if it makes you feel better, she was simply someone with the misfortune of being in the wrong place at the wrong time. Nothing personal."

Peter's index finger brushed against the trigger. He felt the tissue in his fingertip smush as he applied pressure. His vision narrowed, and then filled with an image of Kate lying in the hospital bed. And he recalled her words from their visit to Washington, DC: *"There's no denying that the weapons you make are designed for one purpose...to kill."*

She'd spoken the truth, and it still was painful. He knew that it was his actions, his work to design and build the pulsed-energy weapon, that had caused Kate's injuries. Injuries that would forever change her life.

His anger built into a simmering rage, ready to boil over. *What would Kate say?* It was that singular thought that checked his actions.

"Just give me a reason, Cho." His words were clipped as he fought to rein in his temper. "You'll be doing me a favor."

The gapping maw of the shotgun only seven yards away was intimidating, and Cho seemed caught in indecision. Her weapon was still hanging at her hip.

Peter said, "I've got a load of buckshot in the chamber, aimed right at your chest. You can't win."

She glared back, her eyebrows pinched tight. In her eyes, Peter saw only loathing.

"Raise your hands," he said.

Diesel was standing by his side, teeth bared and head lowered. His entire body was coiled and ready to strike.

Cho's gazed flitted from Peter to the dog, and back again to Peter.

"Easy, Diesel. Stay." Peter's voice was low, his tone firm.

Cho ran the calculus in her mind. She would be firing unaimed shots, and at best, could hope a couple would connect with Peter. Simultaneously, he'd fire, and with the shotgun already aimed, there was no way he could miss. Then there was the pit bull. She'd seen how the dog had savagely ripped her men to ribbons. Recalling those images sent a chill up her spine.

Slowly, her arms relaxed, and the muzzle of the submachine gun lowered.

She raised her hands. "This isn't over. You have no way to leave. No helicopter or truck. What do you plan to do? I'll have plenty of opportunity to kill you. And I won't hesitate."

"It's over," Peter said. "You lost. On your knees."

She lowered her body, still keeping her hands above her head. Peter walked up to her, the aim of the Benelli locked onto her torso. He slowly circled behind her, then pressed the barrel of the gun into her back.

"Now, on your face."

Cho followed the order, pinning the submachine gun under her body. With her arms outstretched, Peter placed a boot in the center of her back and added weight. When he heard a muffled grunt, he knew he had applied enough pressure that she wasn't going to try any moves. He held the Benelli with one hand, and with the other, pulled his Ka-Bar from its leather sheath. He slipped the razor-sharp blade between Cho's back and the gun sling. With a brisk tug, the blade severed the sling. Then he unsnapped the restraining strap on her leg holster and removed the QSW-06 pistol, which he placed inside his waistband.

Peter removed his foot from her back and took two steps away.

"Now, with your hands above your head, roll to the side. I'm going to take that weapon. Diesel is going to watch. And if he sees anything he doesn't like, if he even senses you plan to attack, he'll be all over you in a heartbeat. And I won't call him off. Not until the last ounce of blood has drained from your shredded body."

Cho rolled her body until she was free of the weapon. Lying on her back, hands stretched above her head, her face was only inches away from the red pit bull's glistening, ivory fangs. Her eyes were wide, and the fire was gone.

Peter ejected the magazine from the submachine gun, then cleared the round from the chamber. He tossed the magazine far into the timber. It bounced off a fallen log and vanished from view. He placed the gun next to the stump and then used the side of his boot to drag sufficient soil to bury the weapon.

"Get on your feet. And keep your hands up."

With her hands laced and resting on top of her head, Cho marched forward, with Peter three steps behind, and with the shotgun aimed at her back.

CHAPTER 45

THE WALKING WAS EASY, and Peter marched Cho at a slow but steady pace. They went to his lean-to first, where he gathered his duffle bag, and then down the ridge to the meadow where he'd come face-to-face with the North Korean team. Peter avoided the bodies, instead selecting a location thirty yards away. He ordered Cho to lay face down.

Using a length of paracord removed from his duffle bag, Peter hog-tied her. Satisfied that she was unable to escape or present a threat, he allowed the Benelli to hang from its sling. Next, using the satellite phone, he dialed the one number he knew would be answered anytime, night or day.

"Yes," the masculine voice said.

The caller ID provided no clue as to whom he was speaking.

"Jim. Its Peter."

"You're not calling on your cell phone."

"I'm using a sat phone. I'm in the—"

"I know where you are. We can't talk. I'm going to disconnect and call you back on a secure line."

Commander Nicolaou retrieved a burner phone from his desk drawer. Although the NSA could still capture the conversation, the phone number was anonymous. So his involvement in the conversation could never be proven.

A few minutes later, Peter answered the call.

"We know your location," Jim said. "At least, generally. We pieced it together from the few clues you left."

"Really? You were able to do that?"

"You have good friends. Loyal friends. And they care about you."

"But I didn't say—"

"You said enough. You want to be judicious with your words."

"I understand," Peter said.

He decided to let Jim speak, see where the conversation was going. Obviously, more people knew about his plan than he'd intended.

"Are you injured?" Jim said.

"No. I'm okay."

"Do you understand that I cannot interfere in domestic issues?"

"I do. This is not domestic. Should I assume you know my motive?"

"You should."

"Then you won't be surprised. I have the North Korean agent. The team leader."

Jim's jaw gaped, but he soon recovered his composure.

"In what condition?"

"Uninjured. She's trussed up like a Thanksgiving turkey."

Jim grabbed a pen and jotted notes onto a notepad.

"How many others?" he said.

"None."

For the second time, Jim paused.

"She came after you solo?"

"No."

"What do you need?"

"Well, I could use a lift. Do you think you can borrow a helicopter if I turn the agent over to you? Otherwise, I'll have to march her cross country, north to West Yellowstone. It'll take a couple days."

Jim cracked a big grin. Somehow, his friend never ceased to amaze him.

"I think I can manage that," he replied.

"Good. I wasn't looking forward to the hike." He provided his coordinates to Jim.

"Just sit tight. It might take a few hours. Can we land a helicopter at these coordinates?"

"It's a meadow."

"Roger that." Jim ended the call.

⊕

Jim tossed the burner phone on his desk. Later, he'd remove and destroy the SIM card, then fry the phone's sensitive circuits in a microwave—standard precautions since he didn't yet know how this would play out.

Using his desk phone, he dialed Colonel Pierson. They preferred to use the landline as much as possible since a hardwire tap would be required for anyone to eavesdrop, unlike cellular communications, whose signal could be plucked from the ether by any capable organization.

"Pierson," the colonel said, in a gruff voice.

The hour was still early enough that Jim knew he'd be at his office at the Defense Intelligence Agency in Washington, DC.

Jim got right to the point. "Sir, we have solid intel concerning the whereabouts of a North Korean agent. She's in the continental US, and is a suspect in multiple murders and felony assault."

Pierson said, "And you're telling me this, why? You know as well as I do that this falls under the jurisdiction of the FBI."

"Because the agent has also made concerted efforts to steal the PEAP carbine."

The line was silent for a moment, before Pierson's deep voice picked up again.

"Does this have anything to do with the attempted assassination at the White House?"

Jim said, "I believe it does, sir. The intelligence we have comes from persons directly involved. According to our sources, the leader—a woman named Cho—operates a ring of North Korean agents."

"What do you know about this Cho person?"

"She was captured earlier today, in the wilderness of Eastern Idaho. Presently, she is being held by Peter Savage."

"That friend of yours has a habit of getting into trouble. You can explain later how all this happened. Nevertheless, nothing you've shared even remotely suggests the involvement of SGIT or the DIA. If you haven't already done so, pass along your intelligence to the FBI."

"Sir, the FBI doesn't have the capability to deploy rapidly. We can deploy immediately and take Cho into custody today, within hours. She is being held in a remote location by one man, a civilian. There is no backup. If we don't act, there's a good chance we'll lose her."

Pierson said, "Whether or not that happens, this is an issue for domestic law enforcement. Our charter is not to do the work of the FBI."

"Respectfully, Colonel, we can't allow a North Korean sleeper cell to operate within our borders. We have to take Cho into custody. She's potentially an intelligence goldmine. There could be multiple cells operating incognito. Who knows the extent to which agents of North Korea have infiltrated government and big business. Even if the FBI is able to capture Cho, she would immediately fall into the civilian judicial system. She'll lawyer up, and we'll be completely locked out."

Pierson considered the appeal. He'd recruited Jim from the SEALs to direct SGIT—at the time, a newly formed division of the DIA. The goal of SGIT was to combine top intelligence analysts with a surgical strike team—the best of both brains and brawn. This combination of talents, plus the small size of the organization, allowed for rapid decision-making, and even faster execution.

He knew Commander Nicolaou was right. This was exactly the type of mission that the organization was created for.

Pierson said, "Okay, Commander. I'm granting authorization. Just keep this low profile, understood? I don't want this to be a PR blackeye for SGIT or the Department of Defense. I'll expect your report first thing tomorrow morning."

As was his practice, the colonel didn't wait for an answer before ending the call.

Jim strode down the hall to Lieutenant Lacey's office for a short briefing, with Jim doing most of the talking.

"Call up to Mountain Home. Inform the base commander that I need a Pave Hawk and crew, fully fueled and ready to go within ninety minutes. You have Colonel Pierson's authority on this. They'll be transporting myself and three team members to these coordinates." He shared the slip of paper on which he'd written the longitude and latitude.

Located southeast of Boise, the Air Force base was roughly 225 miles from the Wyoming border, making the round trip an easy hop for the Pave Hawk helicopter.

"This location looks like it's in the Zone of Death," Lacey replied.

Jim nodded.

"You're going after Mr. Savage," she said.

"That's right. And the North Korean ringleader. We'll take the jet up to Mountain Home, then transfer to the Pave Hawk."

Jim left Lacey to make the arrangements. Next, he scrambled the on-call pilot and copilot of the C37A transport—the Air Force designation for a Gulfstream V business jet. The jet was stationed at SGIT Headquarters, located at the McClellan business park in the Sacramento metro area. The former SAC air base boasted a 10,600-foot runway, allowing easy air travel. Jim also ordered Ghost, Bull, and Homer—three of his best operators—to meet him at the armory. In short order, they'd signed out their M27 rifles, sidearms, a full load-out of ammunition, two M67 hand grenades each, plus tactical vests and helmets.

The interior of the cabin was decked out in plush leather-upholstered chairs, with ample leg room, that resembled first-class seating on commercial airlines. The comfort was in stark contrast to conventional military transports. Under other circumstances, the comfortable surroundings might have given rise to a jovial atmosphere. But not now. This was a mission, and the SGIT team was focused on their job.

Jim said, "Your objective is to take a North Korean agent named Cho, into custody. As of one hour ago, she was being held prisoner by our friend Peter Savage."

The entire SGIT team knew Peter from previous missions in which he had become entangled.

Jim continued. "They are at a location in the Idaho wilderness that also falls within Yellowstone National Park. The State of Idaho has no legal jurisdiction. That falls to the National Park Service and the judicial district of Wyoming. We will transfer to a Pave Hawk at Mountain Home Air Force Base. The Pave Hawk will ferry us to the coordinates, then land. We will take custody of the prisoner, and then return, with Mr. Savage, to Mountain Home. This is an in-and-out mission. A snatch-and-grab, except I don't anticipate any resistance."

Bull, the largest and strongest man on the SGIT team, said,

"What about the North Korean agent?"

"She will return under our custody, to The Office, where she will be held until Colonel Pierson gives us other orders. I suspect she will be transferred to a secure military location for interrogation, but that decision is above my pay grade."

Homer said, "Sir, if we don't expect resistance, why are we going in heavily armed?"

A veteran of SGIT, Homer had been recruited from the Army's Delta Force. Like all of his teammates, he was clean-shaven. His dark-brown hair—not quite black, but close—set off his piercing cobalt-blue eyes.

"Contingency," Jim replied. "In case the Supreme Leader wants to prevent Cho from falling into our hands."

Homer nodded. "Rules of engagement?"

"I was about to get to that," Jim said. "We are on questionable legal ground, and the colonel doesn't want an incident that some panty-waist politician in Washington can use to embarrass the organization. Consequently, use of force is only authorized in case of self-defense. So if you shoot, you'd better be damned certain it was justified, because your actions will be dissected under a microscope, and every armchair warrior in the country will be second-guessing your decisions. Am I clear?"

Bull, Ghost, and Homer replied in unison: "Yes, sir!"

CHAPTER 46

AS THE PAVE HAWK APPROACHED the landing coordinates, the air crew spotted smoke from a campfire Peter had lit. The helicopter banked and circled at an altitude of only two hundred feet. Peter stood and waved his arms. The side door was open, and Homer spotted him first.

"There he is." Homer pointed.

Although a stream meandered through the meadow, which was also dotted with small trees, the pilot had no difficulty identifying a suitable landing zone. As soon as the wheels touched ground, the SGIT team jumped out and dispersed. Each man held his rifle at the low-ready position.

With the special operators on the ground, the Pave Hawk lifted off and circled overhead, the gunner ready at the open door.

As a precaution, Jim ordered the team to separate and approach Peter's camp from different directions. He had no reason to believe that any members of Cho's team had set an ambush, but he wasn't going to risk misjudging her capabilities.

Jim set off in a straight line from a hundred yards away. At first, he couldn't see Cho, only Peter, who was standing and still waving his arms. Jim acknowledged with a wave. Only when he was close did Jim see the prone figure that he assumed was the North Korean agent.

Jim called out when he was still a dozen yards away, his voice carrying easily over the muted *whump, whump, whump* emanating from the Pave Hawk circling above.

"Is that Cho?"

Peter nodded. "Thank you for coming."

Diesel was standing alert, wary of the approaching figure. Peter looked down to his companion.

"It's okay, boy. He's our friend."

Jim closed the remaining distance in a few strides.

"It's not every day we're given the chance to bring in a foreign agent operating on American soil," he said.

Jim walked over to Cho, who was laying in the shade of a tree, and visually confirmed that she was securely bound.

He noticed she was gagged. "Her talking get on your nerves?"

"Yeah," Peter said. "After about ten minutes of constant threats, I stuffed a scrap of cloth into her mouth and tied it in place. She tried to bite my fingers."

Jim pointed to the smoldering fire. "Thanks for the smoke. Helped us spot you."

Ghost and Bull approached from opposite directions, and a minute later, Homer arrived.

"Clear?" Jim said.

All three reported no enemy sightings.

"There's three dead tangos back there." Homer pointed a thumb over his shoulder.

Jim looked at Peter. "That your doing?"

Peter nodded. "Also, my laptop is next to one of the bodies. They wanted the design of the PEAP carbine. All the files. It was on the hard drive, but it's wiped and riddled with buckshot. Nothing there now."

Jim said, "How did she find you?"

"Apparently, it started with a guy named Billy Reed. Somehow, he came into possession of the prototype."

"You mean the very same one that was stolen from your company?" Jim said.

"Yes. There was only one. Anyway, Billy told me he had made contact with Cho and offered to sell it. Somehow, that went south, and Cho murdered two of Billy's friends. So he offered to sell it back to me. We were in the process of completing the transaction at my home when Cho showed up with a bunch of her men."

"I'm aware of the police reports. Lieutenant Lacey was briefed by both the Bend PD and the FBI. But according to those reports, the PEAP carbine was never found, and they have you on record stating that Mr. Reed didn't have it either."

Peter raised his eyebrows, then cleared his throat. He scrambled to recall his exact words to Detective Colson, trying not to get tripped up in his lie.

"Billy claimed he had the PEAP carbine, but I never saw it. The North Koreans burst through my front door and started shooting. They had Kate as a hostage. Billy was shot and killed. When Kate tried to escape, she was also shot."

"I'm sorry," Jim replied. "Bull, Ghost, go with Homer and retrieve the laptop and the bodies. Take them to the LZ."

While his team was busy, Jim radioed in the Pave Hawk.

Peter turned his gaze skyward and watched as the large helicopter came in and landed, the rotor wash whipping nearby trees and bush willows. Again, his mind returned to Kate, and Peter wondered now if he would see her again, or if he would immediately be arrested. He knew he'd broken the law by destroying the prototype and deleting all records of its design and testing.

Jim's voice drew him back to the present.

"You know, I'm not sure what you were packing in that holster on your thigh." He pointed to Peter's leg and the now empty holster strapped in place. "And I'm not asking, either. But wearing that is likely to raise questions."

Before the helicopter had arrived, Peter buried the sawed-off shotgun. But he didn't think about the holster. Given its oversized shape, it obviously wasn't for a legal pistol.

"Yeah," he replied. "Good idea."

He removed the holster and tossed it on the fire. Within a few minutes, it was consumed.

"Time to go," Jim said.

While he kicked dirt and gravel on the embers, Peter walked over to Cho. With Diesel watching, he knelt next to her and cut the cord binding her hands. She drew her arms forward while Peter shifted his focus to severing the rope around her ankles.

In a flash of movement, Cho removed a small thrusting dagger from her belt buckle. She rammed it into Peter's leg, unable to reach his torso, burying the blade to the hilt. The blade sliced through muscle, the tip gouging the femur bone.

Peter screamed in agony. He lashed out, attempting to backhand Cho. But off-balance, his motion caused him to fall to his side. Cho held firm to the dagger, extending the laceration down his leg.

Diesel lunged at the woman, clamping his jaws onto her forearm, teeth penetrating to the bone. Then the violent shaking began, ripping flesh and tearing arteries. In one second, his muzzle was awash in red.

Jim extended his sidearm forward and squeezed the trigger, sending a .45 caliber bullet into Cho's shoulder.

Peter pulled away from Cho, then commanded Diesel to cease. Under Jim's watchful eye, the pit bull ended his attack and rejoined his master.

With her arm severely mauled, and a bullet wound in her shoulder, Cho wasn't likely to offer any further threat. Still, Jim refused to holster his weapon. He radioed Bull, the team corpsman.

"Bull! Bring the med kit. Peter's been stabbed. He's bleeding badly."

Bull grabbed the trauma kit from the Pave Hawk and dashed the hundred yards in record time. He was followed by Ghost and Homer.

Peter had removed the dagger and clamped his hands onto his leg. Even so, bright-red blood was oozing out.

While Jim guarded Cho, Bull went to work. He sliced open the pant leg and then applied blood clotting powder, followed by a sterile bandage. He wrapped a layer of gauze around the leg to hold the field dressing in place.

Bull had seen a great number of battle injuries, and had even patched up every one of his team members at least once. He knew this injury was serious, and would require surgery soon.

He hoisted Peter over his broad shoulders in a fireman's carry, and headed off for the Pave Hawk, Diesel trotting by his side.

Homer gathered up Peter's daypack, Benelli, and duffle bag, while Ghost treated Cho's wounds. She was still conscious despite the pain. The two SGIT soldiers flanked Cho as Jim pushed her forward, his pistol barrel never far from her back.

By the time they returned to the Pave Hawk, Bull already had Peter laying on his back with an IV drip in one arm. Diesel was sitting by Peter's side.

Ghost loaded Cho into the cabin and secured her, while Bull placed an IV with strong sedative in her arm. They still wanted her alive, and sedating her was the safest way to transport her back to Mountain Home.

"How are you?" Jim said to Peter.

"Never saw that coming," he replied. "Hurts like hell."

"I gave you a painkiller with the IV," Bull said. "You'll be feeling better soon."

Peter slept most of the way back to Mountain Home. But not Diesel. The ever-loyal pit bull remained alert, ever-wary of the people surrounding his master.

CHAPTER 47

SITTING IN A WHEELCHAIR next to Kate's bed, and dressed only in a hospital gown, Peter had his leg propped up on a stool. When he had told his nurse—a young man named Tylor—that he was going to the next floor to visit his fiancée, Tylor understandably protested. After all, the laceration in Peter's thigh, all the way down to the femur, had been sutured less than two days ago. It would take time to heel, and unnecessary strenuous movement could pull the wound open.

But Peter had made up his mind, and nothing short of physical restraint would stop him.

With a sigh, Tylor rounded up a wheelchair and escorted his patient to Kate's room.

Entering Kate's room, Peter's nose was overwhelmed with a mix of floral scents. Five large bouquets of flowers surrounded her bed. Peter hobbled to the closest arrangement and read the card: "To Kate Simpson. Wishing you a full recovery." It wasn't signed.

Peter checked the other bouquets as well. Only one card

was signed, indicating that it had been sent by the employees at EJ Enterprises.

Kate had a mystery admirer.

Now, sitting in the chair, Peter gazed upon Kate's face while she rested. He felt at peace being close to her. Still under the effects of his own pain medication, Peter drifted in and out of restless sleep, his eyelids closing for minutes at a time, only to snap open when his head fell to the side.

It was late morning when Kate moved a hand—the first sign that she was rousing from her sleep.

"Hello, beautiful," Peter said.

At first, Kate didn't say anything. She just gazed into Peter's eyes. When she did speak, her words were thick with emotion.

"I didn't think I would see you again." She began to cry.

"I'll never leave you. I'm sorry to say it, but you're stuck with me."

She smiled. "That suits me fine."

Peter leaned to his side and wiped the tears from her face. Then he brushed a stray lock from her forehead.

"When they told me you went away, I knew what that meant—that you'd gone off to fight those people..." she drew in a breath and exhaled, "...to fight those people who did this to me."

Peter nodded.

"I knew you would." She spoke with a steady voice, having regained her composure. "You know, you're an easy man to figure out."

"I am, huh?"

"Like reading a newspaper."

An IV was still inserted in her arm, restricting her movement. But with her other hand, she reached up to rub her fingers against Peter's cheek. Her soft, warm touch felt good to him.

"You're a good man. Loyal. Honest. Principled."

"I'm not who you think I am. I've done things. Bad things."

"I know. I remember a saying from an English nobleman. Something that was taught in my history class. It goes something like this: 'The only thing necessary for the triumph of evil is for good men to do nothing.'"

"Edmund Burke."

"My professor shared this quote and pointed out that it's just as true now as it was two hundred fifty years ago. Anyway, you're a good man, Peter Savage. And sometimes, good men must do bad things to stop evil deeds."

"The real world is not so black and white," he said.

"I know that. But the message is still true."

Peter found comfort in her words, although he wasn't ready to forgive his own actions. He still vividly recalled the faces of those he'd killed. Their images haunted his sleep. He was cursed by second guesses. *What if I'd only done something differently. Did I have to kill them?*

Kate suddenly seemed to notice that Peter was dressed in a hospital gown, and she fingered the lightweight cloth.

"Why are you wearing this?" she said, fearing the answer.

Peter pulled himself upright in the chair, then raised the gown, exposing the bandage on his thigh.

Kate gasped and placed her hand over her mouth.

"It's not that bad," Peter said. "Just a few stitches, really."

"What happened?"

Peter retold the events from the Zone of Death, and finished with Jim's arrival and then Cho stabbing him in the leg.

"She could have killed you," Kate said.

"But she didn't. And that's what matters. Cho is in custody now. She's no longer a threat to us."

"That's why you went there, isn't it? So you could kill her."

Peter nodded. "Yes. I'm not proud of that, but it's the truth.

After what she did to you…and she threatened Ethan and Joanna. And us. She wasn't going to stop."

Peter cleared his throat. He found it hard to confess his sins, but he knew he must, and hoped Kate would forgive him. She had to fully know who he was.

Peter continued. "I lured her to the Zone of Death. I knew she would bring her team. They wanted the secret design of the laser weapon, so I used that as the bait. I knew she would come, and when she did, I planned to kill her."

"But you didn't. You said you turned her over to the government."

"Yeah. She was just standing there. We were close, and I had her in my sights. I could have pulled the trigger, and I doubt anyone would have ever found the body. Between the wolves, bears, coyotes—I don't think there would have been anything to find, other than a few scraps of clothing."

Kate said, "Why didn't you…"

"Shoot her? God knows I wanted to. She's an evil woman, and she deserves to die. But then I imagined you standing there next to me. And I thought about what you would say. And I couldn't. I couldn't pull the trigger."

"So I'm your conscience?"

Peter shook his head. "No. But you help me listen to my conscience." He wrapped his hands around Kate's. "You're the best thing that has happened to me, and I can't bear the thought of losing you. You've made me think hard about what I've done with my life, decisions I've made. There are some I wish I could do over again."

"Nonsense. You're talking like a crazy man. You've raised two wonderful children who are now responsible adults. You're the most kind and honest man I've ever met. You protect the innocent, and you've never hesitated to defend your friends or your country. You also run a successful business that provides good jobs."

"Yeah, jobs making weapons to kill people."

"Peter, stop beating yourself up. I wish I could take back those words I said in Washington. I didn't mean to hurt you."

"No, you're right. I can do better—"

"Knock, knock," a nurse said, standing in the doorway. "How are you feeling?" she asked Kate.

"Okay. Better than yesterday."

"I have good news. The doctor is pleased with your recovery. If this trend continues, we should be able to discharge you in a few days."

"I'd like that. Lying in bed all day is not my idea of fun."

The nurse walked Kate and Peter through the treatment plan for the next few days. They would continue to gradually reduce the amount of pain medication Kate was taking. So far, she'd been responding well. Later, a physical therapist would come by and discuss a plan for Kate to help her regain mobility in the amputated leg, and ensure adequate blood circulation. As the swelling reduced, they could fit her for a prosthetic. Since the amputation had been below the knee, the prognosis for fully regaining mobility—walking, even running—was encouraging.

The nurse then turned her attention to Peter. "As for you, I'm told we have your discharge paperwork ready. Let's get you back to your room so you can dress, and we'll get you out of here."

CHAPTER 48

WALKING ON CRUTCHES, AND WITH his leg still bandaged, Peter entered the lobby of St. Charles, accompanied by Todd. He waited his turn at the business office.

"Next," called a lady behind a desk.

Peter took a seat. "I'm here for Kate Simpson. She's scheduled to be released."

While the necessary paperwork was printing, Peter removed his checkbook and found a pen.

"Just sign here." The lady indicated several lines. "All done. I'll call the nursing station, and they'll bring her down."

"But isn't there a bill to pay?" Peter said.

He knew Kate didn't carry much medical insurance. She couldn't afford it on her salary.

"No," the lady replied. "Everything has been paid in full."

"How can that be? I would rather just pay the deductible and copay now."

She looked over the payment history again.

"No. Looks like another party already made those payments. Nothing is due."

Peter returned to the lobby with Todd.

"I don't get it," he said. "The business office told me someone already paid the bill."

Todd chuckled. "Count your blessings."

"You don't know anything about this, do you?"

Todd held up his hands in conciliation. "Nope. Probably a Good Samaritan who heard about Kate's injuries on the news."

Five minutes later, Kate was brought into the lobby in a wheelchair. She was smiling broadly, and Peter was overjoyed to be taking her home.

At the curb, he helped her into Todd's truck. The nurse folded the wheelchair and placed it in the back, although the physical therapist encouraged Kate not to use the chair unless she developed sores under her arms from the crutches.

Upon arriving at Peter's condo, he and Todd helped Kate up the stairs.

"That wasn't too hard," she said.

Then she thanked Todd for his help.

Diesel greeted Kate with a wagging tail.

"Hey there, boy. How are you?"

She lowered herself onto the sofa, laying the crutches on the floor. Diesel sniffed them thoroughly, then sat beside Kate while she rubbed his head and neck.

Peter busied himself warming chicken noodle soup in the kitchen.

From the great room, Kate called, "I'm so happy to be out of the hospital."

"Me, too." Peter dished up a bowl and carried it to her. "I missed you."

The doorbell chimed, and Peter walked to the door, with Diesel by his side. When he opened the door, he was greeted with a floral arrangement so large it obscured the person holding it. Peter took the flowers and thanked the delivery person.

"Oh, there's three more arrangements. They took up half the van. I'll be right back."

Peter watched the delivery person retreat down the stairs. At the curb was a white cargo van, and on the side of the vehicle was the name All Season Florists. He knew it to be a local shop, but he was still on edge.

He commanded Diesel to stay and guard while he took the first bouquet inside.

After the delivery person set the last arrangement down on the porch, under Diesel's watchful eyes, he said, "That's the last one."

Peter thanked him, and then carried the flowers into the great room.

"These are beautiful," Kate said. "Who are they from?"

Peter raised his eyebrows. "Don't know. There's no card. But I assume they're for you."

"Not a flower guy?" Kate said.

"Not so much. My preference leans toward Roadrunner and Wile E. Coyote balloons."

"I think someone spent too much time watching Saturday morning cartoons."

"It seems you have a secret admirer. All these flowers. And at the hospital, too."

"I have no idea," Kate replied. "I wonder why they didn't sign a card?"

Peter's phone rang. He checked the caller ID. It was Jade.

"Maybe I know." He answered the call.

"Hello, Peter. It's Jade."

"Hi, Jade. I have you on speaker. I'm sitting next to Kate."

"Did you get the flowers?"

"Yes, they just arrived."

Kate said, "Hello, Jade. Thank you so much. They're beautiful."

"I've been in touch with the hospital, and they said you were going home today. How are you feeling?"

"I'm doing well. Thank you."

Peter said, "Jade, did you have anything to do with the medical bill?"

"Oh no. I hope there wasn't a problem. I spoke to someone in the business office, and they assured me that everything was taken care of."

"There was no problem," Peter said. "Thank you, but there's no need—"

"I know what you're going to say. And you know my uncle. He insisted. Everything is taken care of. He instructed me to hire the best physical therapists to work with Kate for as long as it takes. And when you are ready for a prosthetic leg, they will fit you with the best available."

Kate said, "Jade, I don't know how to thank you. I mean, we haven't even met, and—"

"I was looking forward to meeting you at your wedding. Tell me, have you rescheduled a date yet?"

Kate felt her face flush. "Not yet. Soon, I hope. I want to be walking without crutches."

They talked for another twenty minutes, Kate and Jade sounding like long-lost friends, or even sisters. At the end of the call, Jade promised to come to Bend in a month and go shopping with Kate.

"Just be prepared," Peter told Kate, once the call was over.

"Prepared for what? Jade seems very nice, and I'm looking forward to meeting her."

"It sounds like you two hit it off fine. But understand, she is the niece of the Sultan of Brunei—perhaps the richest family in the world. She will insist on paying for everything. Be gracious, because if you refuse her offer, you'll hurt her feelings."

Peter's phone rang again. It was Jim. Peter rose and walked

to his study. He didn't want Kate to be upset by the conversation.

Jim said, "I wanted to let you know that Cho is under military custody. She's already providing useful intel."

"What about the cell she was running in Boise?"

"Thanks to you, that cell no longer exists. But she had connections to other sleeper cells. We're working that in conjunction with the FBI. From the bodies you left behind, we are beginning to construct a detailed picture of who these North Korean agents were, and how they arrived here. It appears they all came into our country under student visas, using fake passports. The FBI will be working for years to plug that security loophole."

"I hope so," Peter said.

"There's another matter I need to discuss."

Peter tensed, knowing this was coming.

"I understand," he said.

"Really? You haven't heard me out yet."

"I'm sorry. I did what had to be done. And I'm willing to accept the consequences."

"Destroying government property is how Colonel Pierson phrased it. The PEAP carbine was developed using funding from DARPA. It didn't belong to you or your company."

"I removed those files from the company server to prevent Cho from stealing them. With only one copy in existence, I was able to draw Cho away—"

"Which set the stage for my team taking her into military custody. It was a brilliant strategy. Even impressed Lieutenant Lacey. And that's damned difficult to do. It was actually Lacey who explained this coup to the colonel and convinced him that no charges against you were warranted."

"I...I don't know what to say. Thank you. I didn't expect leniency."

"We have bigger problems now, and sacrificing you doesn't

make any sense. I know you did what had to be done, and what was ultimately in the best interest of the United States. It's not often one gets to put the genie back into the bottle."

"Sorry?" Peter said.

"The proverbial genie—knowledge. In this case, knowledge of how to build the PEAP carbine. I think we are all rightfully concerned about the power of that weapon. We've seen it in the wrong hands, used in an attempt to overthrow our government. I, for one, would prefer to forget that it ever existed. And with the only prototype missing, and the design destroyed, I suppose that decision now falls to one person—you."

Peter said, "For the record, I see that work as my greatest failure."

Jim asked about Kate, and about Peter's leg wound. He passed on his best wishes for Kate, and was about to end the call when a final thought came to mind.

"Oh, almost forgot. Lacey was also impressed by your selection of the Zone of Death to execute your plan against Cho and her team. She found the legal arguments compelling for that narrow strip of land being a place where one can get away with murder, literally. Tell you the truth, I think she was just a bit disappointed that we won't see that theory tested in the courts."

"You mean there won't be any charges against me for killing Cho's team members?"

"Self-defense. And given these were foreign agents from a hostile regime, the FBI is more than a bit embarrassed this all happened in the first place. Hell, I wouldn't be surprised if you get another medal from President Taylor."

Peter leaned back in his chair. So much weight had been removed from his shoulders. His entire body relaxed.

He replied, "I can't begin to tell you how happy I am to hear that."

"I understand. Take care of Kate. She's good for you."

"I will. And thank you."

The call ended, and Peter returned to the great room. Kate was lying on the floor next to Diesel. The red pit bull was on his back, and she was rubbing his chest.

She looked up at Peter. "Is everything okay?"

Peter nodded, then sat on the floor next to Kate. He reached out and held her hand.

He knew they had a lot of work ahead to heal, physically and mentally. But there was nothing he wanted more than to be with Kate.

Finally, he said, "Everything is wonderful, because I'm with you."

EPILOGUE

DECEMBER 9

THE THIN DUSTING OF WHITE on the ground marked the first snowfall of winter. It hadn't been cold enough to freeze the pond next to Aspen Hall at Shevlin Park—formerly a fish hatchery—but that would come soon enough.

Standing before a wall built of dry-stack lava stone, Todd Steed faced an audience of less than two dozen guests. Peter, dressed in a gray suit and a Jerry Garcia necktie in bright splashes of red, purple, and blue, stood facing the guests. A red carnation was pinned to his lapel.

When the background music stopped, several heads turned toward the back of the hall. The opening cords of *Never Stop* played over the PA system, and then Kate appeared at the entry. Wearing a long white dress that followed her shape, a veil over her face, and carrying a bouquet with red carnation highlights, she stood there, gazing down the long aisle. As the lyrics spoke of never-ending love, she noticed Peter's lips quivering. She, too, felt the emotion expressed so honestly by the song.

Then she began walking at a measured pace, working hard to maintain her composure. Everyone in attendance knew the importance of her steps was profoundly more than completing this customary part of the marriage ceremony. Kate had worked tirelessly over the past six months to walk again. Supported by Peter, a small circle of friends, and a group of dedicated professionals, she'd vowed to walk down the aisle.

Jade's uncle, the Sultan of Brunei, had insisted on hiring a team of the best physical and mental therapists. He paid generously to relocate them to Bend to provide dedicated support to Kate. His Majesty also paid for the best prothesis money could buy. It was fitted to Kate's leg only a month earlier.

At first, she found it hard to find her balance without the tactile feedback from a foot. But she learned quickly. And now, dressed in the gown she'd selected six months ago, she was living her dream.

She arrived next to Peter, just as the lyrics ended. Todd gave them several moments in which Peter held Kate's hands and gazed deeply into her eyes. He shuffled his feet to edge closer to her.

Todd spoke slowly and clearly, the words easily heard by the audience. But Peter barely noticed them—he was enraptured by Kate's beauty.

Peter slipped the ring onto Kate's finger, and she reciprocated. And then Todd said a few more words, followed by, "You may kiss the bride."

Peter raised her veil, leaned forward, and gently met her lips.

Following the recession, Peter and Kate received congratulations and blessing from the guests. Then the single women, including Jade and Kate's friend, Abby, formed a small cluster as Kate threw the bouquet. It was caught by Abby, only because she had an inch longer reach than Jade.

A DJ played a variety of music, heavily weighted toward 80s rock—Peter's favorite—mixed with Jimmy Buffet and contemporary country. A spread of food was placed on three folding tables, with beer and wine served by a bartender.

Gary Porter, his wife, Nancy, and Jim Nicolaou approached Peter and Kate after they finished their first dance.

Jim said, "It's good to see you again, Kate."

She smiled. "Our first meeting in Washington seems so long ago."

"It was. A lot has happened since then. I'm very happy for you." Jim turned to Peter. "For both of you."

"Me, too, buddy," Gary said. "I hope this means you'll take it easier."

Peter tipped his head and raised an eyebrow.

Gary said, "You know. No more playing Rambo."

Before Peter could reply, Jade slid in next to Kate.

"You look absolutely radiant," she said. "I don't think there was a dry eye when the processional song played. That was so touching."

"Thank you," Kate replied.

"Tell me, did Peter help you pick that song?"

"No," Peter said. "It was a surprise. But I couldn't have picked a more appropriate song." He was looking into Kate's eyes.

Gary raised his glass. "A toast to the new couple. We are so happy for you. And I think I can speak for everyone in wishing you both a lifetime together to share each other's love."

"Here, here," Jim said.

After a pause that stretched almost into awkwardness, Kate looked at Gary, and then Jim.

She said, "Well, I still want to know what you've dragged my husband into."

Jim tensed, sensing an accusation coming.

But then Kate said, "I know there are stories. And now that I'm family, I have a right to know."

She finished with a crooked smile.

"Oh, I have many stories," Jade said. "Let's have lunch when you're back from your honeymoon." She gave Kate a conspiratorial wink and grin.

"Where are you off to?" Jim said, happy to change the subject.

"We," Kate looped her arm through Peter's, "are flying to French Polynesia the day after tomorrow, for seven nights on Bora Bora."

"Wow!" Gary said.

"Hey." Nancy looked at Gary. "How come you've never taken me there?"

"Tell me," Jim said. "Is it true? The rumors I'm hearing?"

Peter said, "If you mean, am I selling the business, the answer is yes. Haven't found a buyer yet, but that's the plan."

"I understand. But still, I'm sorry to hear that."

"I'm not," Gary said. "We've had a lot of close calls. I mean—"

Peter's phone rang. He was going to let it go to voicemail, but noticed the number was from the UK. He turned away from the group and answered.

"Hello. This is Peter."

"Hello, Dr. Savage. You may not remember me, but my name is George McIntire. We spoke some time back. I'm the customer service manager for Rolls Royce." The British accent was thick.

Peter smiled, knowing what was coming.

"Yes, Mr. McIntire, I do remember you."

"Jolly good. And please, call me George. First, I wish to congratulate you on your marriage to Miss Kate Simpson. I understand it was a lovely ceremony."

"Thank you, George."

"Not at all." George cleared his throat.

Peter turned to face the group, and now all eyes were

focused on him.

He said, "Would I be correct that Miss Jade put you up to this call?"

"No, no. Not at all. His Majesty, the Sultan of Brunei, insisted I call you directly. He said it is a matter of a proper wedding gift, and that I was to speak with you and your lovely bride."

Peter's lips drew back in a wide smile. "George, I'm going to put you on speaker. Kate is standing next to me. Jade is here, too."

"Wonderful. Miss Simpson—err, Mrs. Savage—it is so nice to make your acquaintance, and I look forward to meeting you in person at the Goodwood factory."

Peter said, "George works for Rolls Royce."

Kate's eyes grew large, and she raised her eyebrows.

"But, we're going to—"

"Oh no, it's okay," Jade said. "My uncle's plane will fly you to London after your honeymoon."

"London? What…"

"I told you," Peter said, referring to a comment he'd made to Kate about the sultan's generosity.

"Mrs. Savage," George said, his tone soothing, "rest assured that we will be with you every step as your select the features of your Rolls."

"My Rolls?"

"Yes. We have several models to choose from. Although, I might suggest the convertible Dawn. Naturally, each is bespoke."

Jade said, "You'll have so much fun. I've worked with George on four cars, including the Wraith for Peter. And of course, we have to go to the theater in London."

Kate was at a loss for words, so Jade carried on.

"My uncle has insisted I go with you. We'll stay at the Piccadilly Ritz, if that's okay?"

"But…" Kate was still stunned.

Jade said, "Diesel can come along, too, just like last time."

Peter said, "You'll have a great time, Kate. Trust me."

George cleared his throat. "Getting back to business…there is also the matter of your Wraith, Dr. Savage."

Caught off guard, Peter fumbled for words. "Uh…my…what about the Wraith?"

George said, "I understand that it may be in need of…shall we say, repairs."

A pang of guilt shot through Peter as he recalled the demise of the majestic automobile.

"I think that's an understatement," he replied.

"Hmm. I see. Then we have no choice but to build another automobile for you as well."

"No, George. Please, that's not necessary."

Jade said, "When I told my uncle that I thought you might have wrecked the Rolls, he insisted that George build another for you."

"Miss Jade is correct, Dr. Savage. His Majesty, the Sultan, can be most insistent. And when it comes to automobiles, I would never try to dissuade him. He is a very good customer."

Kate leaned toward Peter's phone. "Thank you, George. My husband and I are deeply grateful."

"You are quite welcome, Mrs. Savage. We look forward to your visit to Goodwood. I will have my assistant follow-up with you first thing in the morning."

As the call ended, Kate wondered if she was dreaming. So much was happening so fast.

She told Jade, "Please express my deepest appreciation to your uncle."

"From me, too," Peter said. "I'm embarrassed that he knows I wrecked the last Rolls."

"Sometime, you'll have to tell me the whole story," Jade replied.

Kate said, "And me, too. I'd like to know."

Peter rolled his eyes and looked at Jim.

"Hey," Jim said. "That adventure of yours had nothing to do with activities carried out by SGIT or national security. I can't help you."

Gary and Jim chuckled as Peter felt the weight of two pair of eyes focused on him.

"Okay," he said. "I'll tell you. But it's a story for another time."

Jade said, "We have to discuss your travel itinerary. My suggestion is to fly straight from Tahiti to London."

"I don't know." Kate looked at Peter. "We have to come back for Diesel."

"Oh no," Jade said. "I've taken care of everything. You can bring Diesel with you."

"How can that be," Peter said. "I mean, there are laws that require dogs to be quarantined for several weeks, sometimes months, when entering a foreign country. We're planning to be on Bora Bora for only a week."

"My uncle instructed the Ministry of Foreign Affairs to approach the French government about an exception. Naturally, they were happy to agree to such a minor request for favor from my uncle."

"I see," Kate said. "I don't know how to thank your uncle. And thank you."

"I know how important Diesel is to Peter," Jade said.

"I'll have to call the resort tonight and see if they allow pets," he said. "It still might be a problem."

With a smile in his voice, Gary said, "You're good. I already contacted the resort."

"You called them?" Peter said. "But you don't know where we're staying."

"Come on, buddy. Give me some credit. It's a small island, and there aren't that many resorts there."

"You hacked into the reservation systems of all the hotels?"

"Well, I wouldn't put it that way."

Jim smiled and patted Gary on the shoulder. "You can speak freely. Whatever you did—"

"May have done," Gary said.

"Okay. Whatever you may have done is outside the purview of SGIT."

"Awesome. So yes. Didn't take long to locate your reservation. Then I inserted a memo into your file."

"And what does the memo say?" Peter said.

"Just that the French Ministry of Foreign Affairs has explicitly requested Diesel be allowed as an honored guest during your stay. After all, he is the first and only dog to receive the Presidential Medal of Freedom."

"I don't understand," Kate said. "If the sultan already received permission from the French Ministry of Foreign Affairs for Diesel to enter without quarantine, why did you have to forge a memo and insert it into our reservation file?"

"Simple," Jim said. "Contingency. Government bureaucracies all too often move at glacial speed. It was actually Lieutenant Lacey who came up with the idea. It was her suggestion."

"I see," Kate said.

"You guys are always looking out for me," Peter said.

"Someone has to," Gary replied.

"You probably didn't realize it, Kate," Jim said, "but when you married Peter, it was a package deal. We're more than his friends. We are all brothers. Our bond was forged in combat."

Kate pulled Peter to her side. "They say the measure of a

man can be gauged by the company he keeps." She looked into Peter's eyes. "You have great friends."

"Brothers," Gary said.

"I couldn't be happier for both of you," Jim said. "I know parts of Peter's history frustrate you, Kate. But I'll also tell you that every one of my operators—and they are without exception the finest soldiers Uncle Sam has ever fielded—would lay down their life to save Peter's. Or yours. Because Peter has put his life on the line to save theirs. I never asked for Peter to do that. No one did. Peter did it because it had to be done. Just like President Taylor said—it's not fair."

Kate wiped the tears from her cheeks.

Then Jim faced Peter, placing a hand on his shoulder.

"It's time you stood down. You've lived up to your personal oath to protect your friends, your country. Now you owe it to yourself, and to Kate, to enjoy life together."

Peter nodded. He pulled Kate into an embrace and whispered in her ear.

"I give you my word. You and me forever. I love you."

AUTHOR'S POSTSCRIPT

AS I DUG INTO THIS THEORY, including reading the original paper, titled *The Perfect Crime*, authored by Brian Kalt (viewcontent.cgi (msu.edu) and Brian C. Kalt—Wikipedia), I decided this had to play prominently in a future novel. Just how this would unfold was still a mystery at the time.

The facts surrounding the Zone of Death, as laid out in this story, are true. A sliver of far Eastern Idaho is, in fact, within the boundaries of Yellowstone National Park. Idaho ceded its legal jurisdiction to the Wyoming District when Idaho was admitted into the Union. The same is true for Montana, as a small portion of Southern Montana is also within the national park boundaries.

Once these facts are understood, the remainder of the legal theory falls in place. Assuming a serious crime, one in which the defendant has the right to trial by jury, is committed in the Zone of Death, constitutional problems immediately arise. The trial must be held in the state in which the crime occurred, and the jury must also be drawn from the state and judicial district in which the crime transpired. Since no person resides in the Idaho portion of Yellowstone, we have a significant barrier to prosecution.

A few years after Brian Kalt published his first paper on this topic, he published a follow-up article ("Tabloid Constitutionalism: How a Bill Doesn't Become a Law," by Brian C. Kalt :: SSRN) describing his efforts to encourage Congress to close this loophole. The paper is fascinating, and maddeningly frustrating. I encourage anyone with interest to read the full paper, but the short version is that Congress has no appetite to fix the problem. In fact, some members of Congress even questioned if there was a problem, since no serious crimes had occurred in the Zone of Death, and therefore Kalt's theory was just that—a theory. Clearly, no lawmakers wanted to proactively close the loophole, preferring to take a wait-and-see approach.

The theory was almost put to the test with a poaching case, but the defendant pleaded out rather than going to trial.

Admittedly, the small geographical size and lack of permanent population in the Zone of Death makes it unlikely that a serious crime will occur there. But the probability is not zero. It seems that, many times, when we tempt fate and play the odds, undesirable consequences occur.

Unless, and until, Congress takes action to split those portions of Idaho and Montana out of the District of Wyoming, or redraw the state boundaries for Idaho and Montana (unlikely), this situation will continue to exist like a buried landmine, primed to explode when an unwary passerby steps on it.

ABOUT THE AUTHOR

DAVE EDLUND IS THE USA TODAY BESTSELLING author of the award-winning *Peter Savage* novels, and a graduate of the University of Oregon, with a doctoral degree in chemistry. He resides in Bend, Oregon, with his wife, son, and three dogs (Lucy Liu, Dude, and Tenshi). Raised in the California Central Valley, Dave completed his undergraduate studies at California State University, Sacramento. In addition to authoring several technical articles and books on alternative energy, he is an inventor on 114 U.S. patents. An avid outdoorsman and shooter, Edlund has hunted North America for big game, ranging from wild boar to moose to bear. He has traveled extensively throughout China, Japan, Europe, and North America.

www.PeterSavageNovels.com

THE PETER SAVAGE SERIES

BY DAVE EDLUND

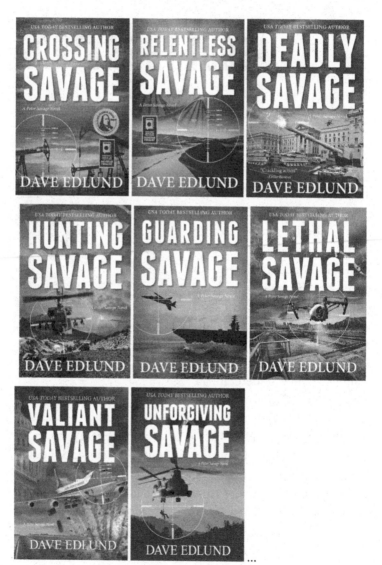